SOLE CHAOS

WILLIAM ODAY

William Oday, February 2019
Copyright © 2019 William Oday
All rights reserved worldwide

ISBN-13: 978-1-942472-19-3

Cover by Christian Bentulan

Edited by Walt Hunt

EXTINCTION CRISIS SERIES

Recommended Reading Order

SOLE CONNECTION, a Short Story

SOLE PREY, a Prequel Novella

SOLE SURVIVOR, Book 1

SOLE CHAOS, Book 2

SOLE REFUGE, Book 3
Coming Soon!

Any Order Works

THE TANK MAN, a Short Story

THE PLUNGE, a Short Story

Never, never, never give up.

— *Winston Churchill*

1

BANG!

The forty-five caliber bullet exited the muzzle at a speed of over a thousand feet per second.

Less than a second later, it punched through the gnarled bark of a Sitka Spruce tree , sending out a shower of splinter shrapnel.

The splinters buried into the ear and cheek of the enormous red-haired man whose head was inches to the right of the point of impact.

To his credit, he didn't flinch.

But Charlie knew that every beast could be broken. Could be trained to obey.

He holstered the forty-five he'd taken from the hunter he'd killed the day before and spat on the glowing embers in the campfire. It hit with a sizzle and a puff of white smoke. The wind gusting over the top of the mountain peak hit the fire and the embers flared brighter.

Charlie sucked in a deep breath of clean, cold morning air. His lungs prickled in a pleasant way. The bright scent of evergreen lingered as he let the air seep out of his nose and mouth.

Even after what must've been the war to end all wars, a body could still get a breath of fresh mountain air. Only on a slice of heaven like Kodiak, Alaska.

The rising sun burned orange behind the distant brown gauze curtain hiding the heavens. Been like that since the nuke went off five days ago.

Musta been more than one. The days of dropping one nuke and that being the end of it were long gone.

World War III had happened.

Nothing else made sense. Not from what he'd seen going on in the town at the foot of the mountain.

No matter. Destruction held the seeds of new beginnings. Just like a fire burning through a forest.

He turned back to the man tied to the tree. "I get it. You're the strong, silent type. I like that."

Charlie had found him half-dead and gibbering like a lunatic. Course he hadn't found him tied to a tree. That was his doing on account of having to break him. But whereas the man couldn't stop yapping before, now he wouldn't say a word.

He'd gone quieter than a nun at a nudie bar.

Charlie strolled over to his captive with a friendly smirk hanging lop-sided on his face. "Thing is, I don't need you to be the talkin' type. What I need is for you to be the obeyin' type."

The large man's gray eyes flashed defiance and Charlie knew the job wasn't done yet. Not by a long shot.

That was fine.

More than most, Charlie enjoyed doing things the

hard way. Even when the hard way wasn't the only way, he sometimes chose it.

Charlie leaned in, inches from his face and looking up at an angle that would've put a crick in his neck if he'd slept like that. He was a big un, no doubt. "I'm gonna ask you again. What's your name?"

Repetition was part of the training.

The large man's auburn beard twitched like an overgrown bush with a raccoon running through it.

But still no reply.

Charlie shrugged, a silent acknowledgement that he understood the deal.

The hard way, then.

He lowered his right hand to the Bowie knife sheathed at his hip and unsnapped the button. In a single, fluid motion, he drew out the twelve inch blade and held it in the air between them.

Not a flicker of fear passed through the other man's eyes.

Charlie would've hollered with approval if it wouldn't have interfered with the training. Like dealing with the BlueTick Coonhounds he'd bred and trained since the age of eight, you had to make it clear that there was a time for play and a time for training.

And the better a dog was trained, the more time there was for play.

This dog had yet to be brought to heel.

Yet being the operative word.

Charlie passed the blade through the narrow space between their faces.

The man's bare chest bulged as he went for the weapon. He had no chance of actually getting it.

Charlie had been tying knots since the age of three and he knew twice as many as any mortal man. He knew the best ones for building spring traps. He knew the best ones for stretching hides. And he knew the best ones for keeping an impressively strong man tied to a tree.

And that was besides knowing just how much pressure to use in securing his arms stretched backward around the trunk so as to produce exquisite agony in the joints while doing no real harm.

Pain focused the attention like little else.

The art of it was finding the right amount of pain applied at the right moment in time.

Now was one of those moments. It was an opportunity to demonstrate dominance. To reinforce the pack order.

In a flash that caught the larger man by surprise, Charlie's left hand snatched through the thicket of red hair and yanked at the man's right ear. At the same time, the blade sliced through the air precisely where he intended.

Right on the bridge of tissue connecting the ear to the head.

And the razor sharp edge sliced through it like a red-hot brand through fresh snow.

His left hand came away with the severed ear as a tiny fountain of blood spurted through the air.

The man roared and, again to his credit, it came out thick with fury rather than fear.

Charlie let himself grin this time. Nothing wrong with letting the man know he was enjoying himself.

Because he was.

Blood flowed down the bearded man's neck, shoulder,

and into the thicket of hair carpeting his exposed chest. What must've been his shirt hung in tatters from the hardest-working belt Charlie had ever seen.

And growing up in the Iron Mountains of eastern Tennessee where some folks thought drinking was more a lifestyle than a pastime, he'd seen more than a few.

The only thing bigger than the one-eared man's barrel chest was his round belly. That bulk would be a lot harder to support in this new world.

Calories weren't gonna be spilling off the grocery store shelves anymore.

And that was just fine by Charlie.

People had gone soft.

Too much comfort and convenience.

Well, not anymore.

Charlie sauntered over to the fire and turned in profile so the man could see. He placed the severed ear on the flat of his knife blade and lowered it onto the coals.

He waited patiently for the meat to cook.

There wasn't much meat in an ear, so it didn't take but a few minutes on each side to finish the job.

The rich scent of roasting flesh filled the air.

Charlie's stomach grumbled and pinched. He was hungry, but he was no savage. No sick and twisted cannibal type that neighbors always said was a nice young man after the truth came out.

No, he was just a man that understood how to deal with an animal. He'd been doing it all his life and he'd never failed. Well, every once in a while you ended up with a dog that wouldn't take to training. Those were shot.

This one would be too if breaking him didn't bring him around.

Charlie hoped it didn't have to go that way. He had a feeling the man could prove to be wonderfully useful. He was a local. And he clearly wasn't used to being on the wrong end of abuse. So that meant others knew and submitted to him.

There was currently an opening for second-in-command and Charlie had a hunch this behemoth would fit the bill.

Charlie plucked the medium-rare meat off the blade and blew on it to cool it down. He glanced over and caught the man's wide eyes. "Good. I see that I finally have your attention."

He kept blowing.

When the meat had cooled enough to not scald his tongue, he tore it in half and popped a half into his mouth.

Damn thing was rubbery as all get out.

But he wasn't eating for pleasure so he kept at it until he finished it.

The man's beard parted where his mouth hung open.

That was a good sign.

But the real note of progress showed in his eyes.

The fear.

The submission.

"I'll ask you again, what's your name?"

"Alexei. Volkov," the man replied with a wincing eye on the side with the missing ear.

Charlie nodded like he knew it all along and had just been waiting for the man to admit it. "Well Alexei, it's like this. I like the looks of that town at the bottom of the hill.

And I expect with all that's going on that there's no reason I can't have it."

Alexei stared at him in silence.

That was good. That was an appropriate time to be silent. The beast was learning.

"I got screwed out of a million dollars. I was going to win it. None of the others stood a chance. Losing it made me very angry until I realized I'd been thinking too small. Money comes. Money goes. But power? The power of life and death over thousands? That's the power of a king. Kings don't need money because they already own everything."

He pushed the remaining meat at Alexei's closed mouth.

"Open."

Alexei hesitated.

"Now."

His mouth opened.

Charlie shoved the portion of cooked ear inside.

"Eat."

Alexei closed his mouth and chewed.

"Chew your food, now. Thirty times for every bite. Just like my Grandma Ida always said."

Charlie waited while he chewed.

"Swallow."

Alexei swallowed and his face contorted into a grimace of disgust. He finished swallowing and spat to the side. "Who are you?"

"Folks call me Charlie Bog."

Alexei's eyes widened in horror. He muttered something through his beard. The same thing over and over, but not loud enough for Charlie to hear.

"What are you mumbling there?"

Alexei's mouth snapped shut and he shook his head.

"Speak."

"Chernobog."

"Chernobog?"

Alexei nodded.

"Who's that?"

Alexei looked away. "You. You are the dark god of my ancestors. I know it."

Charlie shrugged. "Maybe."

Hell, who was he to get in the way of a little useful superstition?

"Even so, that name's a little old world for me. We're gonna be friends and my friends call me CB."

Alexei muttered something, and while Charlie didn't know much about other languages, the accent definitely had a Russian ring to it.

"You're gonna help me, Alexei."

"How?"

"You're gonna help me get every low life and dirtbag in town in line. I need an army of men willing to do the dirty work. And it starts with you."

Charlie slipped a glove on while making his way back to the fire and then pulled his knife off the coals. He returned to Alexei and offered a comforting look. "This is gonna hurt."

He raised the knife and pressed the flat of the blade onto the bleeding wound that used to be Alexei's ear. Flesh sizzled and popped and the stink of burning hair filled the air.

Alexei screamed in anguish and his head slumped forward.

In a flash, Charlie whipped the knife at the ground. Exactly one rotation later, the point stuck into the moist ground with the blade buried halfway up.

Charlie left the unconscious man and walked over to the nearby ridge.

Far below was the town of Kodiak.

Just waiting for him to take it.

2

FLORENCE BICKLE tapped her foot on the floor, doing her best not to notice all the glares aimed in her direction. The hum of nervous conversation echoed around the room. The cloying heat of too many bodies packed into too small a space had her arm pits sweating. The scent leaking out of her winter jacket should've been enough to drive people away, except they all smelled the same or worse.

Where the hell were Earl and Jim?

She'd promised to arrive early at the town meeting and hold two open chairs up front for them. But that was before the two old geezers decided to take their sweet ever-lovin' time in arriving to claim the two conspicuously open spots.

"Are these taken?" said a woman with a baby on her hip and a child clinging to the other hand.

Flo would've cursed the two old men if she could've. But she'd never been to voodoo school or anything beyond high school. Between marrying and having a baby right out of school, opportunities and her hadn't been on speaking terms.

Not that she was complaining.

Her son, Rome, was the sun in her sky.

Sure, he had his problems. What teenager didn't?

But he was a good boy with a good heart.

And she prayed to God every night that the world falling apart wouldn't change that.

Despite hating it, he was at home right now taking care of Bob. That alone was a testament to his character. He'd wanted to leave Bob at the hospital. And before that, to leave him bleeding out in his motel room at The Weary Traveler. And either would've been the smart thing to do.

A person who'd just stolen from you and left you vulnerable in a dangerous situation didn't deserve a second thought. Certainly not a kind thought.

But Flo wasn't the type to ignore someone in need.

Most folks might've thought that was being a good person. With her, it was a character flaw.

She was drawn to the wounded bird.

To helping where help was needed most.

"Excuse me," the mother said. "Are these taken?"

Flo couldn't deny her. The woman's bloodshot eyes, dirty clothes and frizzed hair made it plain as day that she wasn't coping well with the aftermath of...

Of what exactly none of them were sure.

Flo yanked her scarf and purse off the two seats and was about to offer them when the woman got pushed aside.

"Out of the way," Earl growled.

Jim shuffled up behind him. "Thinking of stealing the

seats that was rightfully ours, huh?" The fuzzy white caterpillars he had for eyebrows twitched at the woman.

Flo helped them both sit down while apologizing to the woman.

The mother cast a furious look at all three of them before stomping away.

"Thanks for taking so long," she said. "Half the people in here want to lynch me for holding on to empty front row seats."

The deep crevices in Earl's etched face shifted, like tectonic plates grinding together. "We're old. What do you expect?"

The caterpillars above Jim's deep set eyes wriggled. "That's right. We're old and we could die any second! You young uns wouldn't understand."

At forty-nine, Flo was no spring chicken. Still, anyone would feel young compared to these two grouches. She rolled her eyes before taking her own seat. "How many times have I heard that? And yet, you're still breathing and causing me problems."

She added the last part after noticing that Earl was already knocking back a gulp from his hip flask.

Jim's trembling hand hovered in the air, waiting for his turn.

Before everything had gone crazy, these two had been everyday regulars in the diner for over two decades. In that time, they'd consumed enough coffee and whiskey to supply a large army.

In the open space in front of them, Mayor Okpik approached the podium. She brought the microphone close to her mouth and then shook her head, pushing it away. "Can I have everyone's attention?"

The commotion in the room didn't change. If anything, it got louder.

Chief Stuckey approached from behind the mayor and raised his hands. "Quiet down everyone!"

That didn't do much either.

"Shut your traps, people!" he bellowed. A thick mustache hung below his nose like the bristles of a push broom. The chief wasn't known for being a people person in normal times. And his blood-shot eyes and scruffy beard affirmed the story that these weren't normal times.

The room settled down.

Mayor Okpik's tight lipped smile at the chief hinted at something between them. She turned with grave eyes and looked over the mass of people packed into the lobby of the Afognak Center. "Thank you everyone for coming today. I know it's been hard since the event five days ago."

"My family's running out of food!" someone shouted.

"My daughter's sick and the hospital won't give her medication!"

Okpik raised her hands and patted the air to quiet the outcries. "I understand there are problems that need immediate attention. Everyone up here is doing their best," she gestured at the line of people seated in chairs behind her, "to keep our town running. But we all know that this is no ordinary emergency."

"Did the Chinese nuke us?" someone shouted.

"Or was it the commies?" someone else yelled.

"The Chinese are commies!" the first voice replied.

"I meant the Russians!" the second voice replied back.

Flo turned around and looked across the sea of faces facing the front. They were scared. Desperate. Angry. Unpredictable.

She glanced at the emergency exit in the corner behind the seated city officials. If things went crazy, she could make it out no problem. Helping Jim and Earl get out wouldn't be so easy though.

They didn't do fast.

They hadn't done fast in thirty years.

Whatever. They'd get out one way or another.

And she wouldn't draw the nine millimeter Beretta tucked under her jacket unless absolutely necessary.

Partly because that wasn't the kind of person she was. And partly because Chief Stuckey would probably shoot the first person he saw pull out a gun.

These were uncertain times.

Shoot first. Ask questions later.

Maybe it wasn't the official take yet, but it sure felt like it would be soon.

Earl nudged her shoulder and held out the flask. "Want a nipper? Be good for you."

She shook her head. "No. Not for the last ten millions times you've offered, and not today either." Long ago, she'd been happily married. So long she barely remembered. She and her husband had been regulars at the bars downtown. Lived it up. And not long after that, she lost her husband and marriage to alcohol. She wasn't going to judge others about it, certainly not these two, but that didn't mean she was ever going to allow it in her life again.

Mayor Okpik was saying something and Flo realized she'd missed whatever it was.

"...all out nuclear war. And anyway, it doesn't matter who started it. The rumors we're hearing on shortwave are that every nuclear capable country got involved and unloaded their arsenals."

"Jesus save us," someone nearby whispered.

Flo doubted Jesus had anything to do with putting mankind where it was, and she wasn't all that sure he'd show up now to help clean up the mess.

"We believe nearly every major city in the United States is gone. Targeted by multiple warheads and wiped off the map. Untold millions gone in a blink of the eye."

Flo sucked in an involuntary breath.

All of those people? Gone?

Millions?

Tens of millions?

Okpik raised her hands to again quiet the room. "We've been unable to confirm the operation of government at the national and state levels. As far as we know, it's just communities like ours trying to hold on and figure this out. Which brings us to another problem. We suspect that sooner or later, radioactive fallout may–"

A frantic shout from the back of the room cut her off. A skinny man with greasy hair shoved his way down the side aisle. "My stuff's been stolen. All of it! Gone, it's all gone!"

Flo recognized him as he lurched to a stop in front of the mayor. His gangly frame, stringy hair and unhealthy pallor hinted at a hard drug addiction. Hinted was probably not a strong enough word.

Ronnie Dean. The repugnant owner of The Weary Traveler. The very motel where she'd found Bob after a failed suicide attempt.

Mayor Okpik touched his shoulder. "Ronnie. What happened?"

"Some low-life, no good SOB stole all of my food! Every last bit! I got nothing left. I'll starve to death." He turned to the crowd. "Your stuff ain't safe, everybody!"

Everyone started shouting at once. A few people on the fringes broke off and disappeared outside.

Ronnie turned back to Okpik and grabbed her arms. He yelled in her face but the ambient conversation was too loud to hear what.

The mayor tried to say something, but Ronnie grabbed her mouth and squeezed. Hard. He yelled again.

An instant later, Chief Stuckey landed a thunderous blow to his chest and hammered him to the floor. The chief wrenched his lanky arms behind his back and cinched his wrists in handcuffs.

Ronnie screamed as Stuckey hauled him to his feet. "Leave me alone! I ain't the criminal! I'm the victim!"

Stuckey passed him off to a deputy. "Throw him in with the others."

"Chief, the cell block is way over capacity."

Stuckey cursed under his breath. "Lock him in the bathroom if you have to. I'll deal with it when I get there."

The deputy dragged Ronnie away as Chief Stuckey worked on getting everyone to quiet down. He eventually did and the mayor finished her brief update on what they knew so far.

As people began filing out, Stuckey appeared at her side. Hey, Flo."

"Hey, chief. How are you?"

"Been better. You?"

"Same."

"Listen, would you mind coming down to the station some time today?"

"What for?"

"We have your statement on how you found that Outsider that tried to kill himself at Ronnie's hotel. We just need to dot a few I's and cross a few T's to finalize the paperwork."

"Paperwork after the end of the world?"

Stuckey snorted. "Yeah, trying to keep things normal as much as possible."

Flo didn't love the idea of having to go out again. The town was slipping toward chaos. But it wouldn't do to hole up like a hermit and try to ignore the rest of the world. Community required effort. And that was truer than ever when things took a turn for the worse.

"Sure thing, chief. I'll drop by this afternoon."

3
———

Taking care of a man who'd just tried to kill himself was a complicated business. On the one hand, he was weak and the nurturing side of Flo wanted to nurse him back to health. On the other hand, he had stolen her pistol and snuck out of the apartment in the middle of the night.

And to top it off, he'd left the front door unlocked. While the apartment complex wasn't normally a dodgy or dangerous place to live, these weren't normal times.

Flo counted out the prescribed antibiotics and shuffled over to the man lying on her couch. She extended her open hand and a glass of water in the other. "Bob. Wake up. You need to take these."

His eyes fluttered open and he stared up at her in confusion. It took a second for comprehension to take hold. "Oh. Thank you."

After he took the meds, Flo set the glass back on the kitchen counter. She stood with her back to him, biting her jaws shut to keep quiet.

But finally realized she couldn't.

She spun around and Bob was watching her with a tired look on his face. He was in no condition to defend himself.

Flo bit down on her lower lip. How could she think of herself as a generally good person if she did what she wanted to do?

"What is it, Flo?" Bob asked.

She threw up her hands. Battling with herself was exhausting and she was done with it. She crossed her arms and nodded, confirming that she was indeed tough enough and cruel enough to do it. "You have to leave, Bob. You can't stay here."

His eyes dropped to the worn carpet. "I understand." He started to stand up and winced in pain.

She rushed over and helped him lie back down. "I don't mean immediately! My Lord. Be careful. I mean once you're well enough to get up and around. Then, I need you to leave."

Bob looked up at her with dull eyes and sunken, pale cheeks.

Nearly bleeding out apparently took the sheen off a person like little else.

"Okay. I promise I'll do it."

Flo nodded and then headed for her bedroom. Better to not be around him. The pity fighting the fury was more than she could stomach. As in it literally gave her a stomach ache.

"Florence."

She paused without turning back.

"I want you to know I'm sorry. I know what I did was wrong."

A long silence followed.

What?

Did he want her to forgive him and hug him and tell him everything was okay and that they could all live together like Three's Company and he would be the kooky old Mr. Roper or something?

No.

He'd put her son in danger and that could not be forgiven.

Even if she wanted to do exactly that.

Her belly pinched tight.

Ugh.

She was so weak.

"Is that all?" she said as she looked over her shoulder.

"And I wanted to thank you. I haven't done that yet. Thank you for saving my life."

"You're welcome." She smiled coldly, approving of the chill coming across through the words.

"I know you don't have any reason to believe or trust me, but it's changed me. Almost dying. I don't want to be the man I've always been. I feel like I survived for a reason."

"Is that all?" she asked again.

"Yes."

She took a step toward her bedroom when the front door lock clicked and the door swung open.

"Help me out here, mom!" Rome said from the entryway.

She turned and stared in shock at the grocery bags filling his huge arms.

He stumbled inside as she tried to direct the impending avalanche toward the kitchen table that sat halfway in the kitchen and halfway in the living room.

The bags just made it as cans of black beans, corn tortillas, cans of soda, wheat bread, a jar of Grey Poupon, and other items spilled out.

"Where did you get all this?"

Rome grinned and, in that instant, she saw the chubby-cheeked little angel that he was ten years ago. He might've been sixteen, six-three, and over two hundred and sixty pounds, but he was still her baby.

Rome adjusted the ridiculous Delta Luvr baseball cap he loved to wear and that she hated with a passion.

Why did he have to choose a hat with a sexy, half-naked cavewoman zombie girl on it? Disgusting. And inappropriate. But he was sixteen and she'd learned long ago to choose her battles.

"I heard about a market in the old warehouse on the south side near the marina. I checked it out and sure enough, there was one. It was crazy! People with stalls set up and selling and trading all kinds of stuff. Like a flea market."

Dazzled by the pile of supplies covering the table, it took Flo a second to get to the next logical question.

But any mother would've got there soon enough.

"So, how did you pay for all this?"

Rome took his hat off and knocked off some imaginary dust.

"I asked you a question, young man."

"Don't worry about it, mom. I got it. That's all. It's fine."

Flo opened her mouth to demand an answer, and she would've if this had been a normal day in a normal life, but it wasn't. And the bounty spilling over the table more than doubled their dwindling supplies.

It was an unexpected blessing and sometimes it was better not to ask. This time, at least.

Rome pulled out an apple from his coat pocket and handed it to her. "Here. Have a bite. It's the last of the fresh stuff." He pulled out several more and set them on the table.

Flo took a bite and the tangy sweet juice dribbled down her chin. She chewed and swallowed. "What do you mean last of the fresh stuff?"

"No ships have come in since the event. Nobody is expecting more to come any time soon. Those are straight from Wesley Smith's apple tree. He was charging an arm and a leg for them, but he cut me a deal."

Again, the *how* question popped into her mind, and again she set it aside.

Another bite of the apple made her jaws ache from the sweetness.

"Is there an apple for me?" Bob asked from the couch.

Rome looked away into the kitchen. "Did someone say something? I can't tell. It sounded like a fart coming out of a donkey's ass."

"Romero! Do not use that language in my house."

"It's an apartment, mom."

"Don't get smart with me, young man. The world may have gone to hell in a hand basket, but that doesn't mean my home will. Do you understand?"

Rome shrugged. "Sure."

Flo took an apple over and handed it to Bob. While he was a guest in their household, he would be provided for. But hopefully not for much longer.

"Mom!" Rome yelled without looking in their direction. "Don't give that bastard our best stuff!"

"Romero Andrew Bickle! No more language like that!"

"Sorry. I'm just saying," he picked up a can of pickled jalapeños, "give him this. It's food."

Flo sighed. It was time for her to head to the police station. "Rome and Bob, I have to leave to meet with Chief Stuckey."

Rome faced her with wide eyes. Fearful. Concerned, at a minimum. "Why?"

What was he thinking right now?

Anyway, that mystery would wait for another day. "I have to go finalize my statement about what happened with Bob."

"You mean the loser's failure at suicide?"

Flo frowned at him and shook her head. Bob may have been, well, Bob, but that didn't make it okay to treat him like dirt. "About the suicide attempt, yes."

"You shouldn't have to go. He should," Rome said as he pointed an accusing finger.

"I'll go," Bob said.

"Both of you, shut your mouths," Flo said with growing irritation. "I'm going. This isn't a debate."

Rome kept his mouth shut and adjusted his hat.

Flo involuntarily glanced up at it. The curvy woman was either the sexiest zombie not alive or else a very down on her luck porn star. She hated the thing as much as ever.

"I need to trust that you two will get along while I'm gone. Can you do that?"

"Absolutely," Bob said.

Rome crossed his thick arms over his thicker middle.

Weight had always been an issue for him. Just another thing for her to feel guilty about.

Flo kicked the thought aside. "At least promise that you'll leave him alone."

"Fine. Whatever. I'll stay in my room. As long as donkey balls doesn't bother me, we'll be fine."

"Thank you," Flo said as they both shuttled groceries into the kitchen cabinets.

When everything was put away, she grabbed her purse and considered whether or not to slip the 9MM Beretta into it. It was the middle of the afternoon and though things had gotten rougher in general, it wasn't like it was the wild west with people getting gunned down in the streets.

Not yet, at least.

Besides, she was going to the police station, the safest place in Kodiak.

She pulled her son's head down and kissed his cheek. Standing at the open door, she looked back and forth between them. "Just be civil. I mean it."

And then she was off.

4

The walk from her home through the north end of town to the police station proved to be uneventful. Most of the cars that had been killed by the electromagnetic pulse still occupied their final destinations on the streets. The EMP had turned them into landmarks like the surrounding buildings.

There was the black Ford F250. Still looked fine, as if someone had decided the world was their parking spot.

There was the cherry red Hummer H3. Though it now had all the windows busted out and tires missing. Even the one on the back.

She could've driven the old brown Ford Pinto, but she didn't want to waste the gas. She used to hate the Pinto Bean. That was their nickname for the ugly old car. But now that it was one of very few cars that still worked, the rust brown junker had turned into a prized possession.

She arrived at the police station and entered through the open door. She entered the small lobby and the front desk that was usually occupied was empty. The large area of desks to the left held the fifteen officers that constituted the entire police force of Kodiak, Alaska.

Chief Stuckey was going over something with the rest of them, but stopped when he noticed Flo. He passed the discussion to a deputy and walked over.

"Hi, Florence," he said as he extended a hand.

She shook it and patted it with her other. "You must be busy these days."

His lips pressed together and his bushy mustache hid the upper one. "Yep. This town is holding on by a thread. And I don't have enough deputies to keep the peace if things really go sideways."

His eyes opened wide as he caught himself. "Uh, that's not information I'd like spread around."

"Of course not. I don't want trouble any more than you do." She gave his hand a squeeze and pulled away.

"Why don't we head into my office?" He led the way through the hallway to the right. "We're going over new procedures in light of the situation. It's a tricky thing enforcing the law during a period of increasing lawlessness."

They entered his office and he shut the door. He gestured at the chair in front of his desk. "Have a seat. Can I get you water or coffee? No wait. No coffee," he said as he shook his head. "Old habits die hard. Water?"

"Yes, thank you," she said as she accepted the bottle. In times like these, there was no sense in saying no. "So, is Ronnie locked up in a bathroom somewhere?"

Stuckey chuckled. "No, he's back at large. The mayor didn't want to press charges so I gave him a stern warning about being an idiot."

"That's too bad."

"He'll probably end up in here again, but I'm glad he's gone for now. We're way over capacity as it is. We haven't resorted to bathrooms, but we did have to clear out a couple of closets to make room. I know that may sound like old school Alcatraz, but I don't know what else to do. I can't give a pass to people breaking the law just because we don't have the space to hold them."

"No judgement here, Chief."

"I know, Flo. I'm trying to convince myself more than anything. It's getting harder and harder to keep things running smooth."

"Well, at least you don't have to write so many speeding tickets," Flo said trying to lighten the mood with a joke.

"True, but then we don't get the revenue either."

Ha! She'd always known speeding tickets were more about the money than the punishment. At the very least, the revenue was part of it.

"There's not much speeding, but there's a lot more of other things. Worse things."

"Like what?"

"Breaking and entering. Domestic violence."

"Really?"

"Yep. Normal people are getting desperate and doing stupid stuff. We've caught half a dozen folks trying to steal food from their neighbors. People that would've never done something like that before."

He opened a manilla file on his desk and shuffled some papers around. "And that's not counting the usual lowlifes and scumbags that consider it their job to ruin this town. Those types are coming out of the woodwork."

Flo took a sip of water. "I'm sorry to hear it, Chief."

Stuckey took a deep breath and rubbed his eyes. "What am I doing? This isn't your problem. I'm sorry. Anyhow, here are the forms I need you to look over." He pushed them across his desk. He clicked the tip of a pen and set it next to them. "We need your signature on—"

BOOM!

An ear-splitting explosion tore through the air. The walls shook and dust rained down from the ceiling tiles.

Flo doubled over, covering her ears and pinching her eyes shut. She gagged on a breath of choking dust.

Stuckey appeared at her side and took her by the elbow. He yelled something.

But there was no sound to his voice.

Only the ringing in her head.

He yelled again and she read his lips.

Come on!

She nodded and let him pull her up.

He threw open the door and a cloud of white dust billowed inside.

Like a January blizzard.

She couldn't see more than a few feet to any side.

Stuckey pulled her forward and she let herself be led. This was his place. He would know where to go whether he could see anything or not.

They stumbled through the grainy fog for what felt like forever.

She bumped into him as he abruptly stopped.

Only then did she notice their surroundings.

They were in the middle of all the desks where the meeting had been going on.

She glanced up at the light pouring through the missing roof.

Dust swirled up and out as the air outside vacuumed out the small space.

Stuckey let go of her and dropped to his knees to check something.

Flo looked over his broad shoulders and sucked in a quick breath.

One of the deputies-what was her name? Tammy?-lay on the floor with half her face peeled away. Pale white bone showed where the cheek and chin should've been. Her lips were gone revealing bleeding gums and missing teeth. The woman's jaw quivered as blood spilled out of her mouth.

Flo lurched to the side as her stomach heaved. She swallowed hard.

Stuckey spun her around and yelled in her face. His thick mustache was powdered white like Santa Claus.

He yelled again but Flo couldn't understand.

BOOM!

Another explosion slammed into her side and flung her across the room.

She hit something, pinwheeled, and crashed into a wall.

Something cracked inside her.

Something deep. Something vital.

The world tilted back and forth.

She took a breath and gurgled instead.

Stuckey appeared above her with blood leaking out of both ears. A gash at his hairline poured blood down into one eye. He swiped it away and hauled her up over his shoulder.

She bounced along as he stumbled outside. Every jostle sent a shockwave of agony through her chest and head.

The air cleared and she realized they were outside on the street.

Stuckey gently laid her on the pavement with his jacket under her head.

Her head fell to the side and she caught a glimpse of the police station.

Of what used to be the police station.

It was gone. Most of it, at least.

More rubble than structure.

A person ran out from the alley next to the ruins. He hurried across the street. Another followed and soon a dozen or more had fled across the street and disappeared between the buildings on the other side.

Another man appeared.

Even with her vision swimming and going dark, she recognized this one.

Alexei Volkov.

She blinked as darkness overtook her.

Something was wrong.

She tried to figure out what, but the answer eluded her.

Then it came with horrifying clarity.

She couldn't see, hear, or feel anything.

Even the painful ringing inside her head was gone.

5

EMILY WILDER stood at the window peering out over the hospital parking lot and the ocean beyond. A brown haze hung high in the afternoon sky. It should've been beautiful scenery, but it wasn't. Even an island with the natural splendor of Kodiak appeared diminished and depressing.

She touched the silver heart pendant that hung from a slender silver necklace around her neck. It had been her mother's once. Long ago. So far back it felt like someone else's life.

"Emily, please don't go."

She turned to face Marco. The sight of his battered body in a loose hospital gown made her heart twist. "I have to."

"I just don't understand what you—"

"She might still be alive, Marco. If there's even one chance in a million that she is, I have to take it."

Marco's lips pressed together in a tight frown. His

concern for her tried to melt her heart, tried to weaken her resolve, but she didn't let it.

Now was not the time for dwelling on what might've been.

Not with an ill grandmother back home who could be alive and enduring who knew what. And if she was dead, Emily wasn't sure she wanted to go on as the last remaining member of her family.

There came a point when any rational person had to consider that maybe it wasn't worth it anymore.

Having lost her mother and father at such a young age, family was more precious to her than most. And her grandmother was all she had left.

Marco reached for her hand and she let him take it. Strength and warmth seeped into her. He cupped her cheek with his other hand. The tenderness in his eyes made her heart race and her head spin. "Chief Stuckey said they found out San Francisco is gone. What are the chances that Oakland survived?"

Emily yanked her hand away and fought to regain her footing. She was going, and that's all there was to it. She pulled away and turned back to the bleak scene beyond the window. "There's a boat leaving the marina tonight for Anchorage. If I have any chance of catching a ride south to Seattle, it'll be from there."

Marco sidled up next to her and a crisp soap scent mixed with something deeper, wilder. He brushed a lock of hair behind her ear.

His touch made her heart skip a beat.

She was acting like a giddy school girl.

Pathetic.

She gritted her teeth and did her best to focus on the journey ahead.

"I'm sorry," he said. "I just don't want you to get hurt."

An ache in Emily's chest made her want to give in. To surrender to him. "I know," she said as she turned to him. She rested an open palm on his chest and tried not to notice the firm, sculpted muscle under the thin gown. "Marco, in another time, in another world, maybe we could've—"

"Don't say it," he said with a lopsided grin. "I refuse to be dumped by a girl I'm not even dating."

Emily laughed. A short hard laugh that came out as more of a snort that she hid behind a self-conscious hand.

His eyes grew serious again. "So you're going out on an ocean voyage with none of the gear that keeps sailors safe in the modern day. No radar, GPS, emergency locator beacon, SAT phone, nothing."

Emily shrugged. "Guess so."

Marco closed his eyes. "Great. Just great."

Emily gently punched his chest. "I'll be fine. This may come as a surprise to you, but people have been navigating the oceans of the world for thousands of years before our technology arrived."

"Yeah, and it was a lot more dangerous then." He paused. "Hold on. I've got something for you."

He shuffled over to the tattered backpack that he'd gotten when the reality TV show *Sole Survivor* had begun. She had one just like it... somewhere.

Marco dug through it. "Here it is!" He pulled out a short plastic tube with a cord attached to it.

"What is that?"

He opened the loop and raised it above her head. "May I?"

"You may."

He lowered the loop and let the tube hang on her chest. "It's a water-activated emergency light. Must not have microchips or whatever inside that the EMP fried. I know because I accidentally dropped it in the sink and it nearly blinded me. If it gets wet, it'll light up a super bright yellow. Turns off automatically when it dries out."

Emily turned it over in her hand. "Cool. Where'd you get it?"

Marco grinned in that way that did no good for anybody. "Scavenged it off that crashed Coast Guard chopper we spent the night in."

She remembered. She wouldn't soon forget his warmth pressing against her as she slept.

Mostly slept.

Kind of slept, due to the distracting warmth pressing against her backside.

The thought of leaving that warmth forever made her chest tighten. They would soon be no more than memories for each other.

She let the light rest on her chest. "I have something for you, too." The decision made before she decided against it. She dug through her pack and pulled out the mints tin.

"I get it. I haven't brushed my teeth today."

"It's not that." She opened the lid and unfolded the cloth to reveal the black G-Shock watch her father had given her long ago. One of a matching pair. The other had disappeared with him when he never returned. It hadn't left her wrist for over a decade.

Until the band failed while she was doing the show. She'd placed it in the tin for safekeeping.

She held it up and glanced at the time. Still working fine.

A part of her didn't want to part with it. But that part was hanging on to the distant past.

She put it in his hand and closed his fingers over it. "This is for you. So you can count the minutes until we see each other again."

They both knew those minutes would go on forever.

He looked at it and smiled. "I'll use my watch band to fix it."

"That would be good." It was the right decision. It warmed her heart to know that he would treasure it just as she had.

"Thanks," he said as he drew her into an embrace.

She rested her cheek against him.

His strong arms wrapped around her. Supporting her. The hard muscles making her insides flutter.

"When are you leaving?"

"After sunset. The captain wants to make the journey at night to avoid problems."

"What kind of problems? Wouldn't it be better to be able to see where you're going?"

"Not according to the captain. He's worried about pirates."

"I don't think there have been any Jack Sparrows roaming the seas for at least two hundred years."

Emily looked up and rolled her eyes. "Not the drunken, bow-legged kind. The kind with guns and the willingness to use them now that law enforcement isn't right around the corner."

The smirk melted off Marco's face as he remembered it was no joke at all. With no radios to call for help or aircraft to locate and effect a rescue operation, traveling on the high seas would once again be deadly dangerous.

Marco bit his lip and Emily could tell it was everything he could do to stop from asking her again to stay.

She pulled away. She couldn't get this close. She might give in.

A moment passed and the empty space filled with an awkward silence. One that didn't belong between them but wouldn't leave now that it had arrived.

A bump in the sheet on the hospital bed popped up. The bump slid up the sheet and Oscar scurried out onto the pillow. The adorable little weasel faced the door and tilted his head, listening. His shiny black marble eyes didn't blink.

"Hey, Oscar. Have a good nap?" She said as she reached out to scratch under his chin. She flinched when he nipped her finger and hissed before turning back toward the door.

With rust brown fur and a cream colored belly, he was cute. She had to give him that. But he was the grouchiest little stinker she'd ever met. Marco naming him Oscar made perfect sense.

Marco reached over and Oscar allowed the contact. He arched his head as Marco apparently found a good spot behind his ear. "Hey, buddy."

The weasel darted to the edge of the bed, and reared up on his back legs. Alert and tense.

Someone screamed in the hall outside.

Another voice shouted back.

Emily hurried over and eased the door open. She

didn't want to shove her head out if there was another robbery going down.

She peeked out enough for one eye to peer down the hall.

Nurses and doctors and even civilians were pushing mobile beds inside with red-soaked bodies in each one.

"Marco! Come on! Something's happened!"

6

They left Oscar with the door closed and hurried down
the hall toward the nurse's station and the ER beyond. A
nurse appeared from around the corner and nearly ran
them over with the empty bed she was pushing. "You two!
Get this gurney outside! More wounded are waiting to be
brought in! Now!"

"Got it," Emily said as she and Marco took the bed
and steered it down the hall and out the double door
entrance to the drive through.

A single doctor shouted instructions to a couple of
nurses who hurried between numerous gurneys,
assessing each patient's state. He lifted the blood-soaked
blanket of a man that looked to be wearing the tattered
remains of a uniform.

The doctor grimaced as he shook his head. He flipped
through a stack of green, yellow, red and black tickets in
his hand, tore off a black one and tied it around the
patient's wrist.

Three old trucks sporting more rust than metal were

parked in the drive-thru. A giant of a man that Emily recognized as Chief Stuckey jumped out of the bed of one of the trucks.

"Over here!" he yelled at them.

They rushed the gurney over as he hefted a limp body out of the bed of the truck. He carefully set the woman on the bed and adjusted her lifeless limbs.

"What happened?" Emily asked.

"Bombs at the police station. Two. Get her inside!"

She and Marco hustled the woman inside. White dust had partially plastered over a coating of blood that covered her completely.

Her hair.

Her face.

Her chest.

Her stomach.

Her limbs.

Everywhere.

It didn't seem possible for there to be that much blood.

They left the chaos outside and went straight back into the chaos unfolding inside.

The nurses had recruited a few of the civilians to help out. One was performing CPR on a victim. Another held a blood bag in the air as the nurse inserted the needle into the inside of the victim's elbow.

"Doctor!" Marco shouted. "Hey! Over here!"

She looked up and nodded. "Be there in a minute!" she shouted as she examined the person on the gurney in front of her.

The woman on their gurney moaned and blood bubbled out of her mouth.

"It's okay," Emily said even though it was a lie. "You're gonna be okay." She reached down and pulled the woman's sticky hair out of her eyes. She used her sleeve to wipe away the plaster covering her face and froze when a wipe revealed a cheek missing skin.

Yellow bone glistened through a pool of crimson.

Marco moved closer and took the woman's hand in his. "This is Flo, from the diner!"

Emily realized in horror that he was right. She hadn't recognized the brutalized body as the saucy woman from the diner, but he was right.

"Flo," Marco said as he patted her hand. "You're going to be okay. Just hang on." He looked at the doctor still working across the room. "Doctor! We need you over here. Now!"

The doctor finished tying a red tag around a victim's wrist and looked up. "Coming!" A few seconds later, she skidded to a stop.

Her experienced hands glided over Flo's body and under the fragments of what remained of her clothes. Her eyes pinched shut and her lips pressed tightly together.

Emily grabbed her sleeve without meaning to. "What? How is she?"

The doctor opened her eyes and shook her head. "I'm sorry. I'm so sorry." She flipped through a rainbow of tags until she got to the black ones at the back.

She wrote something on a black tag and tore it off. The stretchy rubber band attached to it snapped. She pulled the rubber band around Flo's wrist and made sure it cinched tight. The doctor started to turn away.

"What are you doing?" Emily asked, even though she already knew.

"Doctor! Over here!" one of the nurses shouted as she leaned onto a victim's chest with all her weight. Blood fountained up and splattered on the floor.

"I'm sorry," the doctor repeated as she hurried over to another victim that apparently had a better chance than Flo.

Marco kissed Flo's hand. "You're an amazing woman. I don't know you that well, but I know that."

Flo's head flopped to the side as she focused on him. Her eyes dilated as a weak smile crossed her face. "I liked you..." blood gurgled out of her mouth. "... from the start."

Marco forced a smile. It was the fake yet sincere smile of someone who pities the tragedies of another. "Just hold on, okay?"

Flo licked blood from her lips. "Too late for that. Tell my son—".

Her eyes blinked shut and stayed that way for what felt like forever.

Emily glanced up at Marco and they shared a sorrow that only a moment like that could create.

"I love him," Flo said through more blood gurgling out of her mouth. "I love him to the moon..."

Emily touched her shoulder, gently, not knowing where or what might cause her pain.

A single tear, clear as water and wet as rain, welled up out of the corner of Flo's eye. It broke free and streamed down her temple, clearing a trail through the white coating of dust, before it disappeared into the bloody thatch of her hair.

"And back," Emily finished for her. She leaned down and kissed the damp streak. As she backed away, Flo's eyes caught hers.

The loss echoing through them stabbed into Emily's chest.

And then she was gone.

Eyes as empty as glass marbles.

Beautiful, yet hollow.

Glistening with gathered tears that would never spill.

Flo was gone.

7

The full moon hung on the horizon, diffused behind a perpetual gray gauze curtain. She was late.

Maybe too late.

Maybe already missed the boat.

Leaving Marco and the tragedy at the hospital behind hadn't been easy. She'd left a part of her heart back there.

But that was the life she'd always known. Slices of her heart left to die as those she cared about were ripped away.

This was no different.

And a cold, hard part inside her chest welcomed it.

She'd made it all the way to the south side of town, slipping from shadow to shadow, avoiding the few people that happened across her path at this late hour.

Emily rounded the building which opened onto the marina beyond and breathed a sigh of relief.

The old fishing boat she'd signed onto was still there. Dark silhouettes hurried back and forth on the dock next to it, pulling lines up and tossing them on the deck. The engine revved and the pale ghost eased away from the dock.

Emily broke into a sprint, shouting as she ran. "Wait! Wait for me!"

The engine slowed as a hushed voice responded. "Quiet down!"

The boat continued drifting away, the space between it and the dock growing larger with every second.

Emily hit the end of the dock at a full sprint and launched into the air.

She flew over the three feet of dark water separating her from the boat and made it. Her momentum slammed her into a dark figure on the deck.

"Whoa, now!" the man said as he absorbed the impact and kept her from breaking an ankle or worse. "And who are you?'

"Emily Wilder," she said through winded breaths. "I made arrangements with the captain."

She recognized the thick beard tinged with gray and thick glasses covering dark eyes.

He nodded as he let her loose. "So I did. Welcome aboard. Didn't think you were going to make it."

"Neither did I."

He looked backward over his shoulder. "Come on now! Let's get this rust bucket moving!"

Emily worked to slow her breathing. "I thought we were supposed to be quiet."

"Yeah. You are. But I'm the captain. I can damn well do what I please." He laughed gruffly and spun away. "I said get us underway!"

Who he was yelling at, Emily couldn't see.

He opened a side door to what passed for the bridge

and yelled something more colorful. An imaginatively descriptive insult that could've won a poetry contest if it hadn't been so laced with vulgarity.

The engines sputtered, roared for a few seconds, and died.

They clicked off, sputtered again, roared like a hurricane, and died again.

Great. She was on a boat to nowhere.

The door to the bridge flew open. The captain stomped out and turned toward the back of the large fishing boat. "If I have to come down there, heads will roll!"

The engines sputtered again and this time caught.

The boat lurched forward and Emily grabbed a hold of the rail or else would've landed on her backside.

"That's better," the captain muttered as he returned to his station.

The vibration of the engines echoed up through her boots as she stared out over the dark water beyond the marina. The captain had told her they'd hug the shore before clearing Kodiak and then head north into the open ocean. If all went well, they'd be safely at Anchorage by day break.

It was the "if all went well" part that worried her.

She walked to the front of the boat and leaned out over the side.

The pale moonlight reflected off the white water peeling away from the boat's side. The marina shrank into the distance as they got underway.

Emily dropped her pack by her feet. She took a deep breath and wondered for the hundredth time if she was doing the right thing.

Or if she was a complete and total idiot.

Why was she so determined to get back to Oakland?

That was easy.

Her grandmother.

The only family she had left.

But did she have a chance of actually making it?

Saying it was a long shot was giving it a sheen of optimism that it logically didn't have.

She wouldn't give up. She knew that.

But that didn't mean she'd make it.

And what if, against all odds, she somehow did get back home?

What did she expect to find?

She pushed a stray lock of hair behind one ear. The cool ocean breeze chilled her cheeks and nose. She inhaled deeply and enjoyed the cold filling her lungs.

What if Oakland was gone?

Just like San Francisco.

Just like so many other cities around the world.

Emily slammed her fist into the railing and, too late, realized it was a dumb idea when her fingers came back ringing with pain.

Thinking about what might or might not happen didn't help anything.

She was on a boat.

A boat that would get her one step closer to home.

And if, by some miracle, she actually made it back to her apartment in Oakland, then she would know the truth.

The reality of whether or not she was alone in the world.

She'd lived most of her life knowing what it meant to

be alone. Knowing that she could depend on no one but herself.

To allow her heart to feel was a dangerous vulnerability. One she avoided by necessity. Her heart had but one soft spot left.

Her grandmother.

And that small, unprotected spot was enough to bring her home.

Or to die trying to get there.

8

BOB RANDY turned over on his side and the slicing ache in his stitched wrists jolted up his arms. He groaned, despite not wanting to draw any attention from Rome. Aside from the discomfort, it was the overwhelming weakness that sapped his energy. Doing the smallest thing required the greatest effort.

Losing a ton of blood did that to a person.

The inside of his nose itched and he would've picked it if he wasn't already so exhausted from turning over. Instead, he settled for crinkling his nose a few times.

The feint stirrings in his bladder promised a trip to the bathroom in the not too distant future. That was gonna be fun. And without Flo to help him, the trip to the toilet was going to be like doing the Iditarod for a normal man.

There was no chance he was going to ask Rome for help. He'd rather open the stitches in his wrists and finish bleeding out before doing that.

Besides, the boy wasn't going to help.

Misery loved company, but what if the company didn't love you back?

The boy in a man's body sat at the small round table that straddled the apartment's kitchen and living room. There wasn't enough room for it to properly fit in either. "The voice that sounds astonishingly like gas exiting a donkey's butt should know that I don't care."

Bob bit his lip as he finished the quarter turn from his back.

The couch was more boards than padding and wasn't all that different from sleeping on a workbench.

But still, Flo didn't have to let him stay here. Nobody could've blamed her if she'd refused to let him come near her home again. But she'd taken him in.

And here was infinitely better than his room at the roach-infested hotel called The Weary Traveler.

It should've been renamed to The Desperate and Dead Tired Traveler.

That would've more accurately described the kind of person who would choose to stay in a room like he'd had.

And that was before he'd spilled a few quarts of his blood all over the bed and floor in a pathetic attempt to end his own pathetic life.

How in everything holy had he ended up here?

Half-dead and somewhat recovering on an uncomfortable couch in Kodiak, Alaska? Lying a few feet away from a fat kid that would prefer he died than take up another second of his or his mother's time.

How?

His life had been so much better than this!

Not so long ago, he was more powerful than Steven Spielberg, for Christ's sake!

He was Mr. Hollywood, pulling in millions and choosing the stars that would be accepting next year's Oscars.

First Barflies and then Schwartzfeld.

Two of the most successful, long running network series ever created!

All his doing!

Who else had thought of the bar where everybody knew your name?

Who else had thought of creating a show about nothing?

No one else. That's who.

Bob's temples pulsed as his heart pounded through constricted veins. The room swayed as a wave of dizziness washed over him.

He laid his head on a lumpy pillow and slowed his breathing.

As his breathing and pulse steadied, he watched Rome doing something at the table. It took a few minutes, but he eventually felt well enough to not pass out. He gritted his teeth and sat up.

Lancing pain shot through the stitched wounds in each wrist. Though he managed to get through it without making a sound this time.

He took a drink of water from the cup on the coffee table.

Rome's eyes darted over and back to whatever he was doing. "The mouth that's drinking my family's water should find another family to leech off of."

Bob swallowed a few gulps and let his head clear. The minute change in altitude nearly had his balance swimming again. After it cleared, he decided to say something.

"Listen Rome, I—"

Rome held up a hand with the palm facing toward him. "The sound that reminds me of two goats getting it on needs to shut up."

Bob shook his head.

It had been like this all day since his mother had gone.

With her here, Rome was somewhat civil. With her gone, not so much. That he hadn't picked Bob up and thrown him out the door was something.

Not a lot.

But still something.

Every time Bob had tried to extend an olive branch, it had been met with a flaming torch.

So Bob decided on a different approach.

"What are you working on? Looks like improvised defensive measures for the home."

Rome's hands froze in mid-air. He turned to Bob with narrowed eyes. "Are you telling me you know about defensive measures for the home during a zombie apocalypse?"

Bob nodded. "I know some."

Rome rolled his eyes. "Yeah, right."

Bob sensed an opening. He knew a few things from a failed zombie tv series that he'd pushed over a decade ago.

Bad timing on that one. It got cancelled halfway through the season. *Zomburbia*. Seemed like a catchy name for a series set in an apocalyptic suburbia, but the Nielsen ratings didn't come through. And then a few years later, *The Walking Dead* took off like a rocket.

Timing was everything in life.

The right angle at the wrong time was the same thing as the right woman at the wrong time.

Neither one was going to get in bed.

Bob scanned his memories of that series and landed on a thought he knew a kid like this would appreciate. "Well, what's the easiest way for a zombie to break into a house?"

Rome shook his head like Bob was an idiot. "Duh. The windows."

Bob nodded, and almost smiled. The kid was warming up. "Exactly. Boarding them up is the obvious thing but that's probably not a good idea with no electricity and already fairly dim light coming from outside."

"Okay. So?"

"So, you take a two by six and hammer nails through it. Then you have to place it correctly. If you have a shrub or whatever outside the window, you put it below the window with the sharp points up. There are different ways you can secure it, but you get the idea."

Rome's eyes slowly widened. "That would seriously hurt. Nails through the bottom of your feet? Oh man!" He made a face like he'd just stepped on the board. "That's awesome!"

He set down the roll of duct tape in his hand. "You like zombie stuff?"

Bob nodded. He didn't. But whatever. "I produced a series a long time ago about a zombie apocalypse in suburbia."

Rome nodded with enthusiasm. "Cool. What was the name of it?"

"Zomburbia."

Rome laughed so hard he choked a few times. "That's

awful. I mean unbelievably stupid. Who would watch that?"

Despite himself, Bob chuckled. "Yeah, in retrospect, it probably could've had a better name."

"Not probably," Rome said as he stood up. "Definitely." He headed for the front door."

"Where are you going?"

His easy demeanor stiffened. "What? Are you my mother?"

Bob raised both hands and winced at the twinge in his wrists. "No. Just wondering. That's all."

Rome's broad shoulders relaxed. "Going to get some boards and nails from our storage closet out back. I like your idea. Be back in a few."

Bob didn't respond as the kid wasn't looking for his approval or even a comment.

A few minutes later and Rome marched back through carrying a load of lumber and a bucket full of tools. He set everything on the floor and got straight to work.

After working for a while in silence, he looked up at Bob. "You ever heard of a tv series called The Edge of Survival?"

Bob nodded.

Of course, he had.

Who hadn't?

Where the writing for *The Walking Dead* had left the fans moaning louder than the zombies in recent years, *The Edge of Survival* had burst onto the scene and grabbed huge numbers. His boss, old boss now by the looks of things, had gotten pitched on it several years ago and turned it down.

And he'd regretted missing out on that cash cow ever since.

It was one of Bob's favorite stories to bring up at lunches with other disgruntled employees at the network.

"Yeah, I know it. Haven't watched more than a few episodes, but what I did see was good. Great storyline. Action-packed and twisted in the best way."

Rome nodded. "Yeah, I loved it. For three years, I watched every episode the minute it came out each week. Every episode except for the season three finale. I purposefully waited because I had to miss the first half. I was going to watch it on Saturday night and savor every beautifully horrible minute."

He shook his head and continued pounding nails through a board.

Bob waited.

And waited some more.

"So what happened?"

Rome slammed the hammer down at a nail, missed it and smacked the flat of the board. "I missed it! I missed the freaking season three finale! And now, with the EMP and global nuclear war or whatever this is, I'm probably never going to get to find out what happened! Never!"

"The show was based on a book series. Didn't you read those first?"

Rome shook his head in disgust. "I don't read books for fun, man."

Bob managed to force a bubbling laugh into a cough and clearing of the throat. "That's too bad."

"Yeah, it really sucks. Mason's daughter and her boyfriend were sentenced to be hanged at Alcatraz while the crazy cult priest guy was going to do the final blessings. You know he was going to do something messed up."

Someone banged on the door.

Rome jumped up and disappeared into Flo's bedroom. He returned with the black nine millimeter Beretta that Bob had stolen less than two days ago. Rome flashed him an angry look before moving to the door.

More banging from whoever was outside.

Rome stood next to the door with the pistol at the ready.

"Rome! You in there? It's me, Chief Stuckey."

9

The banging continued as Rome remained frozen. The kid must not have been certain whether or not he recognized the voice.

Bob waved at the door. "It's him. Open it."

Rome whisper-shouted back, "Shut up, old man!"

Through the door, Stuckey continued. "It is me, Rome. Please open the door. I've got news about your mother."

Rome tucked the pistol into his waistband and hurriedly unlocked and opened the door.

It swung open and the enormous form of Chief Stuckey filled the frame. "Mind if I come in?"

Rome stepped to the side and muttered something.

Bob considered the two men standing next to each other. They said everything was bigger in Texas. Well, Alaska made Texas look small.

Stuckey entered, taking in the dim interior with a sweep of his eyes. He turned back to face Rome, and his eyes dropped. He shook his head while reaching for

Rome's pistol. "Don't ever tuck a gun there. For the love of the girl that may someday be your wife. I've seen idiots shoot their balls off doing that."

"Oh, okay," Rome said with a horrified look on his face. The horror passed and the concern returned. "Where's my mom? She's been gone all day. She went to see you this afternoon and hasn't been back since. That was five or six hours ago!"

Stuckey placed a hand on the boy's shoulder. "I know, son. I have terrible..." He swallowed hard as his mouth clamped shut. "Terrible news. Your mother is no longer with us."

Rome flung the hand off his shoulder. "What do you mean 'No longer with us?' Where did she go?"

Stuckey's eyes fell to the floor. "She's dead. I tried to save her, but she'd lost too much blood."

Rome's face lost all color but one.

The one that remained when all meaning leeched out of life.

The pale oval floating in the dim light looked like a ghost. An empty, bloodless thing. A hole tore the oval open near the bottom third. "How? She was just here a few hours ago. How could she be dead?"

Stuckey shook his head as he watched the tornado of emotions taking over the boy. "Someone bombed the police station. Two bombs. One of them went off when your mother and I were nearby."

Bob remembered they'd heard something that afternoon. They'd wondered at first but then written it off as a jalopy back-firing.

Rome slumped and Stuckey guided him into a chair at the kitchen table. "A bomb? My mother?

What?" He stared at his hands like they weren't his own.

Stuckey pulled a chair out and sat down beside him. He glanced at Bob an instant and then back to Rome. "I got her to the hospital as fast as I could. But it was too much for her. She passed a short time later."

Silence smothered the room.

The type of silence that scratched you raw like sheet of sandpaper.

Huge tears spilled down the boy's cheeks.

Bob stood and shuffled over to him. "I'm so sorry."

Stuckey nodded. "I am too. She was a wonderful person and brought so much to this community."

Rome shook his head as the tears splashed onto the table top. "She can't be dead. She can't be. I just saw her."

Stuckey reached across the table and squeezed his shoulder. "I know there's nothing I can say or do that will help, but if you need anything, let me know."

Wracking sobs jerked Rome's body in sudden, violent spasms. "Need anything? I need my mother!"

Snot dangled from his nose as he continued shaking his head, refusing to accept the new and terrible future.

"I'm so sorry, Rome," Bob said in a soft voice.

And to his relief, he truly was.

His chest felt like someone had dropkicked his heart. Flo was the kind of good Samaritan that rarely existed anymore. She'd saved his sorry life, even after he'd stolen from her and ran away like the selfish coward he was.

Rome swiped at his eyes and face. "Where is her body? I want to see it."

Stuckey nodded understanding. "It's at the hospital."

Rome bolted up and grabbed his pistol from where

the chief had set it on the table. "I'm going to see her." He turned toward the door but Stuckey held out a hand.

"Whoa. Hold up a second. Let's leave the weapon here. I don't need you walking around with a loaded pistol feeling the way you're feeling."

Fury flashed through Rome's eyes as he took a step back to keep Stuckey from grabbing the gun.

Stuckey raised both hands. "Easy! I've got an old truck that has been requisitioned for police service. I can drive you there. Let's leave the pistol here."

Rome's eyes darted to Bob. "Not a chance. It goes with me."

Stuckey glanced over to Bob with a question in his eyes.

A question Bob had no desire to answer.

That was who he used to be.

He was different now.

Not like a new body and brain.

Well, maybe like a worse body and a better brain.

Or something.

Bob jumped in with a solution before things went wrong. "Chief, how about you hold on to the gun while you're taking Rome. Then, you can give it back to him whenever you drop him off."

Stuckey nodded. "Good idea." He carefully watched Rome's movement, especially the hand holding the gun. "That work for you, Rome? It'll be with us the whole time."

Rome stared with suspicion. "So you won't take it for good?"

Stuckey shook his head. "Not a chance. I just want to hang on to it while we visit the hospital."

The tension in Rome's body eased a little. His shoulders slumped and the hand holding the gun dropped a couple of inches. "Fine." He held the gun out with the muzzle pointed at the floor."

"Thank you, son. I appreciate what you're going through."

A spasm of hate flashed through Rome's face. "How could you possibly understand what I'm feeling?"

The chief coughed into his hand and then wiped it on his pants. "Because those bombs took out the entire Kodiak police force. People I've known, worked with, and been friends with for over thirty years."

He wrapped an arm over Rome's shoulder. "We're all hurting, son."

"Yeah."

"You ready to go right now?"

Rome grabbed an insulated jacket draped over a nearby chair. "Yeah. I'm ready." He turned to Bob before heading to the door. "Don't touch anything. I swear to God I won't be as forgiving as my mother."

Stuckey sent another confused look Bob's way.

Bob put his right hand over his heart. "I promise you I will be here. And I won't touch a thing."

Rome threw open the door and stomped through.

And in fewer minutes than was fair for a kid so young, he would see his dead mother.

He would know she was gone forever.

A dull ache clenched at Bob's chest. He squeezed a hand over it.

Just like his own father had clutched at his chest when his heart had failed and he'd collapsed and died at the feet of the boy Bob used to be.

10

DR. ZHANG YONG laid in his bunk with the covers pulled over his head. The soft hum of the air exchanger masked the silent heaving of his chest. Wet tears streamed down his temples and soaked into the thin pillow. Another sob and his torso clenched tight.

Despite his anguish, he refused to let so much as a murmur escape. Nothing that might alert anyone passing in the halls outside to the depths of his condition.

He winced as the bottom sheet caught on the stitches at his hairline and pulled at the wound. It was mild pain resulting from the fall he'd taken in the collider ring before stepping through a time gate. A wound that was two days old for him, but that had happened over ten years ago in this world. It hurt, but it was nothing approaching the anguish in his soul.

Hari Ganesh was gone.

Only a day had passed since his death. And yet thousands of years had also passed.

They said time healed all wounds.

But what if time wasn't bound in one direction?

What if old wounds could be revisited?

What if a second chance made it possible to avoid the wound in the first place?

That's what Hari had done. And yet his effort had created a new wound. Substituted one for another.

It was like the scales of life required balance. Hari had stolen the weight of Zhang's death and then repaid it with his own.

One lived.

One died.

The grief weighing on Zhang's heart would've dragged him down into a morose, insufferable abyss had it not been for Hari's last words.

The world needs you! Now more than ever!

Upon arriving in the present day, he'd discovered the world did indeed have great needs. But he was no savior. No messiah. He had no answers for the ruin that humanity had brought upon itself.

Who was he kidding?

Save the world?

He didn't even know how to lead the project. He was now the de facto director of Project Hermes and he had no clear idea of what to do next.

Visionary plans and leadership had always been Hari's role. He'd been in charge since the project began. And Zhang had always been a capable and trusted assistant. Always the follower. He'd always given his best as much out of scientific curiosity as out of a personal obligation to Hari for all that the older man had done for him. Hari's death didn't negate that debt.

That alone kept him from crawling into a dark hole somewhere and waiting for his flesh to wither into dust.

He hadn't slept last night after returning to the facility. He didn't expect to sleep tonight either. His thoughts circled again and again around the final minutes of Hari's life.

He'd been a friend, a colleague, a mentor, a father in many ways. And in the end, he'd even been his personal savior.

A short-faced bear had been seconds away from attacking Zhang and Hari had offered himself as a sacrifice.

And a sacrifice he'd become.

The sickening crunch of cracking bones haunted his waking dreams.

The comms panel in his room beeped. For such an advanced facility, the hardwired communications network was exceedingly rudimentary. No display. No way to tell who was calling.

He considered not responding. Hiding in the dark in his room like a child. A vision of Hari's face, frowning with stern disapproval appeared in his mind.

Zhang wiped his eyes with the blanket and sat up. His movement caused a dim light in the ceiling to turn on. He coughed several times to clear his throat of mucus and hoped that when he did speak, his voice wouldn't crack or otherwise give away his emotional state. He reached over to the panel and tapped the answer button.

"This is Doctor Zhang."

"Sorry to disturb you, doctor. This is Captain Whitaker."

"What can I do for you, Captain?"

"Sir, I've got the team assembled and provisioned. We'll be ready to move out at first light. Have you had time to consider what we discussed?"

Zhang's mind was so numbed with grief, it took him a second to remember.

Oh, yes. Captain Whitaker had suggested they send out teams to get readings on several of the nearest time gates. A preliminary data-gathering mission. Zhang had agreed on the spot.

It was what Whitaker had suggested next that tripped him up.

That he take a team through the nearest time gate to investigate what was on the other side.

Zhang had immediately vetoed the idea, and he wasn't about to change his mind now.

"Captain, I don't think it's a good idea."

"I understand your reservations. I do. But we've got numerous gates to other times, and possibly other worlds as far as we know, in our own backyard. The closest is half a click from our main entrance. That's a serious security risk. Who knows what might come through any minute."

Zhang knew what might come through. A giant bear that could remove a man's head with a single bite.

"Doctor, I'm talking about a simple reconnaissance mission. Get in, take a look around, and get out."

"What about what happened to Hari? Do you want more people to die?"

His voice hardened. "Of course not. And Dr. Ganesh would be alive today if he'd waited for his security detail."

A moment of tense silence passed.

"I'm sorry. I know how much he meant to you."

"Then you'll understand why I'm reluctant—"

"Sir, we're professionals with the training and equipment to carry out the mission. I wouldn't suggest it if I didn't think it was important."

This was why Zhang wasn't a leader. He didn't want to make the tough calls, one way or the other. He didn't know what was best.

"Fine. Do it."

"Thank you. I'll let you get to sleep now. Whitaker out."

Get to sleep?

He was about to lay back down when comms beeped again.

What did Whitaker want this time? To drive a column of tanks through the gate?

Zhang punched the answer button. "What now, Captain?"

"Sorry?"

A different voice. A woman's.

"Who is this?"

"It's Collins in Operations. I know it's late, but I have something I need you to see."

Zhang pinched his eyes shut. All he wanted to do was disappear. And that was the one thing he couldn't do.

"I'll be there in a few minutes."

He clicked the line off before a reply came through.

A few more than a few minutes later, he arrived in Operations and saw that only a skeleton crew was on duty at this late hour.

Collins must have heard the door because she looked back and waved him over.

Zhang stopped at her terminal, looking over her shoulder at the monitor.

"The topside antennae arrays on the island have come in with the latest weather forecast." She traced a finger along a curved line overlaying a map of Alaska and the ocean to the west. "See this?"

"Yes, of course." Zhang failed at trying to hide the irritable bite in his voice.

"This is our best projection of a weather front coming in from the southwest." She slid her finger over a timeline, swiping backwards through the last few days. "It's coming directly from Tokyo and it'll be here in approximately two and a half days."

"What do you mean *approximately*?"

"Well, we're only getting data from the hardened arrays on the island. We have no satellite data or supplementary data from the region of Japan. We're combining our data with historical weather patterns for this time of year to run a forecast simulation. This is the result."

"So, it's a guess?"

"It's a good guess. It could arrive a little early or a little later than our projection. But there is a high probability that it will arrive."

Zhang let out a slow breath.

Tokyo was a pile of carbonized ash. They'd picked up that much from various shortwave transmissions sent out by independent HAM operators. And assuming the reports were true, a storm system passing over it would suck up huge amounts of radioactive particles.

And in two and a half days, it was going to unleash those same particles on the town of Kodiak.

Not enough time had passed to render it even remotely safe.

Anyone exposed to the fallout would be in trouble. Depending on how much and how concentrated it turned out to be, they could be looking at a mass die off starting within days.

There were six thousand people in that town.

Six thousand lives that were two and a half days away from a nightmare worse than the one they'd just survived.

11

MARCO MORALES sat up in the hospital bed and stared out the window at the dim, cold sunrise. The sun returning for another day was usually something to celebrate. It had been a constant and recurring relief for mankind for hundreds of thousands of years.

But today, it brought only misery.

Emily was gone.

Out on the ocean somewhere.

Dead or alive.

He would never know.

A squeak from beneath the bed sheet drew his attention.

He lifted the paper-like sheet and saw Oscar curled into a ball. His tiny paws twitched as he probably dreamed of stealing more of Marco's bait.

How many grasshoppers had the little stinker stolen? Enough to cost Marco a few meals. That was for sure. And the way the little scamp popped them into his mouth and crunched down like potato chips. Marco had been furious the first few times. All before they'd decided to become partners.

It felt like he'd met the cute, little grouch a lifetime ago.

Before the world ended.

During a reality TV show game where the winner went home with a million dollars.

And he'd needed that money as much or more than any of the others.

But now, none of that mattered.

He'd never see home again. Never see the green rolling hills west of Baker, Montana that had been his family's land for generations.

As much as that hurt, and it twisted in his gut, losing Emily hurt more.

Marco eased his hand down and gently petted the sleeping weasel. At least this guy hadn't abandoned him.

Marco's lips curled into a snarl as he caught himself using that word.

Abandoned.

A lingering coal of resentment warmed his belly.

His ex, Justine, had dumped him less than two months ago, but that was definitely so long ago that it no longer mattered. His heart ached for Emily.

But were his feelings for her genuine? Or were they just the needy grasping of a broken heart on the rebound?

Again, it didn't matter because both were gone. Justine had gone to Los Angeles. She, like it, was probably nothing more than toxic dust now.

And Emily was probably lost at sea. Or sunk. Or

murdered by pirates out to take advantage of the lawless world.

"Come on, man!" He punched the bed in disgust and the weasel bounded into the air screeching like mad. He landed on all fours with his tail erect and ready for an attack. "Sorry, buddy."

He threw his legs off the side and was about to stand when a sharp set of fangs pierced his finger. "Ouch!"

Oscar looked up and bared his teeth, hissing.

Marco pinched the bitten pinkie. "I said I was sorry. Jeez."

The weasel hissed again and then burrowed under the pillow until all that remained was a twitching tail. Then it too disappeared.

Marco shook his head. "You're pushing your luck around here. You may just wake up someday and find yourself on your own. I'm just saying."

A muffled hiss responded from below the pillow.

Marco laughed and felt a flood of tension drain out of his chest. The truth was that the weasel was now his best and only friend.

What kind of messed up life was that?

He shuffled toward the bathroom to relieve a full bladder. It took a minute to get going but then felt like it took an hour to finish up.

He went back to the bed, but then decided to stretch a bit before climbing back in. He reached for the ceiling and his back and shoulders complained from the abuse of the last several days.

Not to be left out, his feet were sore and his legs ached. He leaned over and touched the white tiled floor. The muscles in the back of his legs screamed like he'd run two marathons yesterday. He exhaled slowly, accepting the discomfort and dropping deeper into the stretch.

A painful pounding in his head made him cut the exercise short. Like a headache on steroids.

He stood up, rubbing the side of his head where the pain seemed to be centered.

BANG! BANG!

BANG!

Gunshots.

Not loud enough to be directly outside the hospital room door.

But definitely inside the building somewhere.

He scanned the room and located his unstrung bow leaning up in the corner. A quiver with several arrows hanging off the chair next to it.

In seconds, he had the bow strung, an arrow nocked and the quiver slung over his shoulder.

A chirp from the bed and he saw Oscar with his head poking out from beneath the pillow.

"Stay put. I'm going to check it out."

Oscar wriggled out and leaped from the edge of the bed onto Marco's shoulder. His tiny claws scratched across Marco's skin as he found his balance.

"Can't you ever listen?"

Oscar squeaked and nipped at Marco's earlobe.

Marco eased the door open. Through the two inch crack, he peered down the hall toward the nurse's station.

Strange.

Nobody was there.

There was always at least one person behind the desk and usually a few.

"You're not going," Marco said as he separated the weasel from his gown. Tiny claws broke free like a strip of velcro coming apart. He tossed the screeching weasel onto the bed and slipped into the hallway.

The door closed before the weasel made it back.

Marco kept close to the wall with the bow raised and ready.

Shouting in the distance made him freeze and swing the bow back and forth as he searched for a threat.

Nothing.

A nurse ran into the hallway coming from the ER. She screamed as she spotted Marco.

BANG. BANG. BANG.

The white fabric of her shirt turned red as she pitched forward and crashed to the floor.

The man who'd shot her came into view.

Marco sighted the bow and let fly.

TWANG!

A second later and the arrow punched into the man's body. He stumbled back, staring in disbelief at the shaft extending from his chest. He started to grasp the shaft and collapsed.

Marco nocked another arrow and hurried down the corridor toward the ER wing beyond. To where the few survivors from the bombing were being treated.

Screams and shouts echoed down the hall toward him.

He pushed through the double doors as more gun shots cracked and more screams followed.

He pivoted around a corner with the bow raised, sighted a man pointing a gun at a doctor and let fly.

The arrow hit him in the neck. The doomed man

gagged and choked as blood poured out of his mouth. He spun around trying to grab at the shaft. He fell off balance and slammed into a nearby wall. The impact smashed the side of the shaft and tore his throat open.

He fell to the floor clutching at the crimson gushing down his front.

Marco had another arrow nocked before the doomed man realized an arrow was lodged in his throat. He pivoted further around the corner and spotted another man on the far side of the ER that he recognized.

The man threw open the curtain to a treatment bay, lifted his pistol and fired two shots at whoever was within.

Bullets pinged off the wall next to Marco's head.

He ducked back into cover.

How did he know that murderer?

The metallic scrape of a curtain being thrown back was followed by two more shots.

He was murdering the survivors of the bombing.

Marco charged out of the hall with the bow raised and ready.

Shots fired and bullets punched through the air where his chest had been an instant before.

He sighted the man with greasy, stringy hair and let fly.

Another man carrying a rifle happened to step into the flight path and the arrow took him in the ribs.

He stumbled, clutching at his side while the man with stringy hair realized he was under attack.

He spun toward Marco and his black eyes flashed as he fired.

Marco dove behind a long desk and rolled to a stop.

He had another arrow nocked and pointed at the corner where any second the man would show.

One shot to the eye would do it.

He waited with the arrow drawn.

And then he remembered the face.

That guy had been one of the contestants on *Sole Survivor*. What was his name? He couldn't remember and it didn't matter.

Wait.

Charlie.

Charlie from Tennessee.

He remembered because Charlie had asked him if he knew anything about training dogs. After Marco had said not much, he'd replied that it wasn't so different from training any other beast.

And that had been the end of their conversation because it hadn't taken any longer for Marco to realize they weren't going to click.

So what was Charlie doing murdering these people?

The doors leading to the ER crashed open and Chief Stuckey barreled through. The pump-action shotgun in his hands went off a second later.

The wet sounds of mangled flesh hitting the floor the proof that he'd hit his target.

He racked the shotgun and fired again, cycling through several rounds before ducking back behind the corner for cover.

He looked down and saw Marco pinned down into the cover behind the desk.

Screams and gunfire filled the air.

Stuckey yelled to Marco. "On three!"

The upper edge of the desk blew off into fragments as a rain of bullets ripped through it.

Marco ducked lower and nodded.

Stuckey slammed several shells into the loading tube of the shotgun and then yelled the count.

On three, he shifted around the corner blasting targets right and left.

Marco pushed off and made it across to him.

They both took cover as a storm of bullets pounded into the opposite wall, sending fragments of tile and drywall exploding into the air.

The avalanche of gunfire didn't slow down.

Semi-automatic rifles. Hand guns. The deeper boom of at least one shotgun.

There must've been a dozen people firing on them from around the corner.

Stuckey grabbed Marco by the collar and dragged him back through the double doors and hallway beyond. "There's too many of them! Come on!"

12

Marco followed close behind as the chief led the way out of the front entrance to the parking lot beyond.

They ran outside and over to a green truck with Kodiak Police spray painted in white on the side. The old beater must've been forty years old and obviously wasn't a regulation vehicle in the fleet.

Stuckey pulled Marco down behind the tailgate and started shoving shells into the shotgun. "What the hell's going on in there?"

Marco shook his head. "I think they were killing the survivors from the bomb."

Stuckey's eyes went wide and a shell dropped to the pavement. He hastily retrieved it and slotted it home. "Who's doing it?"

"I'm not positive, but I think I recognized one of them. His name is Charlie. He was on the survival show I was on."

The doors at the front entrance shattered from a

gunshot and the crunching of footsteps over glass followed.

Marco peeked around the corner and saw more than a dozen armed men standing on the other side of the parking lot. Charlie stood in front of them all. Nearest to him on his right stood a huge man with a wild copper beard that looked like an animal clinging to his face.

Marco recognized him. The man driving the truck with the trailer and two four wheelers. The man who might've shot them were it not for Emily taking him out.

How did he survive those strange hunters?

The truck had crashed and Emily had pulled Marco to safety, leaving the man to his fate. It appeared his miraculous survival hadn't come without injury though because a pale bandage wrapped around his head covered one ear.

"Red," Chief Stuckey said in a voice seething with rage. "I shoulda killed him a long time ago."

Another man carried a woman over his shoulder and stopped next to Charlie.

Red pulled the limp figure off and held her up with a single arm encircling her chest.

Charlie raised his pistol and touched the muzzle to her temple. "Chief Stuckey! I know you're out there!"

Stuckey muttered a dark curse.

"Come on out and let's have a talk. I think you and me could figure out a mutually beneficial situation."

"I'm going to kill both of them," Stuckey hissed. And I'm going to make it hurt for as long as possible first."

"No?" Charlie shouted as he looked around the parking lot at the vehicles sporadically parked here and there. "Okay. Here's my backup offer. Come out right this second or this fine deputy of yours is going to meet her maker."

Stuckey started to rise, but Marco pulled him down. "Get down! They'll kill you and you know it. That woman is going to die. There's nothing you can do to change it."

Stuckey gritted his jaws and bared his teeth. His face shook with fury.

But he didn't make a move to leave.

"Okay, then," Charlie shouted. "This is your decision."

BANG.

The sound of a body thumped onto the pavement.

Stuckey's hands shook as he gripped the shotgun so hard Marco wondered if he actually might bend it in half.

"You did that, Chief Stuckey!" Charlie yelled. "That was you. Now, the sooner you come around to my way of doing things, the sooner you'll start saving your people."

Marco grabbed Stuckey's jacket at the shoulder. "We have to get out of here. If we try to take them now, we're dead. It's that simple."

Stuckey's eyes didn't indicate he'd heard. They focused on nothing in the distance.

"Come on," Marco said. "We survive this and we can come at them later."

Stuckey still didn't move.

Marco knew he would charge out of cover any second and take out as many of them as he could before they shot him down.

And as heroic a death as that might've been, it wasn't going to help all the other people of Kodiak.

Marco grabbed Stuckey behind the neck and cranked his head over until their eyes locked inches apart.

"Don't die for nothing! Too many people need you."

The fog in Stuckey's eyes cleared and he nodded.

"You ready to run for it?"

Stuckey nodded.

"On three."

Marco counted it down and they both bolted at the same instant.

They dropped over the ridge and slid down the slick grass embankment as bullets zipped overhead.

They hit the street below at a run and didn't slow down until they'd made it to the building across the street and had ducked around the corner.

They both pushed back against the brick wall and sucked in deep breaths.

Marco recovered and checked for signs of pursuit while the chief caught his breath.

The street leading to the hospital parking lot was quiet. It didn't look like they were being chased.

"Marco," the chief said through wheezing breaths.

Marco shuffled back to his side. "You okay?"

"Thanks for that. For stopping me."

Marco nodded and left useless words unspoken where they belonged.

Stuckey squeezed his eyes shut and rubbed them with one hand. "That demon just killed Marjorie. She only joined the force this Spring. Had her whole life ahead of her."

His chest spasmed as he coughed. "They're all dead. Every last person on the force. All except me. How is one man supposed to protect this town from savages like that?"

Stuckey stared at the ground, shaking his head, dazed and murmuring to himself.

Marco didn't know why he did it.

Some things didn't require much thought.

Or explanation.

He faced the chief and squeezed his shoulders. "We aren't gonna let that madman take this town. Are we?"

13

EMILY stood at the railing of the stalled fishing boat, staring out at the curtain of darkness coming their way. The edges of the approaching storm cut hard lines into the relatively lighter surrounding morning sky.

A gust of chill wind whistled over the rail, needling her face and stinging her eyes. She inhaled and the cold seeped into her chest.

Even with so many layers on, the wind managed to tunnel down to her bare skin and cause her arms and legs to break out with goose bumps. A spray of mist hit her lips and she licked away the briny water. The wind dried the moisture on her lips making them feel ready to crack and bleed.

She kicked the side of the boat and cursed. How long had they been stuck here dead in the water?

They hadn't made it more than a couple of hours out of Kodiak before the engines sputtered, choked, and died. The crew had been working on it all through the night and into the morning.

What could possibly take that long to fix?

Did the engines melt down into puddles of metal sludge?

The one time she'd asked the captain for a progress update, he'd cast her a glowering look that made it clear he'd sooner throw her overboard than answer questions from the cargo.

The door to the interior quarters opened and a middle-aged man walked outside. He joined her at the rail.

She'd met him the night before. Another passenger like her trying to get somewhere. What was his name?

Erik. Erik Cox. That was it.

Said he used to be a history professor somewhere. Out east. Washington DC, maybe.

"Hey Emily, how's it looking out here?" Tall and lanky and moving like a willow tree, he reached for the railing as the boat rolled over a big wave. "Whoa!" he said with surprise.

Emily gestured from left to right, from one end of the approaching storm to the other. "It's coming fast. And I don't like our chances if we can't get this heap moving."

He swallowed hard and adjusted his glasses. "What do you mean? You think we're going to die out here?" His voice broke on the last word. A brittle crack that betrayed more than a little fear.

"Don't listen to me. What do I know? I'm sure we'll be fine." Emily turned away before he could read the truth in her eyes.

"It's just that I have a family I have to get back to," he said. "I can't let them down. I can't..."

Emily took his hand in hers. She squeezed it in a reassuring way. "Hey, it's gonna be—"

The door to the cockpit crashed open and Captain James stomped out. "Do you two have cotton balls in your ears? I been yelling up and down this boat telling people to get their survival suits on! And make sure yours has a survival kit in the chest pocket!"

Emily hadn't heard a thing. Then again, the whistling wind out here made it nearly impossible to hear.

The captain threw his arms up. "So what are you waiting for!"

Erik raced toward the door to the crew's quarters as a big wave hit.

The ship keeled over sending him skidding across the deck.

Emily managed to latch onto the railing as it hit. She held on with all her strength as the world teetered left and then right.

The captain stood his ground on the deck, riding the motion like a cowboy on a bucking bull. He leaped through the air and landed on an intersecting path with Erik.

He reached down and managed to halt his slide. A second later, he dragged Erik to his feet and marched him toward the door.

It opened and one of the crew jumped outside.

Captain James shouted something to him while pointing back at Emily.

The howling wind kept her from hearing anything. What had been infrequent gusts had suddenly grown in strength and duration. It now roared like a beast let loose.

Another wave hit and Emily lost her footing. She managed to cling to the railing and pull herself back up.

Captain James and Erik disappeared through the doorway as the remaining crewman made his way toward Emily.

The deck bucked and rolled, but he was equal to the task. He rode it almost as smoothly as the captain had a moment ago.

Emily had more strength and coordination than most people and she still found herself barely hanging on. Every time she got her feet under her, the deck shifted and sent her sprawling.

Another wave hit and this one tore her grip loose from the rail. She flew through the air, a trip cut short as the crewman wrapped her in an iron embrace. He spun them around and rode the bucking deck toward the door.

After a shifting path that more resembled a sidewinder slithering across sand than people walking on two legs, they made it to the door.

The crewman wrenched it open and shoved her inside. She grabbed the rail on the wall and held on for dear life.

He lifted a foot to follow and the boat lurched to the side.

It wasn't like the sickening roll of a big wave. It was like hitting a giant rock.

The impact flung the crewman away from the door. He hit the deck on his back and the look on his face said it wasn't a soft landing. He sat up, reaching a hand toward her.

And then a river of water swept over him. It slammed

the door shut. The boat tilted again and the door swung back open.

The torrent of water seeped away, revealing the deck but not the man.

"Man overboard!" Emily shouted as loud as she could.

The captain appeared in the narrow corridor that led to the cockpit.

"Man overboard!" Emily shouted again. "He was just there and then a wave took him away!"

"Get your suit on! Now!" He grabbed Emily's jacket by the collar and shoved her backward toward the sleeping quarters.

She stumbled forward and watched in horror as he lunged outside as much under his own control as under the ocean's.

14

A few minutes later and Emily had the survival suit on with the kukri knife sheathed and secured to her hip. She tied the emergency light Marco had given her to the suit and verified that the chest pocket had a mini survival kit, but didn't have time to check what was inside.

She swallowed hard to keep the rising bile in her throat from reaching escape velocity. Fighting to get into the suit in the tight confines of the crew's quarters had her dizzy and nauseous. She needed to see the horizon and breathe some air not reeking of diesel fuel.

She lurched through the corridor toward the cockpit. The surface of the wall under her palm vibrated and shook. The deep thunder of the engines roared to life.

"Yes!" she shouted.

She made it to the small space with the aft door and found Erik stumbling in from the cockpit. "Captain said if any more cargo enters the bridge, he'll personally tie an anchor around their waist and throw them overboard."

Emily almost laughed. She would've but feeling like

she was going to barf at any second put a real damper on her good humor. "What are we supposed to do then?"

Erik shrugged. "Hold tight."

They were both already doing that.

Each stood holding onto a rail as waves pitched the boat back and forth.

The shrieking wind outside the door sounded alive and evil. Like it wanted them dead. Like it wanted nothing more.

Emily swallowed hard again as a wave of queasiness swept over her.

The engines thundered underfoot and the boat spun to the right.

Emily pinwheeled around and slammed her shoulder into the wall.

Something on the deck outside crashed and ended with the long screech of tearing metal.

A crewman appeared a few seconds later carrying a huge crowbar. He wore the same kind of yellow survival suit that each of them had on. He looked at both of them, sizing them up. "I need your help outside! One of the cranes snapped and is hanging over the side."

An enormous gong sound battered the air.

"It's smashing into the boat. A few more of those and it'll bash through the hull. That happens and we'll go down in seconds!"

Emily nodded to affirm she was ready. To do what exactly, she had no idea. And whether she'd end up being more of a help or a hindrance was equally uncertain.

The crewman threw the door open and led the way outside. Emily followed him through and looked back.

Erik stood frozen at the threshold. The eyes behind his glasses were wide with fear.

"Stay inside," Emily yelled over the wind. "You don't have to do this!"

A muffled shout and she turned to see the crewman with the crowbar wedged under a thick bar that had torn free of the deck and was stuck under another section of bent metal.

He waved her over and shouted again.

She turned back to Erik as he stepped outside. The droplets flying through the air coated his lenses and she wondered how he could possible see anything.

"He needs help. Let's go!" he said.

They hurried forward and somehow made it to the crewman.

BONG!

The crane hanging over the side slammed into the ship. It hung from a thick cable like a wrecking ball.

All three grabbed a section of the crow bar and pulled upward.

The tendons in Emily's shoulder popped with the strain. She gritted her teeth and screamed, fighting to give everything and more.

A wave rolled under the ship, but the tension between the crowbar and deck kept all three locked in place.

The metal pole shifted. An inch at first.

And then it broke free.

The bar swung up and out catching the crewman in the chest. It hit like a catapult.

The crewman's yellow covered limbs dragged behind on each side of the pole as it swept him in an arc and then flung him through the air.

He helplessly clawed at nothing as he sailed over-board and disappeared into an oncoming wave.

Emily screamed but the wind swallowed the sound.

The cable holding the dangling crane snapped and it plunged into the frothing water.

The cable whipped through the air with a hiss and lassoed around Erik's middle.

Emily watched in horror as the end of the cable continued around and caught underneath a large metal storage crate.

Erik's eyes bulged as the loop tightened, crinkling the material of the survival suit.

The crate creaked and shifted as a huge wave rolled under the boat.

The cable constricted further, shattering his ribs with sickening hollow cracks.

Another wave hit and the ship leaned over hard on its side.

The crate broke free and slid across the deck.

The loop jerked tight and cut through Erik's torso like a garrote wire. It sliced through his spine and snapped away.

Blood fountained through the air, covering Emily's face and suit.

The two halves of what used to be a man dropped onto the deck and tumbled away as the ship rolled back the other way.

The deck fell away under Emily's feet as a wall of water above rushed down to crush her.

Ice stabbed into her lungs as the saltwater blasted down her throat. A wave sucked her overboard as she saw the ship's spinning props cutting through a ripping rain.

A black wave rose up, impossibly high. A curled hand of death that promised oblivion.

Emily stared up with something like grim fascination.

This was her end.

It wasn't the one she'd imagined.

Not when she left her grandmother in Oakland to have a chance to win a million dollars.

Life didn't always go according to plan.

She knew that better than most.

But this was something else altogether.

She squinted up at the monster cutting across the gray sky.

The peak broke and the avalanche of water crashed down.

The impact drove her and the nearby ship down into darkness.

15

The current spun her head over heels through shades of black and gray. Water shot up her nose and down her throat, choking her as she tried to cough it out. The spinning slowed and she oriented herself to the direction that looked lighter than the surrounding water.

The surface.

She hoped.

She kicked her feet and felt the water slide by as she moved upward.

Hopefully upward.

Wracking spasms shook her middle as she spewed out salt water. The coughs subsided and the salt water was replaced by a growing ache.

A burning need for a breath of air.

She kicked harder, but suddenly felt the water sliding by in the wrong direction.

The gray twilight above drifted away.

Something was sucking her lower!

She glanced down and saw a darker shadow below.

The sinking boat.

And it was dragging her down.

The ache in her lungs ignited into a burn. Like a lit match.

She kicked with all she had left. The feeling of sliding through the water stopped, but didn't switch directions.

The awkward suit made swimming twice as hard and she desperately needed a breath of air.

Energy drained from her legs like a battery with a hole in the side.

And then she broke free of the descending column of water.

The gray above drew closer. Her lungs fought to breathe but she clamped her jaws shut to avoid filling her lungs with water.

As darkness crept in around the edges of her vision, she broke through the roiling surface and sucked in a breath.

Half air and half water had her choking and sputtering again. She sucked in a few more breaths until she felt inside her body again.

And that wasn't necessarily a good thing.

Even inside the survival suit with layers of clothes and thermals below that, the cold water bit at her skin like needles. It numbed her exposed cheeks and made her teeth chatter like a baby's rattle.

A wave lifted her up like a high-speed elevator. It rose impossibly high and then reversed course just as quickly. She plummeted like an elevator with the cable cut.

Her stomach jumped up into her throat and she screamed as she fell. She spun in a circle, squinting through the stinging rain pelting her face.

The ship was gone.

All that surrounded her were churning waves and whitewater tinted gray in the dim morning light.

Alone.

And she'd thought being left alone on the island was the most remote feeling anyone could possibly ever have.

She couldn't have been more wrong.

This was remote.

This was alone.

There was no help coming.

And there was no chance she could save herself.

This wasn't a puzzle to be solved like constructing a shelter out of the available natural resources.

This wasn't a challenge like grinding through another afternoon of foraging for food when you hadn't eaten more than a few mouthfuls of calories for days.

No. That was hard.

This was impossible.

This was hell.

And it served no other purpose than to remind her how insignificant and powerless she was. And that her death would be meaningless and forgotten and even then only granted after sufficient suffering.

Emily fought to stay above the choppy surface while also trying to stay facing away from the driving rain.

But the instant she spun around to put the rain to her back, the direction shifted and a new onslaught slammed into her face, blinding and choking until she could again shift a few degrees away and find temporary respite.

A part of her wanted to let go.

To surrender.

It would be over faster that way.

But a harder, deeper part raged against the inevitable end.

A glowing coal at the center of her soul smoldered ever hotter the closer it got to being snuffed out.

She couldn't quit.

Not even if she wanted to.

There was a raging beast in the depths of her core that wouldn't go quietly. Its teeth gnashed and its claws slashed and it would not die without a fight.

Emily welcomed that fury. It burned through her veins, spreading warmth and comfort.

The shrieking wind yanked her hood back and slapped at her ears. The darkness inside her roared a challenge in return.

Another wave drove her up into the heavens. She clawed at the water, tearing at the beast that ignored her like a gnat battering a mountain.

An instant later, it pulled her down with equal disregard.

She hit the bottom of the valley and kicked hard to keep from getting sucked under.

A darker shadow passed through the depths below.

Something massive.

The ship still on its way down?

The light shifted and shadow bled into the surrounding darkness.

Had she imagined it?

A growing roar behind her pierced through the maelstrom of sound and motion.

She spun around as something hit her like a speeding truck.

It dragged her through the water as she struggled to stay afloat.

After it slowed and her vision cleared, she realized she was still clinging to it.

A fragment of floating timber from the destroyed boat.

She wrapped her arms around it and hung on.

This was it. Her final move in a game where mother nature made the rules and then changed them whenever she wanted.

Emily went where it went.

When it went down, so would she.

16

BOB slipped into his coat and buttoned it all the way up. It must've been around noon, but the weather looked miserable and cold outside the window. It was the first time he'd been up and around for more than a few minutes since his *episode*.

Episode.

That was the euphemism he'd started to call slashing his veins open and hoping to die.

His suicide attempt.

His *episode*.

What else would an old washed-out Hollywood veteran call it?

Bob drank the last few gulps out of his water bottle, capped it, and stashed it in the jacket pocket. Good to have handy in case he ran across a place to fill up. The water at the taps still worked, but he expected it to cut off any second.

He stretched his back to work out the kinks.

No, that wasn't right.

He was officially sixty years old and more than forty of those were hard living. The kinks were there to stay.

He continued rolling his shoulders.

The last couple of days lying in bed doing nothing had added a few more kinks. As he moved, the muscles started to warm up and the aches fade.

The kinks never went away completely, but they could be convinced to soften and relax for a time.

"What are you doing?"

Bob spun around and saw Rome standing in the hallway outside his bedroom. He wore black sneakers, black pants, a black sweatshirt and his favorite cap. It wasn't a cap Bob would wear without someone pointing a gun at his head, but he could appreciate the curvy chick with the tattered clothes.

Bob's eyes fell to the green military duffle bag hanging from Rome's right hand.

"What's that?"

Rome's upper lip curled into a snarl. "None of your business is what it is!"

Bob shook his head. "Okay. You're right. It's just that if you're thinking about going into town carrying that, well..."

Rome tilted his head, waiting for the rest. "Well, what?"

"Well, that's pretty conspicuous. Don't you think? I mean, you're wearing all black and that bag screams *I'm full of drugs or twenty dollar bills!*"

"I don't remember asking your opinion."

"Are you going to drive your mom's car?"

"The Pinto Bean?"

"Yeah."

"No."

"Why not?"

"Because I can't find the stupid key. And even if I could, it wouldn't be a good idea. You probably haven't noticed since all you've been doing is laying around on my couch, but things aren't the same out there. A car driving around is going to attract a lot of attention."

"More than wearing all black and carrying a large duffle bag?"

"Shut up already," he said as he stomped toward the door.

Bob unlocked and opened it.

Rome stopped and cast him a suspicious look. "Why aren't you in your suicide pajamas?"

Bob swallowed hard and clamped his mouth shut. He somehow managed to swallow the biting reply. "I'm going with you."

Rome cast him a *You're insane, old man* look. "Uh, no you're not."

Bob nodded. "I'm your back up. That's all. Probably won't need me and I'm not much good anyway. But something is better than nothing."

"Uh, did you not hear me? You're not going. You're lucky I'm letting you stay here. I'm only doing it because I know my mom would've wanted that."

"She was a good woman."

Rome stepped forward and looked down at Bob. "Don't tell me about my mother. You arrived three weeks ago. You don't know anything about her."

The kid was ready to explode.

Couldn't blame him.

Losing a mother would do that.

"Sorry. All I'm saying is that she wouldn't have wanted you going out alone. I know that much about her."

Rome's pudgy cheeks quivered. He may have been fat, but there was a good amount of muscle hidden in that large frame. If he decided to throw down a beating, there wasn't much Bob could do to avoid it.

After a few seconds of waiting for Rome's fist to flatten him, the boy spun toward the door and marched through it.

He lurched to a stop in the hallway outside. "Fine."

Bob's outlook brightened. He wasn't going to let the kid leave without a fight, a literal fight, and the news that he wasn't going to end up unconscious was both unexpected and welcome.

They made their way out of the apartment complex and down toward the main road. They arrived at the corner and turned south.

Bob looked down the street and gasped.

The town had utterly transformed in the six days since the end of the world arrived.

It was slow at first, but the change was speeding up.

Abandoned cars littered the road. Whereas they'd all looked fine the first few days, they now looked like they'd endured a nuclear war.

Which, of course, they had. But now they looked the part.

A red Ford F150 parked at the next intersection had all its windows bashed out. Only narrow perimeters of jagged shards remained. It sat low to the ground because all four wheels were missing. The passenger side mirror hung limply from a black cable. The hood looked like a boulder had fallen on it. The driver side door was open, but nobody was around.

Bob scanned the street as far as the crest of the hill that concealed the other half of town.

Not a single person could be seen.

People were still walking around the first few days.

Not anymore.

There was an eerie menace in the air as they hugged storefronts and darted through the open spaces. Glass crunched underfoot as they passed the broken window of the local Starbucks. Someone had done a number on the interior.

And not in a home renovation kind of way.

Bob had never liked that charred beans acid water, so it wasn't a big loss as far as he was concerned.

Rome stopped at the edge of the building and peeked around the corner.

Bob stopped behind him. "So what are you going to do with whatever is in that bag?

Rome looked over his shoulder with a gleam in his eye. "I'm going to get as many guns and bullets as I can."

"Why?"

"Because I'm going to kill the bastard that murdered my mother. Come on!" He broke into a jog across the street.

Bob did his best to keep up.

And by best, that simply meant stumbling behind while not passing out from dizziness and chest pain.

"Hey!" a voice shouted down the street.

Rome and Bob both turned toward the sound and stumbled to a stop.

Two men carrying rifles jogged across the street a half a block away.

"Don't move!" one shouted.

Rome took off.

Bob followed right behind.

They made it past the cover of the building on the opposite side before their pursuers could react.

Rome ducked to the side to avoid a bent door frame hanging out over the sidewalk. He cleared it.

But his duffel bag didn't.

The broken and twisted door frame caught the bag, ripped it open, and bricks of wrapped cellophane tumbled out onto the pavement.

Bob accidentally kicked one before skidding to a stop himself. He picked it up and turned it over in his hand.

Beneath numerous layers of tightly stretched plastic, dark green marijuana showed.

"You're carrying drugs?"

Rome was already on his knees scooping up the half dozen bricks that had fallen out.

This kid was an absolute idiot.

Who carried a duffel bag full of weed around town six days after the apocalypse?

Did he think this was a Hollywood movie or something?

This was how you got yourself killed.

And worse, this was how you got the old guy that came with you killed.

17

"Leave it!" Bob shouted as he tried to pull Rome to his feet.

The vastly larger boy shrugged him off as he snatched up another brick.

"It's not worth dying for!" Bob grabbed him again, but it was no use.

Rome shoved the last few bricks back into the bag. He yanked the one out of Bob's hand and was about to stuff it into the bag when a voice shouted.

"Don't you move another inch!"

Bob slowly turned his head and saw the two men with their rifles raised and ready to fire. He glanced back at Rome and saw the kid looking toward nearby alley. "Don't do it. They'll shoot you down."

CRACK!

A bullet snapped by Bob's head, inches away.

"I said don't move!"

Bob froze and was relieved to see Rome did too.

The two men sauntered up and stopped next to

Rome. Both had a hollow emptiness to their eyes and a mouthful of rotten teeth.

Bob had seen their kind plenty of times before. They were always cruising Hollywood Boulevard, looking for the next fix or looking for something to steal to pay for it.

The smaller one wearing a camo jacket and camo rain pants reached out for the brick of weed in Rome's hand. "What do we have here?" he said as he yanked it free. He started laughing as he flipped it over and over in his hand. "Otis, we done caught ourselves a drug dealer!"

The taller man with a long, frizzy goatee hanging off his chin whooped with joy.

The camo'd guy let his rifle hang by the sling and drew a knife from a sheath at his hip. He sliced open the plastic wrap and took a deep breath. "Whoa! This is some tasty nugs, man!"

The taller man pointed his rifle at Rome. "Open the bag."

Rome didn't move.

The man's finger curled inside the trigger guard. "I won't ask again."

"Do it!" Bob said. "Open the stupid bag!"

Rome cursed under his breath, but pulled back the zipper. The contents of the stuffed bag spilled out.

A dozen hard bricks tumbled around like oversized dominoes.

"Holy crap, Otis! We hit the jackpot!" the camo'd man started jumping around like he'd won the lottery.

"Ricky! Gather it all up before anyone sees!"

"Oh, yeah!" He started scooping up the bricks while the taller man moved the muzzle back and forth between Rome and Bob.

From the corner of his eye, Bob saw Rome's hand easing toward the hem of his jacket.

"We gonna be high as planets!"

"Yeah, and I'm gonna be the moon!"

The taller man shook his head. "The moon ain't a planet. And plus, planets are way higher than the moon. Did you learn nuthin in school?"

The camo'd man cackled like a maniac as he continued gathering the bricks. "I learned how to smoke weed!"

The taller man held the rifle with one hand and pulled a metal flask out of his pocket with the other. "This deserves a toast." He spun the cap off as he continued. "Whiskey begins and makes best friends and we'll see what happens when the whiskey ends."

Rome's fingers pulled up the hem revealing a black holster underneath.

Bob had to stop him!

The kid was going to get them both killed.

This wasn't the wild west and he wasn't Doc Holliday, the fastest gun in the west. This was Kodiak, Alaska and the guy pointing a rifle at them would shoot them both before Rome's pistol cleared the holster.

Bob turned back to the rifle. A high-powered hunting rifle only a few feet away and pointing at their chests. Exactly what kind of rifle was beyond Bob's comprehension or concern. All he knew or cared about was that the barrel looked huge and that dark tunnel at the end scared him like nothing else he'd ever experienced.

Bob tried to think of something, anything to stop the inevitable from happening, but he was too late.

Rome went for his pistol.

He yanked it from the holster, but it got tangled in his jacket, binding his hand for precious seconds.

The taller man shoved the end of his rifle into Rome's forehead. "What do you think you're doing?"

The camo'd man spotted the pistol and yanked it away. He held it up to his partner. "Look what we got here."

The taller man growled. "I was thinking of letting you live. Not anymore!"

"Kill this fatty!" the shorter man screamed. "Splatter his brains on the sidewalk!"

The taller man nodded.

Something sparked in Bob's mind.

A lightning bolt of recognition blazed through his brain.

"Wait! What did you say a minute ago?"

The taller man cast him a sideward glance.

The memory sizzled through Bob's mind.

That line.

That line!

That joke!

He'd written it over thirty years ago. He thought it would be a throwaway laugh but something about it caught people. It had become a running gag between two of the main characters on *Barflies*, the owner and bartender.

And the man about to shoot Rome had said the first half. The set up.

Bob knew the second half, the punch line, like he knew his own name. "Until the whiskey ends!"

The taller man's eyes narrowed. "What did you say?"

"Until the whiskey ends! That's the rest of it. Whiskey

begins and whiskey best friends. Don't talk to the wife until the whiskey ends!"

His eyes widened. "You like classic TV series?"

Bob's mouth talked so fast his brain could hardly keep up. "Like them? I made them. I wrote that joke. It's funny because it shows the new bartender, Jimmie, has a lot to learn from the owner and old pro, Don."

"We're talking *Barflies*, right?" the taller man asked.

"Yes, *Barflies*! That's my show. I created it!"

The camo'd man shook his head. "He's lying. That's ridiculous!"

A cloud of uncertainty passed over the taller's man gaze.

"It's true. I promise you."

"What's your name?" the taller man said.

"Bob Randy. Executive Producer. You must've seen it in the credit roll at the beginning of the show." He better have because Bob had fought tooth and nail to get that placement at that size. A viewer would've had to been blind not to see it.

The taller man's eyes opened wide as the end of the rifle lowered. "He's for real. I remember seeing that name because Grampy always made fun of it. He always wondered what kind of Hollywood jackass had two first names for a name."

"Yes! That's me!" Bob said. And the fact that he'd just been insulted didn't cross his mind.

Mostly didn't cross his mind.

The taller man let the rifle point to the pavement. He extended his hand toward Bob.

Bob shook it, wondering if this was merely a brief pause in their imminent execution.

"I want to thank you," the man said as his eyes started to glisten. "Grampy and I watched your show every night the last year of his life."

"I don't remember that."

"Shut up, Ricky! You idiot! You don't remember because you were too young. All you cared about was eating your boogers and pulling the legs off of crickets!"

"Yeah, I was a pretty cool kid."

"You were an idiot and you still are!"

The camo'd man frowned and continued gathering the blocks.

"Anyhow, we watched that show every night until the cancer finally got him." He wiped at a tear forming on the inside corner of his eye. "The drugs had him in a stupor the last couple of months. But on his last day, there it was. Your show came on and it was like he came back for a few minutes. He was himself again while the show lasted. Then it ended. And not long after, so did he."

Bob had no clue what to say to that. Anything that kept them from getting shot sounded right. He went with something safe. "I'm sorry he suffered so much."

The taller man bit his lip. "Me too."

The camo'd man punched him in the shoulder. "Look at you! You're crying like a little girl. Wait 'til mama hears about this!"

The taller man grabbed him by the collar and wrenched the material to the side until it tightened around his neck.

The camo'd guy's face turned red and a vein on his forehead bulged below the skin.

"You ain't gonna say nothing to nobody. You get me?"

The choking man nodded as the vein threatened to pop through the skin.

The taller man released him and then turned back to Bob. "Look, for what you did for my grandpa, I'm not gonna kill you two."

Bob was thanking him before he finished the sentence.

"This is a one time deal. We're square now."

"Got it," Bob said as he glanced at Rome.

He had a snarl on his face, but his mouth stayed shut. Good.

The last thing they needed was for him to blow it with some smart ass comment.

The taller man waved them away with his rifle. "Get going."

Bob started walking, but Rome stayed put. Bob turned back as the rifle pivoted to Rome. Not raised. Still pointing toward the pavement. But in the neighborhood now.

Rome pointed at his pistol. "Can I have my gun back?"

The taller man shook his head. "The weed and pistol are mine." He looked over at Bob. "Word of friendly advice. You and the kid get out of town. CB owns this place now and he don't do kind gestures. You stay and you're going get yourselves killed."

Bob grabbed Rome's elbow and pulled him away. "Thank you. We'll do that."

He managed to pull Rome across the street, back toward the apartment.

They made it a few more yards and then Rome pulled away.

"They stole my gun and my weed! And you let them!"

"Let them? They were gonna kill us. I'm the reason we're still alive!"

"What? I'm supposed to be grateful or something?"

Bob sighed.

Teenagers.

He was way too old for this crap.

18

MARCO pulled the collar of his jacket up to keep the gusting wind out. The afternoon sun hid behind a brown gauze that would've looked right at home in the sky above Beijing.

But not here in Kodiak.

A town of six thousand didn't have enough tailpipes to create smog.

No. The sky had changed since the nukes dropped. The sun no longer brought warmth and energy. Now, it glowed weak and pale behind a blanket of thick dust.

Not that his neck was cold. On the contrary, it was toasty warm due to the little bundle of heat curled over his shoulders and softly snoring inches from his ear.

Marco and Stuckey had circled back to the hospital after the gang had left. Oscar had been furious when Marco opened the door and the two reunited. Marco had felt bad because he knew the feeling all too well. Abandoned by his ex. And now by Emily.

His hiking boots thudded on the pavement as he

lengthened his stride to keep up with Chief Stuckey. They'd just left a pizza joint and successfully recruited its owner to come to the meeting set for that night.

The resistance.

With the police decimated and Marco a deputy with less than a day's experience, the two of them weren't a match for the gang that had nearly killed them at the hospital.

They needed more people.

Citizens who cared about the town and had the back bone to do something about it.

They were walking down Mill Bay Road, keeping a low profile, checking every business as they went. All were closed and locked up, but some still had people inside that came out when they saw Stuckey banging on the door.

They crossed the street, hurried through the exposed intersection, and headed toward the Gas & Go on the opposite corner. Stuckey approached the front door and peered inside.

The glass of the store front was still intact. That was something. A third or more of the stores looked like they'd been hit by mini-tornadoes.

The chief tried the handle, but it was locked. He banged on the glass and again peered into the dark interior.

A voice shouted from above. "Get away from my door!"

Marco looked up and saw a man standing on the roof, looking down with a shotgun aimed at them.

SHUCK SHUCK.

"I'm giving you five seconds to beat it. One—"

Oscar's claws scratched Marco's neck as he scurried onto one shoulder, staring up and hissing.

Chief Stuckey held his hands up as he backed away. "Easy, Henry! It's me. Stuckey."

The man standing on the roof tilted his head and squinted. "Chief! What are you doing creeping around? I almost blew your head off!"

"I'm walking around in broad daylight. That's not creeping!"

Henry trained the shotgun on Marco. "Who's that?"

Chief Stuckey stepped in front of Marco, notably with his hands still in the air. "Name's Marco. He's with me."

Marco waved. "Hi there."

"Is he aware he's got a rat perched on his shoulder?"

"It's a weasel," Marco said as Oscar screeched.

The man cast him a scornful look. "If you say so," he said as he lowered the shotgun.

"Did you hear about what happened to the police station?" Stuckey asked.

The man nodded. "A gas explosion or something blew it to smithereens. That right?"

"No. Not gas. A bomb. Two of them. Killed everyone at the station but me."

"That so?"

"Henry, there's a madman trying to take over Kodiak. He busted out a bunch of criminals in lock up. I think he's building his own personal army."

"You mean that gang that's been running around acting like they own the place?"

"When did you see them?"

"Earlier this morning. They came tearing through here in a convoy of old trucks. Hollering and throwing beer bottles through storefronts as they went. I kept my head down because there were too many."

"More than a dozen?" Stuckey asked.

"Think so. Fifteen or twenty, I'd say."

Stuckey muttered something under his breath. "Well, if we don't do something and do it quick, this town is lost. Will you help us?"

Henry leaned the shotgun on the rim of the roof and dug into the front pocket of his overalls. He tugged out a packet and dipped his fingers inside. He pinched out a wad of chew and stuffed it into his mouth.

Marco waited and watched, the same as Stuckey did.

Like it was some kind of ritual that had to be observed before a decision could be made.

He worked the chaw a bit and then spat onto the roof. With the tobacco apparently settled in, he picked up the gun and looked down at them with a nod. "I reckon you can count me in."

"Chief Stuckey!" a voice called from across the street.

Marco, the chief, and Henry above all pivoted with their guns trained in the direction of the voice.

A woman appeared from a narrow alley between two buildings. She was about to run across the street, but Stuckey stopped her.

He raised his hand. "Gloria, stay over there! Lower your weapons. She's one of us."

"Is that you up there, Henry?" the woman yelled.

"Sure is. Didn't recognize you without the apron on and the hair pulled up in a bun."

"No time for baking since the world ended."

Marco followed Stuckey across the street, both of

their heads on swivels, scanning up and down the street for possible threats.

Stuckey got to her while Marco stopped a few paces back, making sure to keep a space between them in case anyone hidden along the street decided to start trying to pick them off. He kept watch, not liking how exposed they were.

Oscar stood up on his haunches on Marco's shoulder, his nose sniffing and long whiskers twitching in the air.

Chief Stuckey held the woman by the shoulders. "Gloria, what happened?"

Marco saw that her cheeks were streaked with tears.

She choked back a few sobs and answered. "It's Mayor Okpik. She's..."

The chief waited a few seconds while sobs overtook the woman. "What? What happened to Linda?"

The woman wiped away snot dripping from her nose. "She's dead, Chief. Murdered."

19

They followed the woman two blocks south and then a block over to Center Avenue. Henry had left his perch on top of his store to join them. There at the intersection was confirmation of the story she told.

The arm of a traffic light arched out over the street. Like all the other traffic lights in town, it hadn't worked since the EMP hit.

But someone had found another use for it.

Mayor Okpik hung from a rope tied to the pole. The noose visible beneath her long hair and lifted chin.

Gloria pointed up. "I told you! I told you! Someone murdered her!" She stumbled and Chief Stuckey caught her.

"Why don't you sit down on the curb?"

The sobbing woman nodded as the chief guided her down. "I bake muffins. I make lattes. I watch Netflix every night. I'm not made for this end of the world nightmare!"

"Take it easy," the chief said as he returned his focus to the dangling body ten feet above.

A gust of wind whipped down the street and the rope creaked as her body swayed. The wind died and she swung like a pendulum coming to rest.

Chief Stuckey shook his head. "Marco, help me get this down."

Marco surveyed the situation. They didn't have a vehicle. They didn't have a ladder. How was he supposed to help get her down?"

Stuckey slowly circled beneath her, shaking his head as he watched the swaying slow to a stop.

What must he be thinking?

Feeling?

Losing his entire police force.

Now losing the mayor.

The man was tough as nails, but nails could be bent over in half with enough hammering.

Marco slung his rifle around his back and hurried over to the vertical base pole of the street light. "Hold on," he said to Oscar. Taking a deep breath because he knew he wasn't healthy enough to be doing this, he then did it anyway.

He shimmied up the pole with Oscar riding along and then rotated out to the overhanging arm. Clinging underneath with his hands and legs wrapped around the pole, he made his way out to her. He glanced down to see the chief studying the road below the body.

He stood and looked up, his gaze shifted past the body to Marco. "What are you doing up there?"

"I'm going to cut her down like you asked."

Stuckey's lips pursed together in a tight line. "I want you to help me get this scene down, as in on paper and in our minds. We don't have cameras or forensics or anything like that, so the old fashioned way will have to work."

"You want me to leave her like this?"

Stuckey squeezed his eyes shut. "I want to understand everything we can about this crime scene before we disturb the evidence. And then, yes, I want to get her body down."

"Sorry," Marco said, feeling like the new kid on the first day of school. He shimmied back and climbed down to the street.

Stuckey was studying Okpik's toes that weren't far above his head. He reached up and held her foot. "Feel this."

As much as Marco didn't want to, he did as instructed.

"A little warmer than the ambient air temperature," Stuckey said. He twisted her foot and the rest of the body followed along like a solid piece of wood. "A body loses heat at one or two degrees per hour after death. Rigor mortis peaks from eight to twelve hours."

Marco kept his mouth shut and listened. His first lesson in homicide investigative work.

"Look at the pavement below the body."

I did and saw nothing unusual.

"No blood or body excretions. She was killed somewhere else. Maybe ten to fourteen hours ago. Late last night, probably."

Marco nodded because he had nothing useful to add. He'd seen plenty of animals in various stages of dying, death, and decomposition, but he was no homicide detective.

Stuckey pointed at her ankles. "See there? The

bruising and discoloration around the ankles. She was bound when she was alive and blood was circulating."

Stuckey spent the next fifteen minutes going over every detail as Marco and Henry stood guard, eyes scanning the street in both directions. The chief spoke out loud as new observations occurred to him and Marco did his best to commit them all to memory.

At the same time though, he wondered what the point of all this was. It wasn't like the legal system was operational. There would be no trial with a jury of peers to decide innocence or guilt. That was the old world, not the new one.

The new world didn't offer the same comfort, conveniences, or complex realities that made modern life possible.

It was far simpler and more direct than that.

Someone had killed the mayor.

Probably that madman from the hospital, or someone in his gang.

Either way, the only justice that would find them was whatever people like him and Stuckey could dish out.

A life for a life.

Killing for killing.

Marco accepted that, but he wondered if Stuckey did. Was the chief too attached to a concept of law and order that no longer functioned?

After Marco cut her down and Stuckey had spent another few minutes going over her clothes and body, they finally covered her with a sheet Gloria had found in a nearby laundromat.

Henry turned away and spat brown juice onto the

pavement. He turned back and sniffed. "What's our next move, boss?"

Chief Stuckey stood with his arms folded across his barrel chest staring down at the thin fabric draped over the still body. "We're going to kill the man that did this to her."

Henry nodded. "Okay. And how are we going to do that?"

"We need more guns and more people to use them." Stuckey pivoted to Henry. "Can we use your gas station on the north side of town as a meeting point?"

"Sure."

"Good, because I've already been telling everyone to meet there."

Henry's brow lifted, but he didn't say anything.

"I want you to go to every person you know in town. Pass along a message that we're going to meet there three hours after sunset. Only people you're absolutely sure about. And tell them to keep quiet. Fifteen or twenty trustworthy citizens with rifles and a plan ought to be enough."

"You got it," Henry said before spinning on his heel and heading off.

"Hey, Henry," Stuckey said.

Henry looked back over his shoulder.

"Be careful. These people mean business, and I need you alive."

Henry spat a glob of brown juice onto the pavement. "Don't worry about me. I don't die easy."

20

DR. YONG misted the leaves of what was undoubtedly the most precious orchid in the world. It was a clone of the famous Shenzhen Nongke Orchid which had gone for over two hundred thousand dollars at auction many years ago. And the odds were high that the mother plant and whoever tended it were vaporized when the nukes dropped six days ago.

That made this one priceless.

It was the last of its kind.

Not altogether different from Zhang.

He gently stroked the stem as most people might pet a cat. No pets were allowed at Project Hermes, but that didn't remove the innate desire to care for another creature.

He often spoke to it as other people might speak to a pet. Promised it treats if it behaved well. More liquid molasses if it stood strong and tall.

Within the cycles of his daily life, it and Hari were the only two entities that he truly connected with. One was perhaps the greatest scientific mind to have ever lived and the other was a plant. An admittedly rare and beautiful plant. But still, a plant.

A psychologist would've had a field day with that information. But the only person who knew of his affection for the plant was now dead.

Zhang swallowed hard as he touched the underside of a leaf. "Perk up, now. I'm back and I've missed you too." It hadn't been long at all for him, but had been over a decade from the orchid's point of view.

He released the leaf and it drooped again.

The plant probably felt abandoned and alone.

Just as he did.

With Hari gone, even the company of his priceless pet plant wasn't enough to lift his spirits. He was well and truly alone.

He'd lost his wife and child so long ago that he sometimes wondered if they were real or figments of his imagination. After his part in the Tiannenman incident, he and his pregnant wife were supposed to get out of the country.

He'd made it, but she hadn't.

He would've wilted into listless despair were it not for Hari. Their shared passion for quantum physics had brought them together and the bond had become unbreakable after he'd accepted Hari's invitation to join Project Hermes.

Hari had always led, and Zhang had always followed.

But no more.

Hari was dead. Killed by a short-faced bear thousands of years ago. And Zhang was powerless to do anything about it, even though they had the technology to change history. Hari had proven that by saving him.

A part of Zhang wished Hari had left him to die in the distant past. The pressure of the present was too great. Everyone at the project looked to him for leadership. For direction.

Him.

Zhang shook his head in disbelief.

He was not a leader. Not a long time ago when his actions made him lose his wife and son and not now when the future of the human race depended on his steady hand.

Zhang misted the leaves again, watched a water droplet race down the contours and drip to the dirt below. It was one of the few plants allowed to grow in soil. And only because this was his personal plot to do with as he pleased.

The rest of the vast underground cavern was dedicated to growing food for the facility and hence the process was far more utilitarian.

Zhang stood and noticed the creeky ache in his knees. It was always worse down at the lower levels where the humidity was higher, and worse yet here at the gardens level where the walls dripped with moisture.

He gazed out over the endless tracts of carefully divided grow plots. Silver spiderbots moved back and forth, up and down over their individual plots, ceaselessly caring for every single sprout under their domain.

The cavern was the size of several football fields. The massive aquaponics system that grew fish and plants in a symbiotic self-sustaining cycle was a marvel of modern engineering. It didn't offer all the luxuries one might wish for, but it provided all of the necessary nutrients and calories to feed everyone at the facility.

That had been one of many key features that allowed the facility to exist on a small island while remaining virtually unknown to the locals after more than ten years in operation.

Being buried deep underground helped, too.

"Dr. Yong, are you there?"

The tone was clipped, almost panicked.

Zhang grabbed the phone in his coat pocket. While the nearest EMP that went off high in space had decimated the surface below, the hardened infrastructure of the underground facility had protected it for the most part.

"I'm here."

"Doctor, we've got a live feed from Bravo Team. We need you up here. Now."

"On my way!" Zhang said as he broke into a jog back toward the security door that led to the elevators and the administration level hundreds of feet above.

He arrived in the operations room breathing hard and dizzy from exertion. He really needed to get more exercise.

Get any exercise, for that matter.

There just wasn't enough time in the day.

He stumbled inside and grabbed a desk for support. The largest screen on the opposite wall showed a feed from one of the soldier's helmet cams.

The view whipped back and forth that didn't help Zhang's vertigo.

"Do we have an audio feed?"

One of the techs seated at the array of desks answered. "We're trying to lock it down."

The view settled and focused on a nearby time gate. The shimmering kaleidoscope hovering in mid-air had become a familiar sight since he'd returned from his own misadventure into the past.

But he still found it mesmerizing.

A tear in the space-time continuum.

A window to another time and world.

The latter hadn't been conclusively proven or disproven yet. But it was unquestionably a window to another time.

Audio crackled through the air causing Zhang to flinch.

"It's a massacre!" a voice screamed. "They're wiping us out!"

The view bobbled, and whipped left and right as the soldier scanned back and forth and then returned his attention to the time gate.

Another soldier appeared through the shimmering fabric.

Zhang recognized him. Captain Whitaker.

He had another soldier slung across his shoulders in a fireman's carry. He hurried forward with one hand stabilizing the injured soldier and one hand holding his rifle.

He looked into the camera, or rather at the soldier wearing it. "Inez, get back through the gate! We've got wounded and heavy contact on the other side!"

"Sir," Inez's voice cracked with terror, "I can't go back. Those monsters are going to kill us all!"

Whitaker eased the wounded soldier to the ground.

He jumped up a second later and his face filled the screen. Spit flew from his lips and his eyes burned with fury. "You will move out this second or I will put a bullet in your head. Do you copy that?"

The view blurred with vibration as Whitaker shook Inez by the battle vest.

"We're not leaving anyone behind!" Whitaker shouted into his face. He spun Inez around and shoved him toward the gate.

The view bounced up and down, with glimpses of Whitaker to the right, as both soldiers ran back to the gate.

As they arrived, a half-dozen soldiers sprinted through.

Whitaker grabbed the nearest soldier. "Where is everyone else?"

"Dead, Sir! Dead! Those invisible things got 'em! And they're coming for us!"

The soldier broke free of Whitaker's grasp and sprinted away from the gate.

The view on the screen followed him a second and then turned back to the gate as the crack of rifle fire split the air.

"Contact! Fire at will!" Whitaker shouted.

The view returned to the gate as something blurred through.

The ground in front of the gate seemed to waver and shift like a reflection through water. A patch of ground shifted and a dark lizard standing four feet high at the shoulders and at least twenty feet long appeared. It's jaws opened and a long tongue flicked at the air.

Its head turned toward the closest soldier.

And it disappeared.

Not completely. Not invisible. More like camouflage. But far better than the most adept octopus hiding in a reef.

Rifle fire went off like a string of firecrackers.

The ground on the path to that soldier wavered and shifted and then it looked like the ground swallowed the soldier.

The shape of the lizard briefly appeared on top of the soldier as its jaws clamped onto an arm and ripped it off. The part of the lizard's body next to the soldier shifted and turned the mottled green of the soldier's fatigues.

Zhang stared in horrified silence.

And wonder.

He'd never seen an animal that could camouflage itself like that. The ability of the octopus was perhaps the closest. But it couldn't vanish like that. And it couldn't move so fast or tear a man to pieces.

The sound of gunfire drowned out the screams of the dying soldier as the lizard tore him to pieces.

The view shifted back toward the gate and a huge area of the ground seemed to come alive.

Captain Whitaker appeared in view. His eyes were wide and unblinking. "Keep it together, son!" He looked over his shoulder and the view on the screen followed.

The shifting ground in front of the gate settled.

An odd clicking sound echoed back and forth. Then the scene changed.

Another massive lizard appeared. Then another. Then another.

The clicking continued as more and more appeared.

In less than a minute, twenty lizards materialized in the wide space in front of the shimmering gate.

"Oh God. Oh God. We're all gonna die!" Inez shouted.

"On me!" Whitaker bellowed. "Regroup!"

The remaining soldiers retreated to his position as the hunting pack of lizards started forward.

Gunfire erupted as they blurred into cover.

Seconds later, a nearby soldier screamed as a lizard took him down.

The sound of gunfire was soon replaced by the shrieking of dying men.

Of men being eaten alive.

A blur knocked Whitaker to the ground, even as he fired his rifle up into the beast. But it was no use. The creature tore the soldier's throat out even as its own chest exploded into a fountain of blood.

"Noooooo!"

The view shuddered with an impact and spun in dizzying circles as the helmet rolled across the ground.

It came to rest with the camera pointing at the soldier who'd just lost it.

Inez tried to bring his rifle up to fire on the lizard pinning him down.

The lizard snapped it out of his hands and flung it away. Its jaws opened and its head darted down with astonishing speed. It bit down and ripped away the battle vest.

Another bite and the soldier's chest was torn in half. A beating heart dangled from the beast's jaws before it snapped its head back and the crimson muscle vanished inside its mouth.

Still alive, if only for a few seconds, Inez stared up in shock.

Zhang turned away from the screen but heard the gristly end nonetheless.

He turned back as the sickening sounds moved away.

With the view on its side, the camera showed a wide expanse of ground. The lizards were all visible, broken into small packs gathered round each of the bodies.

Like a pack of hungry lions, they fought each other to bite off a share before the meal was gone.

The screen tracking the biosigns of every member of the team showed the same for all of them. Flat lines where there had been the spikes and valleys of beating hearts before.

"Bravo Team is gone, doctor. Not a single survivor."

Zhang pinched his eyes shut.

What would Hari do or say right now?

How would a real leader respond to such a tragedy?

Not being one himself, nothing came to him.

21

EMILY choked and sputtered as salt water blasted down her throat. Her eyes blinked open as she coughed it out. A yellow light blinded her with every flashing strobe.

A wave came in and she briefly floated up a couple of inches before it receded and she settled back into the sand.

She pushed the emergency beacon hanging around her neck out of the way.

She was alive?

She almost laughed out loud, but then spotted another wave rolling in and clamped her mouth shut before it hit. After it reversed course, she struggled to her feet and stumbled forward beyond the water line.

Without necessarily deciding to, she dropped to her knees and sat down hard.

How was she still alive?

A shudder rattled through her frozen body and banged her teeth together. The survival suit kept the water out, but not the cold. Not all of it, anyway.

She swallowed and winced at the sting in her throat. Her throat felt raw like it had been worked over with a power washer, which it more or less had.

The sun hung low in the western sky.

Emily pulled the zipper down on the tight-fitting collar cinched around her neck.

Better.

She took a deep breath.

And promptly started hacking out the last dregs of salt water lingering in her lungs. After the fit passed, she wiped her arm across her mouth.

"Where am I?"

She hadn't realized she said it out loud until the stinging in her throat erupted. She groaned and rubbed her neck.

How was she still alive?

The impossibility of it made her doubt the reality.

Maybe this was heaven.

If so, it sucked.

If there was a heaven, she expected a lot more from it. For one, she wanted to see her father again. Life had lumbered on for ten long years without his presence in her life.

He'd never been that religious, but he was a good man and the best father. If God hadn't let him in, Emily doubted she'd be let through either. Besides, she didn't want to go anyway if he wasn't there.

Another shiver quaked through her. She squeezed her eyes shut and they burned like they hadn't blinked in a couple of days.

She was miserable and cold and starting to feel sorry for herself.

No. This couldn't be heaven.

And as bad as it was, her understanding of hell with all the lakes of fire and sulfur stink and tormented souls made it an unlikely scenario as well.

Which meant only one thing.

Well, maybe it meant a lot of things, but it meant one especially important thing.

She was alive.

She'd somehow survived drowning and ended up on this beach.

Which again brought up an important question.

Where was this beach?

She scanned the tree line a few dozen yards further up the beach. The interior dwindled to darkness not far beyond the closest towering Sitka Spruce trees.

This could be anywhere in Alaska for all she knew. It looked like any number of places she'd been to on Kodiak Island, and she was willing to bet it looked like plenty of other places in Alaska.

She traced the beach in one direction until it curved around a bend maybe a half a mile to the north.

Nothing.

Doing the same in the other direction, she spotted something on a prominent point to the south. It was further in this direction, maybe two miles away following along the shoreline.

Emily pushed up to her feet to get a better look.

Whatever it was still looked like a dark blob on a pale beach.

The details were impossible to make out this far away, but it was big.

Was it a broken off part of the sunken boat?

Maybe an overturned lifeboat?

She couldn't tell from here.

All she could tell for sure was that it wasn't a log or seaweed or some other bit of flotsam from the sea.

And that made it worth investigating.

22

The good thing about walking the two miles to get to the unidentified object was her frozen core had thawed. Another good thing was that the emergency beacon had dried out and so the annoying flashing had stopped.

She had the hood of the survival suit peeled off and the front unzipped to her waist. A cold wind whistled in off the water. The suit was open enough to let in fresh air without sucking away too much warmth.

That part was an improvement on her previous condition.

But it wasn't all rose petals and celebratory champagne because she was thirsty enough to drink rain water out of a street gutter. Her tongue was thick and fat in her mouth. Like a slug without the mucous.

She'd have to find water, and soon.

Maybe she'd get lucky and find some supplies in the washed up debris.

Emily skirted around the point protruding into the

water and arrived at the final stretch of beach to her destination.

And she stuttered to a stop as she saw the thing she'd come to investigate.

It wasn't a fragment of the ship.

It wasn't an overturned lifeboat.

It wasn't anything that would help her situation.

Because it was alive.

She broke into a jog and arrived a few minutes later.

Lying on the beach at the highest point of the outgoing tide was a massive orca whale. Blood gurgled out of its parted jaws. Its black skin dulled by the lack of water. Its eye blinked and tracked Emily as she moved closer.

It must've been twenty feet long with a four foot dorsal fin extending from its back.

Why had it washed up on the beach?

Emily had read about whales sometimes beaching themselves. Nobody understood why it happened. Some theorized that the Navy's underwater sonar system was driving them crazy or damaging their sensitive aural organs or perhaps even damaged their air bladders and made it so they couldn't dive.

No one knew for sure.

As she walked around the whale, Emily saw that there was no mystery why this one was dying. She approached it.

A bite mark showed on the orca's back behind the dorsal fin. A huge chunk of flesh was missing and the pattern showed the jagged cuts of a shark's teeth.

She drew closer still as the size of the wound became clear.

Whoa.

The bite was ten to twelve feet across. And had removed a half moon slice of the orca's back.

No creature would survive that mutilation.

A high pitched squeal made her jump.

A similar squeal echoed in from the water and Emily saw an even larger orca swimming in water that barely covered its back. It had a dorsal fin that reached six feet into the air. It would've reached another foot or two if the whole thing had been there. It looked like whatever got this one also took a chunk of the one splashing through the breaking waves. Several smaller orcas swam in tight circles in the deeper water beyond the break.

The squealing continued.

They were communicating.

Emily started around the back end of the orca to get a better look at the pod in the water when another discovery made her lurch to a stop.

A baby orca protruded from the underside of the dying orca.

It was a mother and baby!

The baby's front half was stuck inside the mother's body.

She realized with a start that it was going to die if she didn't do something.

So she decided to act.

To try.

That's all she could do.

She hurried over to the infant and grabbed hold of its tail.

The tail unexpectedly flapped and sent her sprawling into a face full of wet sand.

It was still alive!

But for how much longer, she didn't know.

Emily scrambled up and got a tighter grip on the infant's tail. She pulled as hard as she could, stumbling back and forth as the powerful tail dragged her side to side. Another pull using all her strength and a powerful flick of the tail sent her sprawling into the sand.

She got up and tried again until she was breathing hard and fast. A wave of dizziness made her pause and grab her knees to avoid keeling over.

The infant wouldn't budge. He or she or it was stuck.

The mother squealed and what Emily guessed by its size and dangerous position in the water was the father answering back.

How could she help them?

Maybe she couldn't.

She hadn't been able to help her own father or mother. What made her think she could do any better for this struggling family?

"Stop it!" she muttered to herself. "The pity party can wait. There will be plenty of time to starve and feel sorry for yourself."

She walked around to the back of the mother, trying to figure out how to get more leverage on the infant.

There was nothing nearby like a tree trunk or other suitable anchor and she didn't have a rope anyway.

Leverage wasn't the answer.

An idea came to her.

And she recoiled.

That was a last chance kind of thing.

She thought for a couple of minutes, trying to come up with a better idea. With any other idea.

The infant twitched. It twitched again and then didn't stop trembling. It wasn't the voluntary movement of a muscle.

It was in trouble.

Emily jumped into action and did her best not to think too much. She drew the kukri knife from the sheath fastened to the small of her back and knelt down beside the mother and baby. She placed a gentle hand on the mother's belly. "I'm sorry."

A lump formed in her throat, making it hard to swallow. She patted the white belly. "I wish there was another way."

Not wanting to waste another second with the infant in distress, she gripped the razor sharp kukri and drove the blade through the mother's skin.

It sank into warm blubber as blood welled out and formed a puddle in the sand.

Emily kept pushing, slicing through blubber and then muscle.

The mother squealed a long, horrifying note that the father echoed from the water.

"Come on," Emily said as she cut deeper yet. When she'd gone as far as she dared to keep the blade from touching the baby, she grabbed the hilt with both hands and began sawing up the belly, widening the birth canal as she went.

The sharp, thick scent on her tongue made her gag, but she kept cutting. Blood spilled over her hands and arms and down her front, coating the survival suit. She was glad she'd zipped it up to her chin before starting or else her clothes would've gotten drenched with the sticky fluid.

She kept cutting as tears streamed down her cheeks.

The mother's squeals broke her heart into a million pieces.

She was killing her.

Yes, the mother was going to die anyway. But cutting her open hastened that death and the guilt was tough to reason away.

Something in the tissue parted and the baby spurted out a few inches.

Emily tossed the knife away and latched onto its trembling tail. She dug her boots into the sand and leaned back as she heaved.

A slurping squish and the infant came free.

It wriggled like a dying fish on the sand.

The mother's squeak rose to a fevered pitch and then went silent. The father in the water carried on squeaking and chirping faster than seemed possible.

"You're not dying on me now!" Emily shouted as she grabbed the baby's tail. She pulled and went nowhere. The baby must've weighed a few hundred pounds.

She jumped over to the other side and then leaned into it. With a grunt, she managed to roll it over a quarter turn. She heaved again and got a half turn.

The advancing water splashed around it as she rolled it another full turn. A few more feet and the advancing wave was deep enough to reach to her calves.

The water rolled in, lifting the baby off the sand. She heaved and pulled the baby into deeper water.

Emily splashed through the hip-high frothing surf, guiding the infant toward the deeper water and its waiting father.

It twitched from side to side, but didn't take off. Maybe it was too weak? Maybe she was too late?

Another wave swept in, hitting it in the face. The infant whipped its tail and shot forward.

The movement threw her backward and splashing into the water. She settled into a floating sit and watched the male orca swimming circles in anticipation.

The baby made it beyond the breaking surf and the father sidled up next to it. A fin caressed and steered the infant toward the waiting pod. The two sank under the surface.

Emily watched the massive dorsal fin of the male slide down and disappear. She stood for a second, but the biting cold water didn't make her want to linger.

As she turned, a huge splash burst through the incoming wave and the massive male exploded through. He skidded to a stop less than ten feet away.

Emily knew she should get out of the water. Get up to the beach where it was safe.

But she couldn't move.

Her limbs were solid ice.

Her heart thumped like a fist pounding through her ribcage.

Every follicle on her scalp tingled with electric current.

The male twisted its head to the side and a huge dark eye stared at her.

It blinked, stared again, and whistled loud enough for her eardrums to hurt.

A wave rolled in and it squirmed to the side, making its way through the breaking surf. Another wave and it pulled free.

A few powerful thrusts of its tail later and it was headed out to join the pod surrounding the baby.

The pod circled round and round the baby as they moved as a group to the south. The dominant male circled around the outside of both, keeping a perimeter watch for any dangers.

Emily stumbled out of the water and up onto the beach. She glanced at the bite mark on the dead mother and a shudder ripped through her.

There was something out there. Something she didn't want to encounter.

23

The fire crackled and spit as it burned the moisture out of the wood. The orange light reflected a few dozen feet onto the beach but didn't penetrate more than a few feet beyond the dense tree line.

Emily held her hands as close to the flames as possible without singeing them.

With all the wood so wet, building a friction fire would've been next to impossible. Fortunately, the mini survival kit stowed in her suit had come up big with a magnesium fire starter and a few other essentials.

A bitterly cold wind whipped down the beach, causing the fire to roar and the heat to get sucked away for an instant.

Her teeth chattered as she waited for the warmth to return.

The gust died down and the heat again licked her palms.

Alone on an island.

A hike up to a nearby ridge had confirmed that.

Lost.

And hungry.

Still, it could've been worse. Her clothes had been freezing because water had leaked in with the survival suit partially unzipped. She'd managed to build a fire at the edge of the tree line and dried her wet clothes. Dried and smoked them, was more like it.

She smelled like a campfire to the core. Like it was a scent exuding from her pores.

She hadn't frozen to death. That was something.

But while she'd survived impossible odds already, they didn't look to be improving any time soon. And with the night temperature dropping fast, every moment that passed was another roll of the dice.

The temperature was dropping fast. It didn't feel like the fire would be enough to get her through to the morning.

She turned away from the heat to review the pile of materials she'd gathered over the last couple of hours.

At least this island had plenty of trees. She'd used the kukri to chop down thick branches for poles and thinner ones for insulation. A simple lean-to with the back and sides walled off would do wonders to trap the heat of the fire and her body once she settled in for the night.

She tried to swallow but it got stuck halfway. Her throat was too dry to function. She'd have to find water in the morning or she wouldn't make it much longer.

Yes, every moment was another roll of the dice.

And mother nature was like a Las Vegas casino because, sooner or later, the house always won.

She let the fire warm her a little longer. The cold that waited a few feet beyond its heat wasn't anything she was rushing to get back to.

There she sat, perfectly balanced between heat and cold. The glowing orange fire casting flickering shadows on the ground.

A little closer and it would burn her.

A little further and she'd freeze to death.

How fragile a human could be.

How perfectly suited to us our environment had to be.

She gritted her teeth and got to work.

The flesh was weak, but the mind was strong.

The will to survive had been honed to a razor edge over tens of thousands of years. The last few hundred years had placed a thin layer of cotton over the top, but nothing more. Below the soft exterior, there remained abundant steel.

Beyond the comfort and convenience that most people considered a birth right in the modern day, there lived a hard reality.

One that didn't care about expectations of privilege or health. That was the stone upon which humanity failed or flourished.

And though many bled and died on that stone, many more survived long enough for the species to evolve.

To adapt.

To fight.

To never quit, even in the face of impossible odds.

Emily heaved up one of the poles and planted it in the sand pit she'd dug. Only a few feet away from the fire and already her fingers were getting numb.

She settled the vertical pole into place and kicked sand around the base to anchor it. After working until her fingers, hands, and limbs were definitely numb, she finally had a basic structure built. Two vertical poles with branch points so even a carpenter could've set a level on it and been impressed.

Okay, maybe not.

But they were close enough to the keep the larger ridge pole straddling them more or less parallel to the ground. With the ridgepole no more than three feet off the ground, it wasn't going to win any comfort awards. But it would keep the small pocket of air warm, and that would keep her alive.

Next was the insulation. The smaller branches hadn't been stripped and so were large fans of twigs ending in a thick layer of pine needles.

She hefted one up and got the end hooked over the ridgepole. With enough of these, she'd have a proper shelter with a warm fire on the doorstep.

The fire crackled in response like a living being.

She glanced over and started when she saw the dying flames. She'd been so focused on the shelter, the fire had burned down and was almost out.

After a few frantic minutes of feeding smaller kindling in and then raising the ante as the flames grew stronger, she again had a bright beast burning.

And it was a beast.

As alive as any animal that walked the earth.

As nurturing as any mother.

As firm as any father.

As temperamental as any heart.

As calculating as any mind.

Emily tried to swallow but the attempt didn't make it past her tongue. A wave of dizziness swept over her and she plopped down to avoid falling over like a felled tree.

She hugged her knees and focused on slowing her racing heartbeat.

A glare in the dark distance out over the ocean caught her attention.

A column of fire climbed into the sky. The hot yellow glow burned into the surrounding black. The light leaked to the far corners of the horizon. It reached higher and higher and then burned itself out.

It vanished as quickly as it had appeared and the shadows reclaimed the night.

Emily stared into the black with the image of the fire still ghosting in her vision.

What was that?

Obviously an explosion of some kind.

Nuclear?

No. It didn't look that big.

What would cause an explosion like that?

Maybe if an oil tanker or refinery or something like that blew up.

Whatever it was, it meant there were people in that direction. Assuming somebody was still alive.

She grabbed a nearby stick and laid it in the sand pointing in the direction where the fire had been. She grabbed a few more and pounded in stakes on each side to ensure the bearing wouldn't be lost by an accidental kick.

An icy wind gusted through, stinging her cheeks.

She had to finish this shelter and tuck in for the night. That would keep her alive until morning.

After that, it was all about finding some water.

And if she somehow miraculously figured out a way to make it off this island, the stick pointed in the direction she'd be heading.

24

BOB grabbed his knees and took a deep breath. The walk to downtown that morning had really taken it out of his already pathetically weak limbs.

"You okay?" Rome said from a few feet ahead. The simple sentiment of the words and the tone in which they were expressed couldn't have been further apart. He scanned the road in both directions for oncoming traffic.

If anyone was out driving at this late hour, they were up to no good. That much was certain

"Come on. It's another block up around the bend on Monashka."

Between heaving breaths, Bob answered. "You do remember that I, one, am old? And, two, almost died recently?"

Even in the dark of night with no moon and few stars bright enough to penetrate the haze, Bob saw the flash of anger streak through the kid's eyes. "You do remember that I, one, don't care? And, two, don't need to be reminded by you of all people about recent events?"

Bob raised a hand in surrender, even as the other clamped harder onto his knee to shoulder the added weight. "I'm sorry."

"We're already late," Rome said as he spun around and continued forward along the road.

There was zero chance Bob was going to hang out alone in the pitch black in an area he'd never been. And that was before considering the possibility of running into one of CB's gang members. They'd gotten wildly lucky to escape one encounter.

They weren't going to get that lucky again.

Bob pushed upright and started off, doing his best to keep pace with a kid that was a quarter of his age. If he hadn't been so overweight, it would've been an impossible task. But as it was, he managed to keep up.

They made it around the bend in the road and their destination came into view.

The Gas & Go on the less frequented north end of town.

They'd run into a man named Henry on their way back to the apartment after escaping the gang members. He'd told them about the meeting tonight and explained that it was a good spot being so far from where CB's gang was holed up at the Kodiak Brewery downtown.

As Rome drew near to the service station, a voice called out in the night. "Identify yourself!"

Bob looked around but didn't see where the speaker was.

"It's me!" Rome said in a whisper shout.

"Who's me?"

"Rome Bickle. Is that you, Henry?"

"Who's that coming up behind you?"

"Bob. The old guy I was with when we ran into you."

"Alright, they're good," Henry said as he emerged from the pitch black shadows in the thicket of towering spruce to their right. A man Bob didn't recognize stepped out behind him.

Notably, both men held high-powered rifles that were casually held at their sides and aimed at the ground.

Guns not pointing in theirs faces was a big improvement considering the events of the day.

Henry clapped Rome on the back. "Glad you could make it, son. We're gonna need every able body we can get." He glanced past Rome and tossed a curt nod to Bob.

"Hello again," Bob said. "Thanks for inviting us."

Henry spat a glob of dark juice on the pavement before turning to Rome. "Anyway, follow me inside."

They headed toward the small store up front when a faint glow swept across the ground. "Someone's coming," Henry shouted. "Get inside! Hurry!" He yanked the door open and ushered them through as a vehicle came around the bend and headlights flooded the area with light.

Bob had to pinch his eyes shut at the sting of the adjustment.

"Get behind the counter," Henry said as he herded them both forward.

The vehicle outside squealed to a stop with the lights pointed at the store and pouring light through the large glass windows. "Hello?" a voice outside shouted.

Henry eased his rifle over the counter, making sure to stay in the shadow behind the cash register.

"Is anyone there?"

Another voice joined the first. "Are you sure this is the

place? How do you know? Isn't there another one of these somewhere? Maybe it's the other one."

"Doctor, let me do my job and you do yours. Now, please get back into the vehicle. Doctor! What are you—"

The bells tied to the front door tinkled as it swept open. "It's unlocked."

The sound of pounding boots approached and the first voice replied. "Get behind me. I didn't agree to this operation with you in the lead."

Henry shifted the rifle over to aim down the aisle where the two men would soon be. He moved his foot as he did and his cowboy boot landed on Bob's pinkie.

A stabbing pain shot up Bob's arm and he grunted before he could stop himself.

The sound of quick shuffling movement. "Who's there?" the first voice shouted as a bright beam of light swept back and forth through the air above them.

"Drop your weapon!" Henry replied. "I've got you dead to rights!"

"Stop!" the second voice said. "We don't have time for this! I am Dr. Yong from Project Hermes. Police Chief Stuckey and I have an arrangement for me to be here tonight."

"Oh, why didn't you say so?" Henry said as he stood up and nodded for Bob and Rome to do the same. "He told me to expect you. Now why don't you do something smart for a change and go turn off your headlights! And park your Rover around the side. You're literally spotlighting our secret meeting, for Chrissakes!"

"Sorry," Dr. Yong replied. "Sergeant Moretti?"

"On it," the large man in a dark blue uniform said as

he jogged outside. The headlights shut off and the vehicle creeped out of sight.

The door to the back room flew open and Stuckey barreled through with a shotgun raised and ready. He glanced a few times between the two groups before lowering his voice. "You must be Dr. Yong."

"That is correct."

Stuckey marched over and shook his hand. "Thanks for coming."

"It was the least I could do."

Sergeant Moretti entered and took up a position beside the frail-looking doctor.

Who was this guy?

What was Project Hermes?

Your typical family physician didn't merit the need for a bodyguard.

Stuckey gestured toward the door at the back by the soda machine. "Everyone's here. I need you to tell them what you told me."

Dr. Yong nodded. "That's one of the reasons I'm here."

25

_____

The utility room at the back of the service station couldn't have been more than twenty feet by fifteen feet. And nearly every square foot was packed with people. Shoulder to shoulder where a movement in one place caused a chain reaction of movements that echoed through the space like a ripple across a pond.

It reminded Bob of the dance clubs he used to take his ex-wife to. She'd loved getting high on coke and then grinding on him all night long.

Not being opposed to either past time, he'd enjoyed every minute of it.

The problem arose when he'd discovered her fascination was more about the drugs and the screwing than it was about him.

When the nukes dropped, Bob had initially hoped his cheating ex-wife and ex-best friend had died in the onslaught. But after surviving six days now after the end of the world, he realized that the worse fate was to continue living.

Dying was easy.

Living was hell.

And it was only going to get worse.

So now, whenever either of their wretched, lying faces bounced across the surface of his mind, he wished them long and miserable lives.

"Scoot over," Rome said as he elbowed Bob to the side. "Not enough room in here for big people."

The stink of unwashed bodies permeated the air, but the acrid scent of cigarette smoke cut through it.

The group filed inside with Chief Stuckey bringing up the rear. He closed the door behind him and frowned when he turned back around. "Who the hell is smoking?"

The two dozen or so people assembled murmured a second before a small voice spoke up.

"Me. Sorry, my vape doesn't work anymore."

Stuckey bulldozed through the crowd until he arrived to face the culprit.

The crowd shrank away from the confrontation and Bob nearly spat venom when he saw the smoker.

The long-haired greasy scumbag who owned The Weary Traveler. The same one that had stolen the pistol. Yes, the pistol that he too had admittedly stolen. But that didn't make the guy blameless. He'd stolen the gun and then threatened to kick Bob out on the street!

Chief Stuckey grabbed the burning cigarette out of the guy's hand. "Ronnie, this is a gas station! No open flames near gas!" He threw it on the floor and ground it out with his boot. "Go out front and help Henry fill up every gas can that needs it."

"What?' Ronnie said as he ran his fingers through hair that hadn't been regularly washed long before the end of the world made it harder to do so. "I wanna know what's happening in this town, just like everyone else here."

"One of us will catch you up, later. Your idiocy has nominated you to be Henry's helper. Go help him."

Ronnie stood motionless, a snarl on his face.

"Now!" Stuckey thundered so loud Ronnie flinched like he'd been hit by lightning.

The coward bolted out of the room.

"Everyone, thanks for coming," Stuckey said as he edged toward the less crowded side where Dr. Yong and his bodyguard stood. "I originally called this meeting to organize a resistance."

"That gang is tearing this town apart! I say we kill 'em all!"

"I heard some fella named CB is the leader. Let's find him and string him up!"

There were shouts of approval and other suggestions of the best way to deal with the gang leader.

Stuckey waved everyone to silence. "That's not why we're here anymore. Bennett, raise your hand."

A man near the back raised his hand.

"I went by Bennett's place this afternoon to recruit him to the meeting. Turned out he had a working HAM radio."

"That's right," the man said. "Had all my gear in a Faraday Cage. Folks called me crazy. They don't anymore."

"Yes, well, he had me listen to a transmission that's changed the course of this meeting." Chief Stuckey turned to Dr. Yong. "Doctor, can you tell everybody what we're facing?"

"Of course," Dr. Yong said with a subtle bow. He turned to face the crowd and scanned their faces.

Bob did the same.

There was a strange concoction of anticipation and mistrust painted on most faces.

"My name is Dr. Zhang Yong. I am the assis... I am the Director of Project Hermes."

"I knew it!" someone called out. "I knew that place was real."

Bennett shrugged. "I knew it was real the whole time."

Dr. Yong adjusted his glasses while the bodyguard scanned the crowd for threats. The doctor continued. "I assure you. Project Hermes is quite real. We are located in an underground complex at the interior of the island. The project has been running for over ten years."

"Yep," Bennett said with a self-satisfied grin. "Knew it. You folks found aliens. Been experimenting on 'em the whole time."

"They found aliens?" another voice said.

"Course they did," Bennett assured him.

"I can't tell you anything specific about our work at the moment," Dr. Yong continued. "What I can tell you is that the facility has hardened electrical infrastructure and, for the most part, our equipment survived the closest EMP released in space six days ago."

"Closest?" someone said. "How many were there?"

"Quiet down, everyone!" Stuckey bellowed. "This is important."

"Thank you, chief," Dr. Yong said with a nod. "The crucial thing is that we have working meteorological equipment and that gear has spotted a problem. Due to the prevailing wind patterns and dominant cold fronts, there is a massive amount of radioactive fallout headed this way."

A chorus of voices broke out.

Bob's wasn't one of them.

He closed his eyes. Of course, there was. No matter how bad you thought it was, it could always get worse. His ex-wife had taught him that valuable lesson. She was like Buddha dishing out all the life lessons, only sexier and perverted and with no moral compass.

"Quiet down, folks!" Stuckey shouted until the assembled mass complied.

"From what we've gathered, a large number of nuclear warheads hit Tokyo, Japan. Likely fired from China and possibly Russia as well. Tokyo is gone. Wiped from the map. And all the radioactive particles that got sucked up into the atmosphere from that catastrophe will arrive here in approximately thirty six hours."

More shouting ensued, until Stuckey again got them all to quiet down.

"So you're saying it's going to rain poison or something on us?"

Dr. Yong nodded. "Yes. It will be a black rain. The soot of a vaporized Tokyo charged with radioactive particles that will destroy any organic matter they come into contact with. Within days of exposure, people will begin getting sick. Radiation sickness is like cancer on overdrive. It will poison your bodies. It will poison your air, your water, your food, everything. Depending on how concentrated it turns out to be, people could begin to die in days or maybe weeks. It's impossible to know for certain. But the danger is real. And it is coming."

Absolute pandemonium broke out. People pushing to get out and go home to protect their families. Others cursing everything under the blanketed sun. Dr. Yong's bodyguard shoved away those that got too close.

So this was how it was going to end.

Bob shook his head. As much as he regretted trying to kill himself, that was probably a better way to go than what was in store.

Stuckey blocked the door while shouting for everyone to shut up and listen. Eventually, everyone did. "Listen, everyone! Dr. Yong has an offer to make."

The doctor nodded. "Yes, I do. The population of Kodiak is six thousand people. While Project Hermes was never made to house that number, we can host as many as needed for a short time. I have made other arrangements for more long term living. For now, you must get as many people as possible to the dock at Ushiankiak Bay by tomorrow night. Our latest projections have the fallout making landfall the following morning. That gives us a buffer of twelve hours to get everyone underground before it hits."

"Where's the entrance?"

"It's inside the power station on Terror Lake. A four mile drive from the dock and we'll have every vehicle at our disposal waiting to transport people to the facility. Space will be precious, so only bring what you can carry."

Murmurs of indignation echoed around the tight space.

Not a problem for Bob. He didn't have squat. Everything he owned may as well have been on another planet. Assuming it wasn't already radioactive dust.

"So, we're just supposed to up and leave everything behind? Our homes and land and property?"

Dr. Yong nodded. "If you want to live? Yes."

There wasn't time for the crowd to digest this latest bit of information because the crack of gunshots echoed in.

Stuckey threw open the door to the front of the store and more gunfire echoed in. "They found us!" He turned to the doctor. "Go out the back door to the alley. It's past the bathroom and to the left."

The bodyguard nodded and pulled his charge in the indicated direction.

"The rest of you," Stuckey shouted, "follow me!"

Being unarmed and generally a coward, Bob had no intention of following, but the current of bodies flooding through carried him along for the ride.

Bob stumbled forward doing everything he could not to fall down and get stampeded. He made it out and fanned out along the shelf running the length of the aisle. Men and women with rifles tucked into their shoulders lined up along the shelf like soldiers in trench warfare.

A dozen trucks in a half-circle were parked on the road beyond the gas pumps outside. All of their headlights lit up the front as bright as day.

Henry was tucked behind a gas pump for cover with his rifle held at the ready. Shafts of light punched through the air around him.

Twenty or more gas cans of various shapes and sizes sat on the ground in the middle of the parking lot. A large circular hatch lay next to the dark hole where a fuel crank and siphon hose lay on the ground.

One end of the hose snaked down into the underground tank while the other end leaked fuel onto the pavement.

Ronnie Dean was nowhere to be seen.

The glass windows shattered as bullets tore through air.

People standing on both sides of Bob returned fire.

The deafening sounds made his ears first ring and then ache like needles were poking his eardrums. He was about to drop down below the lip of the shelf when something outside caught his attention.

A spark on the pavement.

A single flame jumped higher.

A trail that tracked along the spilled fuel toward its source.

The growing orange glow lit up Henry as he made the sign of the cross over his heart.

The fire enveloped the spilled fuel around the crank.

The next instant, there was nothing but heat and light like the surface of the sun.

The explosion flung Bob backward even as it sucked the air out of his lungs.

His head struck something hard and he thought, for the instant before it was over, that he was thankful to go out like this.

It was way better than wasting away from radiation poisoning.

26

MARCO opened his mouth and pain shot through his jaw. He eased it shut and the joint clicked, sending another electric zap through his head.

The butt end of a rifle did that kind of damage.

He started to reach up to massage it, but just as quickly gave up when the tape binding his hands behind his back stopped the movement.

They'd been loaded up into an old school bus that looked like an antique from a cable TV show. Where they'd dug it up, he didn't know. But there was no way it had carted kids around for at least several decades.

At the front of the bus, the driver took a left turn onto Mill Bay Road faster than was safe or sane. The tires squealed and all the occupants, prisoners was more accurate, slid to the right.

Marco bumped into Chief Stuckey. The two shared a bench seat made for three school children and not for two grown men. The contact sent another pain signal jabbing into his brain. He grimaced and focused on not passing out.

Stuckey shifted toward the aisle in a futile attempt to give him some more room.

Oscar was nowhere to be seen.

Did he survive?

Marco didn't know what happened to him after the explosion. There was chaos and people dying and then the gang members loading the survivors on this bus.

Several stood at the front, laughing and jeering and taking turns aiming their rifles at the captives like they were about to spray them all down.

Seated in the last row, Marco and Stuckey were furthest away, but not far enough to escape a hard rain of bullets.

"How's your jaw?" Stuckey said in a whispered voice.

"Don't think it's broken," Marco replied. He spoke through barely parted lips. Anything wider than half an inch invited agony.

"You'll be lucky if not. You got cracked hard."

Marco nodded. That was an understatement. His face felt like it gotten hit by a train. "You don't look much better. Your lip looks like a split sausage."

Stuckey licked his lower lip and winced. "Least I knocked out that bastard's front teeth." He glanced to the front.

Alexei Volkov stood there with a rifle in one hand and his other on the driver's seat for balance. Even in the dim glow of the inadequate overhead lighting, the twisted grimace contorting his bushy beard was obvious. Somewhere hidden behind that beard was a mouth with two fewer teeth.

Stuckey shook his head. "Red's the type you had to be watchful around in the best of times. But now, he's a dangerous animal let loose. One with a thirst for violence and mayhem. I should've put him down long ago."

The bus hit a pothole and the back end jolted upward lifting Marco off his seat for an instant. He slammed back down and his teeth crashed together.

Blinding pain shot through the center of his head.

"You okay?"

The image of Stuckey and the surrounding world seemed far away. Like Marco was looking through the wrong end of a telescope.

"Stay with me. We've got to be ready when the opportunity presents itself." Stuckey pivoted away. "I've got the edge of the tape up, but can't get it off with my wrists pinned together."

Stuckey scooted back until he bumped into Marco. "Can you grab hold of the end and pull?"

Marco shifted around, feeling with his fingers until he found the lifted corner of the duct tape around Stuckey's wrists. He pinched it and scooted forward.

The tape slipped through his fingers.

He scooted back, found it again, and pinched as hard as his fingers could. He scooted forward and felt the tape pull free a couple of inches.

Now, they just had to do that about thirty more times.

The bus stopped before they'd completed half that number.

"It's getting looser," Stuckey said. "Keep going."

The accordion door at the front squealed open.

"Everybody out!" Red shouted as he yanked the man in the first seat to his feet.

"Hurry!" Stuckey said.

Marco had the urge to respond because he was already moving as fast as he could considering he was clinging to consciousness and he had almost no freedom or room to maneuver.

But he kept his mouth shut.

It was less painful that way.

He managed to pull off a few more layers when he abruptly stopped.

"What are you two doing?" Red shouted, towering above them. He had to hunch over from the low ceiling. A flashlight appeared in his hand and clicked on.

Their seat was suddenly bathed in blinding light.

"What do we have here?" he said in a voice that indicated he knew exactly what they had. He grabbed a fistful of Stuckey's hair and slammed his head forward.

The chief's face bounced off the steel bar of the seat in front. A nasty cut across the bridge of his nose gaped open and blood poured out and into his mouth.

Stuckey spat a spray of blood up into Red's face.

Their captor didn't take it well.

He slammed the Chief's face into the seat again. Hard enough this time so that Stuckey's eyes lost focus.

Red leaned down and got into Stuckey's face. His breath reeked of vodka vapors and poor dental hygiene. "CB's going to punish the both of you. In ways you can't imagine."

The glow of light landed across the side of Red's head and Marco noticed the angry hole of pink skin where an ear should've been.

The visual made his stomach flop.

The light moved and the horrific injury dropped into shadow.

Red yanked Stuckey to his feet and shoved him forward through the aisle.

Marco quickly stood and followed as his jaw couldn't take any more abuse. Their eyes drew close as he passed. "Who is CB?"

Red's eyes flamed with excitement.

And something else.

He'd seen it before.

Somewhere.

The memory surfaced.

In the churches of his youth.

In those filled with the Holy Spirit.

The total belief.

The rapturous embrace of the destruction of reason and personal will.

It frightened him then. It frightened him now.

Red pulled him closer until their eyes were so close an invisible current crackled between. "Chernobog. The Dark One."

27

The bus had stopped in the parking lot of the Kodiak Island Brewing Company. The squat single story structure with all glass front didn't seem like a great choice for a defensible position.

Marco followed the other captives through a gauntlet of gun-toting gang members as they whooped and hollered. Several took cheap shots as prisoners filed past, knocking them to the ground and then laughing harder than ever.

An older man took a punch to the gut and collapsed to the pavement. He rolled over onto his back, clutching his stomach.

Marco stuttered a step as he recognized him.

It was Bob Randy! That slimy producer from *Sole Survivor*. The reality TV show that had brought Marco to the island and now, like so many other things, meant nothing and only served as a sad memory of life before the end of the world.

Marco felt zero empathy for his suffering. It was his

fault that Marco was here in the first place. If only that call had gone to voicemail. If only he'd said no. He'd still be back on his family's land west of Baker, Montana. Folks were probably doing fine out there. There were no population centers or military bases nearby so the nukes probably never hit anywhere in the region.

In fact, maybe life would be better for him now. The bank that was trying to take his land probably no longer functioned. All the computer records of what he owed were now nothing more than scattered electrons.

But he'd answered the call.

And he'd accepted the offer.

Which brought him to Emily. He never would've met her without going on the show. Not that it mattered now because she was gone.

It was a lot to process in the seconds that he watched Bob crumpled on the ground in agony. A huge kid helped him up to his feet. He looked familiar, too. Rome. Flo's son.

Now a son without a mother.

Whereas Mr. Hollywood's suffering didn't produce a spark of sympathy in Marco's chest, the boy's loss hit him square in the chest.

He knew what it was like to lose your parents at a young age.

The line shuffled forward through an open space between two parked buses. As soon as the group passed, an old delivery truck fired up and pulled across the open space to close the perimeter.

Marco glanced around as they headed toward the front door.

The place was well chosen as a defensible position. It

backed up to a steep hill and the perimeter of parked school buses created an open interior courtyard. Gang members carrying rifles walked along the roofs of the stationary buses. They moved from bus to bus by stepping across the narrow gaps between the abutted vehicles.

Nobody was getting through that without a tank or a small army of soldiers.

And with the resistance crushed before it even began, this place was basically impregnable.

Gang members threw open the tinted front doors and light spilled out into the frigid night air.

"Keep it moving!" Red shouted as the visual assault slowed the line. He shoved the man ahead of them in the back which set off a chain reaction of stumbling and recovering from those ahead. He turned back and got in Stuckey's face. "You're gonna wish you were dead," he said with an evil grin.

Stuckey's nose bled freely down through his mustache and into his mouth. "You know how this ends, Red. It ends with my hands around your neck, strangling you to death."

Red chuckled. "We'll see about that after CB is done with you." He grabbed Stuckey's jacket by the shoulder and threw him forward.

Marco followed through the front doors into a large open space. The right half of the room had long tables filled with more than a dozen gang members drinking as much beer as they spilled.

That was probably another big reason for this being their headquarters.

With all the grocery store shelves stripped bare days

ago, this brewery must've drawn these idiots in like gnats to sweat.

Their captors guided them to the open area occupying the left half of the room. They shoved them together into a tight huddle of bodies.

Several glaring bright lights close to the back wall completely hid whatever was behind them.

Marco glanced in that direction and quickly shielded his eyes from the brightness. He wondered how they had this much power going. Some kind of rudimentary twelve volt battery system?

A door squeaked open and the gang members erupted in cheers and garbled swearing and cries of support. Whoever had entered stood hidden from view, beyond the blinding lights. The cacophony of voices echoed through the voluminous interior like an amphitheater.

Red banged the butt of his rifle on the floor several times and bellowed at the assembled drunks. "Quiet!"

The room sunk into silence faster than Marco would've thought possible. There was order to this chaos.

A calm, measured voice spoke.

"Well, well, well."

The words spilled out thick with southern drawl.

"Look what we have here. A big group of concerned citizens. Ready to do what's right." He laughed and the facade of civilized reason slipped. There was madness in the high-pitched cackle.

And more than a little.

"Y'all planning something that I should know about?"

None of the prisoners spoke.

"What's wrong? Cat got your tongue? Well, I can fix that in a New York minute."

A shadowed silhouette stepped forward between the banks of dazzling lights.

A man of average size.

Through squinted eyes, Marco couldn't make out much more. But the voice. He knew it.

Charlie from Tennessee.

With shocking speed, Charlie leaped upon a captive in the front. He drove the prisoner to the ground and raked the knife across the poor man's neck.

A bubbling scream of terror.

Crimson blood geysered through the air and splashed onto the wood plank floor.

Charlie sat down on the man's chest. The blade flashed through the air and into the man's mouth.

A gurgling cry.

A pool of blood grew on the floor.

The lunatic lifted his hand into the air. "Now, I've got your tongue!" He put the tongue into his mouth and gnawed off a bite like it was a chunk of beef jerky.

Horrified gasps escaped from several of the captives.

"Jesus," Chief Stuckey whispered.

The dying man struggled a few more seconds and then went quiet and still.

The killer stood and handed the rest of the tongue to Red. He nodded when the larger man hesitated. Red shoved the whole thing into his mouth and chewed.

Charlie turned back to the prisoners. "Now, I'm gonna ask again, and this time, I'm not going to be so understanding if I don't get an answer."

He stepped in front of the lights, partially blocking them.

A halo of illumination glowed around him. A heavenly glow, only this was the devil.

"Hold up a second!" Charlie shouted. He scooted around the group and reached in toward the middle.

The captives melted away like snow near a red-hot branding iron.

He grabbed someone and pulled them out.

Bob.

Charlie held Bob by the collar as he looked around the room. "Look who showed up on my front porch?"

Bob stared at the ground. The fear in his eyes shined brighter than the lights behind.

Charlie grabbed Bob by the ear and twisted hard. The old man yelped and his knees buckled. Charlie dragged him across the floor as Bob scrambled along to keep his ear from getting torn off.

Charlie looked around the room, ensuring he had everyone's attention. "This man owes me a million dollars." He released Bob's ear and let him collapse to the floor. "Are you going to pay me my million dollars?"

Bob held a trembling hand up in surrender while babbling something.

"No? I didn't think so. I'm gonna save something special for you, Mr. Randy." He spat out the name like it was a turd in his mouth.

Charlie returned to the gathered captives, looking them over. "Honestly, I don't want the money anymore. I've got something better."

His gaze scanned over them like livestock.

Marco tried to duck behind Stuckey, but the chief shifted to the side at exactly the wrong time.

Charlie's eyes stopped and eyes locked on Marco. A twisted smile split his face. "I've got this town. And I've got each and every one of you."

28

EMILY sat in the sand at her campsite with her hands inches away from the glowing coals of the fire. The sun had finally cleared the horizon and was starting to add some much-needed warmth of its own.

Her teeth chattered from the chill pervading her core. The night had been long and brutally cold. She'd managed to keep the fire going, but the gusting winds often sucked the warmth away as soon as it hinted at gathering.

She tried to swallow but it got caught halfway as her parched throat rubbed together like sandpaper.

She needed water.

Like never before.

Ironic since she was staring at an ocean full of it. Just not the kind her body needed.

During the weeks of filming *Sole Survivor*, she'd gone without a few different times. But not like this. After it warmed up more, she'd have to venture inland into the forest and pray she could find a water source. With the small mountains dominating the interior of the island, there was a good chance moving water was around somewhere.

What else?

The shelter needed improvement.

And some food would be nice.

A movement on the beach caught her eye.

It was the carcass of the mother orca. It had shifted a few feet down the beach.

High tide was coming in.

Another larger wave climbed up the beach, splashed over the inert body, and then pulled it a little further into the water.

A thought struck her and she jumped up.

Another wave pulled at the body as she sprinted over.

The orca was dead.

It was meat.

She had no idea what an orca tasted like. Probably not good. But it was meat and it was just sitting there.

Well, now inching back into the ocean with every receding wave.

She arrived as a larger wave rolled in, this one grabbed the body and sucked it out a dozen feet.

She should've thought of it earlier.

Emily yanked the kukri out of the sheath at her hip. Somehow, the knife her father had given her so long ago had made it through everything she'd been through. She slammed it into the orca. She leaned into it and pushed with all her strength. The blade bit down to the hilt.

Another wave came in and splashed over the orca, drenching her in the process.

She flinched as the icy water hit and spilled inside the

half-worn survival suit. Her feet and legs were already starting to feel slow and heavy. The waterline up to her knees.

Emily climbed up on top of the carcass as another wave came in. As it sucked back out, the body moved with it. This time in deep enough water to break free of the sand underneath.

The body rolled to settle into a new equilibrium.

She scrambled up the side to stay on top. She accidentally let go of the kukri as she did. She made it to the top and spun around in a panic as she realized what she'd done.

The knife!

It was still there, stuck in the orca's body. The handle bobbed in and out of the water as the carcass steadied.

She had to move fast.

She reached for the knife and the orca started to roll in that direction.

She jerked backward to stop the roll and keep herself from getting dunked in the bone-freezing water.

How was she going to get it then?

She dropped to her belly and laid across the orca's white stomach, perpendicular to its length. She curled around it and kept as much of her lower half on the other side as possible while also inching forward with arms outstretched.

The body lolled back and forth as waves swept by, but it appeared to be working. She stretched the final few inches and latched onto the hilt.

Yes!

A big wave crashed into the body, almost throwing

her off into the water. She yanked the knife free and managed to hang on as the body rolled underneath.

The wave retreated, dragging the carcass deeper.

Emily looked around.

She was floating away from the beach!

She glanced back at the open ocean as the sound of splashing grabbed her attention.

A dark fin protruded from the water.

Was it the male coming back for his partner?

The fin rose into the air as the creature drew closer to the surface.

The thing was moving fast.

Right at her.

And then she noticed something else.

Something that froze the blood in her veins.

Something that stole the air from her lungs.

The fin.

It wasn't the slender, graceful fin of an orca.

It was the blunt triangle shape of a shark fin.

Only this fin rose seven feet above the surface of the water.

29

The hideous fin sliced through the water like a sword, cleaving the surface and sending wakes rolling away at an angle. The creature underneath the fin turned into a dark shadow below the surface. Seeing it at such a glancing angle made it hard to judge the size, but that didn't matter.

The thing was bigger than any shark that had lived in the last two million years could possibly be.

And yet there it was.

Coming at her like a torpedo of ravenous death.

Emily spun around and nearly doubled over in terror.

The beach!

It was so far away!

The inexorable pull of the tide had sucked her out faster than she'd realized. A rip tide maybe?

She squared up to launch herself into the water.

And another wave crashed in.

The carcass jerked and rolled underfoot.

She teetered over and fell face first into the water.

Sea water flooded into her suit. The cold stabbed her lungs and the air shot out. She somersaulted over and over under the water.

The sand below a dark shadow and the sky above a brighter haze, both spinning by like night and day on fast forward.

The movement slowed and she managed to orient herself to the light and surface several feet above. With her lungs prickling like cloth bags full of needles, she kicked off the bottom.

She broke the surface and gulped in a breath. The air helped, but the saltwater that joined it didn't.

Hacking coughing doubled her over.

She kicked to stay afloat.

Another breath.

Choked down and burning like it was bits of shattered glass.

The enormous black carcass of the mother orca bobbed in the water a dozen feet away.

That shark was coming for it.

She had to get out of the water.

She was about to turn away when every shred of connection between her brain and body evaporated.

Motivation. Thought. Process. Movement.

They all stopped.

A frozen instant in time.

A shape rose above the half-submerged orca.

A form so terrifying that nothing could live in its shadow.

A thing that obliterated puny concepts like reason and logic.

Even the indomitable will to survive withered like a weed in the winter. It surrendered to the inevitable.

A broad triangular nose rose high into the air.

Jaws opened wide revealing staggering row upon row of razor teeth. A dozen feet across.

The thing that had taken a bite out of the orca.

Come back to finish the job.

Emily knew she should move. Swim for the beach.

Swim for her life.

But she couldn't.

She couldn't move. Couldn't think. Couldn't do anything.

The beast was a god incarnate.

Death and destruction came with it.

It came down upon the whale with a ferocious grace.

A killing machine operating as mother nature intended.

A design perfected over millions of years and once again unleashed.

The jaws bit down as the hulk crashed into the carcass.

A curtain of water slammed down onto Emily, driving her below the surface. Her back hit the hard bottom. She grunted through the pain that shot through her limbs.

But the worst was yet to come.

The light at the surface above turned to shadow.

The massive body of the mother orca rolled over on top of her, pinning her legs.

Crushing them into the sand.

She knew it would soon be over.

The smooth bulk curved out and above her. If it rolled a bit more, it would cover her completely. The weight would crush her skull like an egg. Her shattered ribs would puncture her heart and lungs.

She pushed her hands up against the dark skin, fighting to keep it from finishing her.

It was like holding your arms out after falling off a building. They wouldn't stop the impact. The end still came.

The black bulk continued to roll, but then stopped as the tide sucked back out into deeper waters.

She screamed as the weight pinning her legs down like a mountain shifted. Bubbles of escaped air floated to the surface.

She briefly wondered if they carried the sound to the surface. If they popped and released her cries into the air.

Through the wavering blur of the moving water, she stared in horror.

The massive jaws again crashed into the body. Teeth larger than her hands tore into the skin and blubber. The weight pinning her down lifted as the shark jerked back and forth, ripping away a gargantuan chunk of flesh.

Clouds of red billowed through the water, quickly turning the translucent blue stinging her eyes into an opaque red.

The carcass slid away as the shark dragged it into deeper waters.

Emily's chest started to expand and her mouth almost opened as her body demanded a breath. Just before her lips parted to inhale, she gritted her teeth together.

Wriggling and squirming, she broke free of the sand. She expected to find her legs pulped and useless, but was surprised to feel the muscles move and respond to instruction.

A wave swept through, tossing her end over end like dirty clothes in the washer.

When the spin cycle ended, she slowed to a stop and floated in an impenetrable red foam. Air and blood and water mixed in equal parts.

With no variance of light and dark to indicate where the surface might be.

It didn't matter.

There was no time left anyway.

Her lungs demanded air.

An intake she could no longer deny.

Her body sucked in a breath and got only water.

Convulsing coughs wracked her middle as it hit her lungs.

The thick taste of metal and salt coated her tongue.

Still, she couldn't give up.

It wasn't in her nature.

The core of her deepest self didn't know surrender.

If it had, she wouldn't have survived all that came before.

The loss of her father.

The loss of her mother before that.

The loss of almost everything that kept a person strong enough to suffer through another day.

She had no quit.

So she kicked hard and dug her hands through the gore.

In what direction and for how long, she couldn't think enough to know or care.

The struggle was deeper than that.

It was about the fight, and nothing else.

The red fog grew darker.

The impenetrable red bled to blue as her head broke the surface.

She heaved and vomit sprayed out and splashed back down.

A wave picked her up and she was too weak to resist.

Her knees banged into sand and dragged across the bottom as the incoming wave pushed her higher up onto the beach.

With what little strength remained, she dug her fingers into the sand and clawed forward.

Waiting and dreading for when the wave retreated and dragged her back and under.

The next thing she knew, something jabbed into her cheek. She blinked hard and lifted her head.

A broken and jagged seashell lodged into the sand with the point up.

She was on the beach. Above the water line.

Above the blood line.

The sand was coated red.

She was covered in the same.

She turned toward the ocean and stared in awe as the massive shark continued tearing the orca apart. A plume of crimson water emanated from the gory site, expanding toward the beach.

What was that thing?

She vomited again and a wave of weakness made her slump to the sand.

It could only be one thing.

Of all the prehistoric creatures that had captured her father's attention, one held a particular fascination.

One that should've been extinct for two million years.

Megalodon.

The largest shark that ever lived.

One so large that it made a thirty foot long orca look tiny in comparison.

One that was apparently patrolling the waters around the island she was stranded on.

30

BOB tried to keep his mouth shut. He tried his best to keep from hurling back a biting reply.

"What? No answer?" Rome spat as much as said at him. The kid's face was beet red from doing his half of their shared labor.

Half was perhaps underestimating it.

Bob wasn't young and not remotely in the best shape of his life even before the near suicide drained him. He wasn't in the kind of shape that made dragging a body several blocks an easy thing.

The body was the man CB had killed last night.

Killed like a normal person might step on a cockroach.

Throat sliced so deeply that only the exposed spinal column kept the head from detaching and rolling away.

Bob pulled on the cold bare foot in his hands, but the body didn't budge.

Not until Rome put his back into doing the same with the foot he was holding did it continue to slide across the pavement. Rome took deep, heaving breaths as they continued.

Bob was spent.

As much from the preceding days as the effort of dragging the body.

That was the special something that CB had saved for him.

And dragging the revolting corpse so far was just half the punishment. Maybe less than half, but he only knew about the other part so far.

"That's the one."

Bob looked back at the guard strolling along behind them.

He pointed at the streetlight diagonally across the intersection. "Make sure it's right in the middle of the road like he said. I'm not gonna get my butt chewed off for you two idiots. And speed it up already. I got better things to do than watch you mangle a dead guy."

Rome glared at him. "It would go a lot faster if you lifted a finger to help."

The man's jaw twitched and his grip tightened around the battle rifle slung across his chest. "Careful. One pull of that finger would put a hole in your forehead."

"We'll do it," Bob said before it escalated. "Let's get it over with. Come on, Rome."

The stubborn teenager dropped the dead man's leg. "What? You're going to order me around, too? No. That's not happening."

Bob choked back another reply and settled for something more diplomatic. "I just want to get this over with, you idiot!"

Diplomacy wasn't a skill he'd nurtured and it definitely wasn't a personality trait.

"I'm the idiot?" If it was possible, Rome's face turned a deeper shade of red. "You're the reason my mother is dead. She wouldn't have been at the police station if it wasn't for you."

"CB set the bomb off, Rome. He killed your mother. Not me."

Rome's nostrils flared more from fury than exhaustion now. "I'm going to kill him."

Their guard laughed. "You're not killing anything, kid. Now, shut up! The both of you! You're worse than a couple of bickering women!"

Rome turned to him and the snarl on his face made it clear that a debate raged inside him. Hot hatred on the one side versus a cold recognition of the deadly rifle on the other.

The stupid kid was going to get them both killed.

Bob reached over and tried to pull Rome back to the task. To focus that fury on something that would keep them alive, for a few more hours at least.

Rome jerked away. "Don't touch me!"

The intervention had the intended effect though. The growing tension and a duel that was only going to end one way cut short.

Rome grabbed the corpse's foot and hauled forward before Bob could help out.

The body slipped off the sidewalk and into the street. The head bounced off the curb and smacked the street with a sickening thump.

Bob hurried over to attempt to help, to add back the ten percent his maximum effort was adding to the task.

They got the body to the street post and dropped the legs like they were bags of dirt. The body deserved more respect, more consideration. But those were niceties cleaved away from society the day the bombs fell.

It was a new world.

A new world in the same way as when the Europeans brought savage domination to the indigenous peoples of the discovered lands.

Power was all that mattered.

Some had it.

Some didn't.

Life was hard for those who didn't.

The guard leaned against a wreck of a car. A black Pontiac Trans Am with a giant gold bird painted on the hood. Like the one the Bandit drove. Must've been someone's pride and joy.

Now, it was a ruined relic from another age. The wheels were gone. The windshield shattered and curled inside hanging over the steering wheel. Bullet holes riddled the side facing them.

Someone must've used it for target practice.

That's when Bob noticed the faded brown stain coating the front fender. A dried brown pool of crust covered the pavement below.

Target practice. But the bullseye hadn't been the car.

The guard noticed Bob taking in the scene. "Yeah, a few days ago we ran into some moron trying to tow this thing away. He made the mistake of mouthing off and then drawing his weapon." He shook his head and chuckled. "Dumb move. Got lit up like a Christmas tree."

So cavalier. So light-hearted about murder.

Bob was no saint. Not by a long shot. A long trail of

coke and hookers could testify to that. But something inside him had changed since surviving his *episode*.

Life was worth something.

What or how much, he didn't know yet.

But it was no longer just a meaningless series of increasingly bizarre and extravagant distractions designed to dull the mind from dwelling on the futility of it all.

Bob turned away before a blurted reply ended up with him joining the guy who'd coveted that Trans Am.

"What are you waiting for?"

A coil of rope landed on the pavement between Bob and Rome.

31

It took Rome several throws to get the coiled end of the rope over the bar extending out over the street. He finally did and the thrown end unravelled down to the street.

Bob swallowed hard.

A boot to his backside sent him sprawling forward for balance.

"I said hurry it up!" the guard said.

Bob heard Rome's whispered opinion of the man's mother and was relieved to discover the man hadn't. He didn't seem like the type that would take kindly to the reference of his mother's similarity to the canine world.

Rome stared at the rope in his hands and then at the pale blue corpse at their feet. His lips twisted in horror. He shoved the rope into Bob's chest. "I'm not doing it."

Bob accepted the unwanted gift. "I guess that leaves me."

Anger flashed through Rome's face. "You're the reason I'm here at all! So, yeah, you're gonna do it."

Bob knelt down beside the hideous thing that only

last night was a living, breathing human being. He tried to ignore the congealed gore across the thing's gaping neck wound.

How was he supposed to get a loop around without touching it?

For that matter, what was he supposed to do if he somehow succeeded?

He had no idea how to tie a hangman's noose.

It was a loop at the end and there were a bunch of coils above that. Everybody knew what one generally looked like. But knowing that was a long way from knowing how to transform a length of rope into one.

Something clicked behind him. He was about to turn to find out what.

"That's the safety on this rifle," the guard said. "If I have to ask you to get moving again, I'm going to put a bullet in your foot, old man."

Bob reached the hand with end of the rope under the dead man's neck. There wasn't enough space in the hollow, so he had to shove it a few times to get through.

The last shove made it while also twisting the corpse's head to the side and tearing open the wound. The parted flesh burped and a cloud of rank stink escaped.

Bob gagged and spun away. His middle pinched tight as it decided whether to hurl his stomach up out of his mouth.

It decided to stay.

For now.

Bob held his breath and got back to it. He reached across and retrieved the end of the rope. He ignored the substance clinging to it and started to tie a knot.

The only one he knew.

The one he tied the shoelaces of his running shoes with. Well, walking shoes for more than a few years now. Okay, whatever. He hadn't laced them up in forever.

In the final years of their marriage, his ex had taken to ceaselessly badgering him about getting more exercise. She'd leave them by his bedside, by the front door, by the toilet.

To improve his libido, she'd say.

Wasn't she worth the effort?

Didn't she deserve to be wanted?

And more, to be satisfied?

Apparently, she did. He just didn't know it was going to be his ex best friend that filled the role.

Bob waited for the burning resentment to ignite in his chest, just like it did every time he remembered that faithless harpy.

But nothing came.

Not even the flicker of a flame.

He didn't know how to take that.

Was it a sign that he was finally getting over her betrayal?

Or was it a sign that his life was so wretched that he didn't care about anything anymore?

He looped the end of the rope through and around and then pulled the end to tighten the knot.

"Really?"

Bob looked up at Rome standing next to him. "What?"

"You're wanna try to hang this body using a square knot? A square knot you didn't even tie the right way?"

The right way?

"What do you mean *the right way*?"

Rome rolled his eyes. "Everybody does it the wrong way. You're actually supposed to do the top loop opposite of what everybody does."

"You mean I've been tying my shoes the wrong way for over fifty years?"

Rome crossed his fleshy arms over his barrel chest and larger barrel belly. "Yeah. And that's never gonna work. Even a regular square knot isn't right for this job." He shook his head like he was talking to the village idiot.

CRACK.

Bob's flinched as the sound of the rifle firing split the air.

"Hang the stupid dead guy already!" The guard yelled with his weapon pointed up into the air.

"Move over," Rome said as he knelt down and yanked the rope out of Bob's hands. He untied it and fashioned a hangman's noose. He finished it with practiced ease.

Bob's eyes narrowed as he stared at the boy.

Rome caught his gaze. "What? I go all out for Halloween decorations. It's my favorite holiday."

Bob lifted the corpse's head while Rome slipped the loop down into place.

He tightened the loop until it closed under the man's chin. "That should do it."

They stood and each took hold of the other end of the rope.

Bob pulled and the rope went taut.

Another pull and the head jerked up and fell back down with a revolting thump. "I could use some help here."

"Uh, yeah," Rome said and then added his superior strength.

In another minute, they had the ghastly thing lifted high and swinging back and forth like a metronome that measured out the rhythm of man's depravity.

Aside from being repulsive, the corpse was heavy. Even with Rome doing most of the work, Bob's heart hammered in his chest. His grip wouldn't last much longer.

"Tie it off at the base over there," the guard said.

"You're a regular boy scout," Bob replied before he could stop himself.

They marched over while the pounding in Bob's ears rose to thundering levels. He was too old for this. His heart was going to explode.

An idea struck him.

Almost made him lose his grip.

Yes.

It could work.

Maybe, anyway.

What did he have to lose?

All that awaited him was whatever torture Charlie Bog dreamed up next. And sooner or later, even that would end in death.

He whispered. "Be ready."

Rome cast him a confused look.

Bob screamed and let go of the rope. He fell to the pavement clutching his chest.

Without Bob's help, the weight on the other end of the rope dragged Rome backward a few steps. He glanced down at Bob and then over at the guard. His eyes flashed understanding. "Help me!" he screamed at the guard.

The guard hesitated but then must've decided he wanted to get this over with because he flipped his rifle around to his backside and ran over. He reached for a hold on the rope.

Rome launched into action, faster than seemed feasible for someone of his bulk. He threw a loop of line over the guard's head and pulled tight after it landed on his shoulders.

He jerked backward and the loop cinched tight. He let go and the heavier weight of the corpse on the other end pulled the guard up into the air.

The guard grunted and kicked wildly at the air as he rose. He stopped when the corpse's feet met the ground.

The guard reached down for the knife tucked into his boot, but missed.

"Come on!" Bob said as he got to his feet.

Rome nodded and the two took off like their lives depended on it.

Because, in fact, they did.

32

MARCO jerked awake and opened his eyes. Or thought he opened his eyes.

There was only darkness.

He'd fallen asleep out on the ridge a few miles from home. It was a new moon and a thick layer of clouds had blanketed the sky, but it was never this dark.

Never a total absence of light.

He started to panic, wondering why and when he'd gone blind. For a long minute, a terrified scream tried to claw its way up his throat.

A whisper echoed out of the darkness.

"You okay?"

He recognized the voice from somewhere.

Inches away and yet so far.

Chief Stuckey.

In Kodiak.

He was thousands of miles from that ridge where he'd asked Justine to marry him. From where she'd stomped his heart out and left him for dead.

Emily.

Where was she?

On a boat somewhere on the ocean.

Alive?

Where was Oscar?

He hoped the little grouch had survived the explosion at the gas station. Maybe he'd returned to the wild and would once again live a normal life.

Marco swallowed hard. It was probably for the best, but it still left an empty space in his heart.

"Marco," Stuckey whispered.

"Yeah, I'm okay. Must've nodded off."

"Must've been dreaming. You were making noises like it was a nightmare."

"I'm fine."

"Good. We have to keep it together. These people need us now more than ever."

It came back now.

Charlie had locked them all up in a stripped bare storage room. Surrounded by concrete block walls with no windows to let in light. There were at least twenty other people locked in with them. Everyone who'd survived the ambush at the meeting. All of the people who'd been recruited because they had the will and ability to resist.

Now captured and imprisoned.

How long had they been there?

They'd been herded to the back and locked up some time last night. After that sick welcome from Charlie.

Was it still night?

More awake now, he noticed the stiff ache in his shoulders from sleeping on the hard concrete floor. He rolled a shoulder. It was the kind of ache that took hours to settle in. It must've been the next morning if not later.

He checked the watch Emily had given him. The green glow blinked on, under-lighting his face.

8:17 AM.

It blinked off.

It was the chunky black rubberized kind. Not a style he would've chosen back in the normal world. But it was now his most prized possession.

Was she okay?

The image of his ex, Justine, jumped into his mind. She'd gone to Los Angeles. The last frown she'd given him before she left passed through his mind.

Her disappointment in him not measuring up to the life she'd wanted to live. The frown that had crushed him and made him feel worthless for so long.

But to his surprise, the memory no longer conjured even the slightest pangs of remorse or loss for what might've been.

Instead, a vision of Emily's warm brown eyes filled his thoughts. The hidden sorrow deep with their fractal patterns. The restrained longing that he wished she'd unleashed.

Where was she?

A muffled clank sounded outside the door as someone unlocked it and then yanked it open with a screech from stubborn hinges.

A flashlight blinked on and a beam of light pierced the air.

Marco blinked through the sudden change.

The light swept around the room, casting a bright

circle of illumination on the huddled forms of the other prisoners.

Marco's eyes adjusted to take in the person holding the light.

Alexei Volkov. Red, as Stuckey called him.

The giant that had somehow become Charlie's right hand man.

Red stomped over and yanked Marco to his feet. He did it with ease, like lifting a child.

Stuckey started to rise to intervene.

Red spun to face him with surprising speed. "Give me a reason. The boss won't mind if I break a few of your bones."

Stuckey's mustache twitched as the anger boiled to the surface.

Marco put a hand on his shoulder. "Be smart. These people need you."

What he didn't say and what he definitely meant was that it also wasn't going to do anyone any good to have the chief squirming in a pool of his own blood, spitting out fragments of his teeth.

In a fair fight, he'd pick the chief against the Russian bear any day. But after the rough treatment they'd all endured after being captured, this wouldn't be a fair fight.

And that wasn't even considering the baton conspicuously attached to Red's hip.

Stuckey lowered himself back to the floor. The snarl never uncurled his lips though.

"I thought so," Red said with a sneer. He jerked Marco to the side nearly making him fall and then shoved him toward the open door. "The boss wants to see you."

33

The guard standing outside the door opened it as Red and Marco arrived. He stepped inside ahead of them and announced their presence. "Hey boss, Red got the kid for you."

Red shoved past and scowled at the man. "I think he can see that for himself, you imbecile."

The man bit his lips together and the air burned with the heat of their meeting eyes.

"You can go," Charlie said from the far end of a rectangular table. "Now."

The man broke the contest of wills and nodded in submission before exiting and closing the door behind him.

Charlie pushed his chair back and stood. He smiled with arms spread wide. "Welcome, Marco, if I remember correctly. Is that right?"

Marco nodded.

"Only a few weeks ago, but it feels like we met in another world. In another age."

"The end of the world can have that effect."

Charlie grinned. "A profound truth, no doubt." He glanced to Red and tilted his head to the door.

"You sure, boss? I don't trust this one."

"Alexei, don't make an enemy of a man who may yet be my friend."

Red didn't respond.

"Do you hear me?" Charlie said as he touched a finger to his ear. The dark threat permeating the question couldn't have been more clear.

"Yes, boss. Of course." He turned to leave, but was frozen by the sharp slap of the next question.

"Aren't you forgetting something?"

"Uhh, I don't think so."

Charlie's demeanor switched from levity to disappointment in a flash. From disappointment to impatience in another. And from impatience to rage in one more. "Remove the handcuffs, you idiot! Now!"

Red shuddered like his testicles had been tasered. "Sorry, boss." He scrambled to cut the plastic cables free. So much so that Marco waited for the line of fire that meant the blade had sliced him open.

It didn't.

The plastic cuffs fell to the floor.

"Wait outside," Charlie said.

Red nodded and hurried out.

Marco watched the interaction in wonder. He'd seen the behavior before. One of the old ranch owners that used to have adjacent land to his acted like that. He was nice enough to people, but he was cruel as could be to the half-dozen dogs that for some reason never ran away from his property.

He'd never liked that guy. And he was a saint compared to the man standing across the room.

Charlie gestured at the table filled with more food and drink than Marco had seen in weeks. Since the morning that the competition began when he and Emily and Suyin had breakfast at Queen's Diner. A breakfast fit for a king and one he hadn't come close to repeating since.

But here.

Now.

This was a breakfast fit for an Emperor.

Especially now that the grocery stores had no more groceries. Now that the convenience stores offered no more conveniences.

A thick slab of grilled salmon with curling wisps of steam rising up set off the waterworks in his mouth. He swallowed a few times to keep his mouth from filling up.

A serving plate piled high with scrambled eggs. The plate next to it piled equally high with crispy bacon. The rich scent of baked bread, the sweetest perfume imaginable.

"Have a seat," Charlie said as he rounded the table and gestured at the chair opposite his own.

Marco nodded and nearly dove into the chair. He didn't care what the crazy man had to say. If listening for a few minutes meant he could scarf down a boatload of desperately needed calories, so be it. He hadn't exactly been living high on the hog during his time in the wilderness. And it hadn't taken long after his return for supplies in Kodiak to get scarce.

Whatever he consumed here would make him stronger.

And whatever the future held in store, strength would be of benefit.

Charlie reach into a bowl, lifted a folded kitchen towel, and pulled out a golden brown biscuit. He set it on his plate and scooped up a ladle full of sausage gravy. He held the ladle under his nose and breathed in. "Not quite like we made at home, but it'll do." He lathered it over the biscuit. "The key is the sausage. The meat has to be spiced and charred just right to keep its form and flavor."

Marco grunted as he speared a slab of salmon with his fork. He bit off a huge chunk and the delicate filet hit his tongue like an explosion. The pleasure was almost painful. Juice drizzled down his chin.

Charlie pointed at the napkin beside Marco's plate. "I realize we are living through the end of the world, but we can still try to be civilized."

Marco nodded as he wiped an arm across his chin.

The merest hint of anger flared in Charlie's eyes and then passed. He reached into a carton of beer and dug out a can. He cracked it open and set it in front of Marco. "One of the benefits to living in a brewery. You a beer drinker?"

Marco swallowed the last of the bite and knocked back half the can in a single go.

Charlie pulled out another for himself, turning the can around and looking at it. "What do you think about all these new style fancy beers? The double IPAs and the sour stouts and all that?"

Marco glanced up at him trying to figure out if he was for real. His stomach grumbled at the interruption in food delivery.

"I'm serious. Me? I'm partial to an ice-cold, full-bodied Coors, but a dark oatmeal stout will do in a pinch." He cracked it open and took a long, slow drink that killed the can.

Marco watched like a gazelle being circled by a lion.

Obviously, this wasn't about sharing a meal and knocking back brews with the boys.

What did this maniac want?

Charlie grabbed another, cracked it open and extended it toward Marco. "A toast. We may not have won that million dollars, but maybe we won something better."

Marco set his can on the table, notably without returning the gesture. "What do you want from me?"

Charlie's jaw tightened as he realized Marco wasn't going to reciprocate the toast. "You know, maybe it's the uptight southern gentleman in me, but it's not polite to refuse a toast. Especially after I've invited you to a sumptuous meal."

Marco wolfed down the rest of the salmon while he could. He had no interest in chatting about beer or anything with this madman. And that lack of interest was likely going to get him forcefully removed in short order.

But hopefully not before he had time to down a few pieces of bacon. He reached over to grab a handful.

A flash of movement and an iron grip locked around his wrist.

He tried to pull away but the lanky man held firm with surprising strength. The grip on his wrist pinched like a steel vice.

Charlie placed a serving fork in Marco's trapped hand. "In times like these, good manners are more important than ever."

Marco accepted the fork and the grip on his wrist released. He transferred a large helping to his plate and began eating.

Charlie gave him a sad smile. "I don't wish to be unpleasant with you. In fact, that's why I invited you here."

Marco made a point to swallow his food before responding. No sense antagonizing a murderer with an odd peculiarity for table manners. "What do you want?"

Charlie's smile perked up as he steepled his fingers together. "Yes, that is the point, isn't it?"

Marco took another bite and waited for his captor to continue.

Charlie sat back in his chair and took a drink of beer. He surveyed everything on the table, ending with Marco. "I like you, Marco. You are a survivor, just like I am. We both entered that contest expecting to win. I believe one of us would have if we'd been given the opportunity to finish the game."

Marco scooped a helping of scrambled eggs onto his plate, being careful to use the serving spoon. If this idiot wanted to wax philosophic while he filled his belly, that was fine. Just so long as it didn't have to be a conversation.

"But a new game is afoot. And we must adapt our idea of what it means to compete and to win. Do you understand?"

Marco nodded, more because he was happy to have a mouth full of eggs than because he actually understood what this maniac was getting at.

"Good. Then you understand that winning now means a great deal more." His expression darkened. "As does losing." The shadow passed. "And I'd like you to be on my team, Marco. The winning team. I could use a man of your skills and determination."

What?

Marco's fork fell from his fingers and clattered to the plate. "You're trying to recruit me? To be part of your gang of thugs?"

The shadows gathered in Charlie's face. "They are admittedly crude tools for the purpose, but I utilize the resources that are available. You could be an important person in my growing organization."

Despite himself, despite the smart thing to do, Marco burst out laughing. He couldn't help it. This petty tyrant wanted Marco's help in running over the people of Kodiak.

He'd never been offered something so strange, something so antithetical to who he was at the core of his being.

Charlie's face flushed deep red. He slammed his fist on the table so hard the plates and utensils and serving dishes jumped. His fingers closed around the handle of a steak knife. "Do not take me for a fool!" He lifted the knife and pointed the sharp point across the table at Marco. "That would not end well for you."

The laugh bubbling up Marco's throat popped.

A knock at the door broke the silence.

"Come in!" Charlie shouted in a fury.

It opened and Red stuck his head in.

"This better be important!" He accented the words with the knife jabbing in the air.

The enormous man looked like a beaten dog as he stared at the floor. "I'm sorry. It's just that the old man and the fat kid have escaped. They somehow got the drop on our guy. I thought you'd want to know imme-diately."

Bob and Rome had gotten away?

Marco tried to hide the smile turning up the edges of his mouth. He almost felt sorry for whoever had let them get away.

Almost.

Charlie's fury turned silent and edged with steel. His chair scraped across the floor as he stood. "Bring him to me."

34

The door opened wider revealing the man responsible.

"Brewster!" Marco said with as much surprise as confusion.

The soldier that he and Emily had run into at the crashed helicopter out in the wilderness. The man that had suspiciously been with the pilot before she died. The man who always made it clear he cared about his own hide more than anyone else's.

"Marco?" His eyes flitted to Marco's plate and the table filled with food.

Red marched Brewster into the room and stood beside him, looking ready to throw a beating on him if he tried anything. That wasn't likely though as the mass of black duct tape encircling his wrists had them locked together and kept him from doing much of anything.

"You two know each other?" Charlie asked.

Brewster jumped in. "We had each other's backs out—"

Charlie cut in, "You shut your mouth." The venom

accompanying the words stung Brewster to silence. Charlie turned to Marco.

Marco shrugged. "Yeah, I know him. I wouldn't say we had each other's backs."

"I saved your girlfriend's life!"

Faster than seemed humanly possible, Charlie darted the few feet over to Brewster and yanked his bound hands up. The blade of the steak knife flash through the air and a single thumb fell to the floor.

It hit the vinyl tile and bounced to a stop. A tiny pool of blood leaked out from the severed end.

Brewster screamed in pain. He tried to pull away but Charlie held him fast.

"I said 'Shut your mouth'." He pointed the tip of the knife at Brewster's mouth to emphasize the point.

Brewster's mouth clamped shut, even as he continued whimpering in pain.

Marco pushed back in his seat, a mouthful of eggs half-chewed and going no further.

He cut off Brewster's thumb!

Like it was nothing.

A blur of blade and suddenly a man was missing a thumb.

Marco gripped the arms of his chair to ensure he stayed seated. Everything inside him urged him to move. To attack the threat while its focus was elsewhere.

He'd been a sheepdog his whole life. Doing his best to protect his family's land, doing his best to protect the endangered ferrets that called it home, doing his best to guard tomorrow by introducing children to the wonder of today.

And a wolf stood a few feet away.

A beast bent on destruction and predation.

If you were a part of its pack, maybe you had a chance. But nobody else did.

He was more than a simple killer.

He was elemental. A being that disrupted the natural order of things. Violence and destruction walked with him. Sorrow followed like a dark cloak.

There was only one way to deal with something like that.

Destroy it.

Without mercy.

Without thought.

The chair lifted off the ground as he unconsciously started to stand. He sat back down as the edge banged into the back of his knees.

No.

Not now. Not yet.

Not with the ogre of a man that was his lieutenant. And not against a man that moved so fast he seemed to move between the seconds.

It would do no good to end up gutted by that same knife, his intestines spilling out onto the worn tile.

Charlie turned to Marco, his eyes registering the tension and indecision in his posture. He paused an instant and then smiled. "I do believe there is some difference of opinion on the depth of that relationship. What do you say, Marco?"

Marco forced his eyes down to the table. To lock eyes with this madman would've sent his body into action. The urge to destroy him would've overpowered everything else. "He's not my friend, but that doesn't mean he deserved that."

"You bring up a fair question," Charlie replied. "He let an old man and an overweight boy get away." Charlie spun back toward Brewster and the man recoiled in terror. "What does failure like that deserve?"

Marco didn't answer.

Red grinned while holding Brewster by the arm, keeping him from stumbling backward. "He deserves to be punished, boss."

Charlie sighed and Red's grin melted like a snowflake in front of a flamethrower. "I wasn't asking you," he said through gritted teeth. He turned back to Marco and extended the knife to within inches of Marco's chest. "I was asking you."

Their eyes locked as a war raged within Marco's soul.

Charlie waited while Marco remained silent. He tilted his head and his eyes widened as if he'd actually expected a response. "Nothing? Okay. We'll go with what I had in mind." Still staring into Marco's eyes, he slammed the knife point first into the wooden table, and then swept his arm across knocking Marco's plate, beer, and a couple of serving bowls to the floor. He stepped aside and bellowed, "Alexei! Put him on his back!"

Red did as instructed, picking up the smaller man and slamming him down onto the solid table. He pinned Brewster down by the shoulders as the condemned man started screaming, pleading for mercy.

Charlie jumped onto the table, whirled around and landed straddled across his chest, with the knife again somehow in his hand.

Marco's jaw dropped open.

The inhuman speed. It didn't seem possible for a man to move so fast. Like a blur of realized intention.

Charlie screamed like a banshee as he dropped forward and brought the knife down.

The tip of the knife stabbed into Brewster's eye.

He wailed in agony.

Marco's stomach clenched so tight he almost lost the meal he'd just eaten.

Charlie raised a flash of silver in his other hand. "This is the kind of shit I live for!" He howled with ecstasy and then plunged the spoon into Brewster's eye socket. A quick flick of both hands and the eye came out stuck to the tip of the knife.

Covered in gore with a bit of the optical nerve dangling off. Blood gushed out of the empty socket, spilling over Brewster's cheek and down into his ear.

Even Red looked uncomfortable. He gulped and kept glancing away every time the magnetism of the horror drew his eyes back.

Charlie leaped off the table and retrieved the severed thumb from the floor. He stood up and held his hands raised. The thumb in one hand and the shish-kabobbed eye on the end of the knife in the other. "Alexei, get him out of here."

Red looked like he couldn't wait to leave as he yanked the shrieking man off the table.

Charlie's eyes burned with malignant light. A darkness that illuminated the evil in his soul. "And Alexei, I want that old man found! Kill the boy. But bring the old man to me."

"Yes, boss," Red said as he disappeared into the hallway.

Charlie strolled back to his chair, sat down, and set the severed thumb onto his plate. He opened his mouth and popped the eye inside. With a careful bite, he pulled it from the blade and bit down.

A sickening pop and clear juice spurted out of his mouth and onto the table. He retrieved the napkin by his plate and dabbed at the fluid dribbling down his chin, looking embarrassed like he'd farted at a formal dinner. "I apologize for the unpleasantries." He carefully spread the napkin in his lap, swallowed, and smiled. "So, what do you think?"

Marco's mouth finally closed, but only because it was preparing to speak. "I think you're insane."

Charlie grinned and winked like they were best friends sharing a juicy bit of gossip. "You're not the first person to tell me that."

35

DR. YONG lifted the bottle of bourbon with trembling hands and watched the golden amber liquid slosh around inside the glass. While searching through Hari's desk last night, he'd found the mostly empty bottle tucked away at the back of a desk drawer. He took a sip and pinched his eyes shut as the liquid fire burned down his throat and added to the warmth already suffusing in his chest.

The first drink, now seven ago, had barely made it to his mouth, so badly shaking were his hands.

The images from the massacre yesterday played through his mind.

An entire team wiped out.

A pack of Megalania roaming the island.

He took another sip and observed the jitters still coursing through his fingers. There wasn't enough booze in the world to wipe out the memory of that horror.

Zhang sat in his mentor's chair and scanned the mess of papers, coffee cups, and other detritus that proved

Hari had once existed. The evidence of a life that now was so much garbage waiting to be swept clean and forgotten.

He would not forget their last few minutes together.

The tragic way they ended.

Not for the first time, Zhang cursed fate for putting him in this position. He was no leader. Ever since he'd raised his head above the masses back at Tiannenman and just as quickly destroyed the lives of those he loved, he'd made it a point to stay away from the limelight.

That had always been Hari's world.

Leading the project.

Dealing with the brass that held the purse strings and were forever wanting more value for their dollars.

Hari had been a genius at keeping all the plates spinning and the project moving forward.

Zhang took a gulp and grunted at the fire singeing his throat. He unscrewed the cap to the bottle and was about to pour out what was left when something caught his attention.

Something in the bottle cap.

A crinkle where he expected the smooth metal underside.

He set the bottle on the desk and peered inside the cap. There was something there. A small square of plastic stuck to the bare metal. Perhaps it had fallen in during the bottling process at the plant and quality control had somehow missed it. He was about to set it aside when a shift of his wrist made the light glance off it in a different way.

In a way that caught something that sent a quiver up his spine.

Almost like a tiny letter H.

He rotated the cap and brought it closer and turned on the desk lamp.

It was the letter Z!

Written in the precise script of Hari's own hand.

Zhang shoved his index finger in to pry it off but he couldn't get his chewed down nail under the edge. He yanked open the desk drawer and snatched out a paperclip. A couple of scrapes with the bent end and it popped out and landed on the wooden desk.

A tiny piece of paper with clear tape that had held it in place inside the cap. He scraped at the backside and it unfolded into a rectangle of white paper half an inch long.

Written in miniature print, and yet unmistakably by the same hand he'd read countless notes, observations and directions over the last several decades was a string of random letters and numbers.

There was no question what it was.

Zhang smacked the spacebar on the keyboard and the monitor blinked on. With hands shaking worse than before, after several mistakes due to his lack of accuracy, he punched in the long code.

He stared at the asterisks at the login screen and took a deep breath. He slowly blew it out and hit ENTER.

His jaw flinched as he expected the failed login screen to appear.

It didn't.

The cursor briefly turned into a circling comet and then Hari's personal desktop screen appeared.

And there, right in the middle, separated from dozens

of folders and shortcuts and application icons was a simple text document. Below the icon said Z.txt.

Zhang's hand shook like a minor earthquake as he moved the mouse to position the arrow over it. He doubled clicked and the file opened.

He was right!

Hari hadn't left him all alone.

Not completely, anyway.

He read the words of his dead mentor. Of the man who had become a father to him.

My dearest Zhang,

If you're reading this, then I am dead. I know that must distress you, but it must also mean that you are alive. And for that, I am grateful. Wherever we go after leaving the flesh, whatever happens when brain and heart cease to function, know that I am happy. For the last ten years, I have wanted nothing more than to see you alive again.

What I have to say next won't be easy to hear. It wasn't easy to write. It is a shame I've held in my heart since the day you disappeared into the time gate.

It was my fault you were there that day.

It was I that left a message hidden under your pillow. It was I that wanted you to get our research out to the wider world.

I was an idealistic fool.

I never meant for it to turn out like it did.

I never meant for you to be harmed.

It will come as small consolation, but know that I worked

feverishly for ten years to return to that moment, to solve the problem of dialing in a time gate with such unerring accuracy.

And it finally worked! I did it!

Please forgive a dead man for his lingering vanity. Pride has always been my biggest failure. Pride that only I could lead this project. Pride that only I knew what was best for humanity.

That pride led to your death.

But maybe you will allow it to balance my account somewhat by knowing that it also led to your rebirth.

In any case, judge me however you will. I certainly have no room to ask for anything more.

And the reason for that is partly from the wrongs I have done to you in the past. But it is also partly from the wrongs I have to do to you in the present.

Judging from the state of the world as it is today, and knowing that you reading this means I was successful with what I will attempt tomorrow, I believe you must be and feel quite alone.

Alone to lead the project forward.

Alone to save mankind.

It is not a fair burden to pass to anyone.

And I know that you have never wanted to lead after the tragedy of your actions as a youth.

It is an injustice that you must accept. I wish that I could be here to share the burden, but I can not.

Listen to me, Zhang. My son, of my heart even if not of my body. Humanity's future depends on you. And though you don't believe it, you are strong enough to see it through.

Zhang wiped away the welling tears blurring his vision,

making the text unreadable. He sniffed and continued on.

Here is what you must do. At the bottom of this file, you will find the contact information for high-level diplomats from around the world. Due to the nature of the calamity that has befallen us, I'm sure it will prove impossible to get through to many of them. But I am just as certain that some are reachable. Our facility was not the only one in the world prepared for this kind of emergency.

You must send an invitation to all governments of the world to come here. We have over a dozen stable time gates on this island. Each government must be given the opportunity to send its people through to colonize the past.

You understand the ramifications of power better than most. Those that accept and journey to the island will not want to share. They will want control of such a precious resource. They will attempt to use force if necessary to obtain that control.

And you must not let that happen.

The past doesn't belong to one nation or one race, but to all mankind. Or as many as can take advantage in this new world.

And so you must issue a threat and be prepared to carry it out.

They will know if you are bluffing, and so you must not.

If any nation attempts to take control of Project Hermes or wrest control of a time gate not allotted to it, then promise that you will destabilize and destroy all of them.

The time gates are our only salvation.

If they want to survive, they will obey.

I know that explains nothing of the particulars. I know it will not be easy. But you stood up to a column of tanks with nothing but shopping bags in your hands. Whether you believe it or not, you are strong enough to do this.

Here at the end, my last thoughts are of you.

Tomorrow morning is the test. If it is successful as I believe it will be, then I will have achieved going back to the minutes before I lost you.

I intend to bring you back alive. Both of us, if possible, but it is you that matters more. What will have been moments for you has been ten long years for me.

Ten years of guilt eating away at my soul. I am no longer the man you knew. I no longer know what I am.

I only know this.

That I love you.

Growing up an orphaned gutter rat on the streets of Kalcutta made my heart hard enough to survive, but it also kept me distant from all who passed through my life.

All except you.

I never had a father and never had a child so perhaps I can't truly know what that relationship means. But I know that I love you like a son. And like a father, I am proud of all that you have become.

You mean the world to me.

You mean all worlds to me.

I will love you forever.

Hari

· · ·

Zhang covered his eyes with his hands. The moisture wetted his palms and trickled down his wrists.

He would do as Hari wanted. Not because he believed he was capable, but because he wouldn't disappoint the memory of someone so dear.

Zhang swallowed hard and wiped the tears away with his shirt sleeve. He scrolled down to the long list of contacts that followed.

He paused on one.

A high-ranking official in the Chinese government.

He would send the invitations. He would do as instructed. And those governments that both believed and had the means would make their way to the island.

But one invitation would be different from the others.

The one to the land of his birth.

If the Chinese government wanted a future for its people, then they would bring something precious with them when they made the journey.

They would bring his long lost wife and son.

36

EMILY stepped back and watched the gray smoke curl up into the air. She used a long stick to shift the blanket of seaweed so that a little more air got to the smoldering fire underneath. It was a delicate balance between keeping the fire going but also smothering it with damp material to get as much smoke as possible.

She shifted things around a bit more until the balance felt right.

Tendrils of dark smoke swirled and twisting together as they rose. It was turning into a good signal fire. With the afternoon skies relatively clear aside from the blanket of smog that dimmed the higher altitudes, it would be visible for miles. If there were any boats nearby, they'd see it.

Which wasn't guaranteed to be a good thing.

It depended on who did the seeing.

But after recovering feeling in her feet and legs from the morning's close encounter with a prehistoric killing machine, she'd decided it was worth the risk.

The Coast Guard wasn't going to be out looking for her. There would be no news broadcasts describing a missing girl and her last known whereabouts.

No. That was before things fell apart.

Things were different now.

She'd be lucky not to die here. Slowly starving and wondering why she was cursed. Wondering why she'd ever left her grandmother alone in Oakland in the first place.

The prize money was the answer, of course. But simple logic didn't make so much as a dent in the dark misery festering in her heart.

If four leaf clovers gave people luck, her life was one long discovery of no leaf clovers. No leaves, just withered stems.

A low rumbling caught her attention.

Great. Just her bad luck. She'd been stranded on an island filled with hungry bears.

No. That wasn't it.

She turned and almost shouted with glee when she saw a fishing trawler rounding the spit of land that jutted out to the south.

Fear followed a second later.

What if whoever was steering the boat wasn't the rescuing-a- damsel-in-distress type? What if the damsel had just called over a new type of distress? The type that came with fists and knives and guns and an eagerness to use them?

There was only one way to find out.

She waved the stick back and forth above her head.

The trawler turned and started heading toward her.

Emily watched with equal parts anticipation and

anxiety. She reached to her hip and unclipped the sheathed kukri. She attached it to the hem of her pants at her lower back. Better not to advertise any advantages she might need. She set the end of the long stick into the fire and laid it on the sand within easy reach.

It was thick enough to pack a punch. And flames on the end would help as a deterrent.

If it was needed.

She hoped it wasn't.

But hope wasn't a good plan.

Backups were.

The trawler puttered closer and she saw a man appear on the deck. He waved and shouted something but the distance and the pounding surf swept the sound away.

Emily waved her hands above her head in wide arcs.

The man waved back.

"Hello!" she shouted. She cupped her hands together to amplify the sound and tried again. "I need help!"

The man waved again and then disappeared inside the pilot's cabin.

She couldn't make anything out through the windows from this distance.

She waited.

The trawler slowed to a stop some fifty yards beyond the break.

What was he doing? She didn't want to swim out there. The water was freezing cold, and she hadn't forgotten the monster from that morning that had nearly crushed and drowned her.

The man appeared again on the front deck and tossed an anchor over the side. He peered after it and must've been satisfied with what he saw as he started toward the back of the boat.

Emily saw it now.

A small dinghy hanging from ropes on the aft deck.

The man shifted it out over the side and lowered it to the water. He waved again before climbing over the side and dropping into the smaller boat.

He seemed nice enough.

Maybe she was being overly pessimistic.

Maybe the world didn't have a plan to make her miserable and knock her down every time she got back up.

Maybe.

The man yanked an ignition cord a few times and an outboard motor puttered to life. He took a seat and revved the engine making it sound like a weed eater on steroids.

The dinghy spun around and headed for shore.

Emily was about to yell with joy...

But it died with a gurgle in her throat.

In the open water out beyond the trawler, a dark shape rose out of the water.

37

In seconds, what could've been initially mistaken for a swimming seal or something equally harmless became clear.

A wide triangular fin cutting through the water, spilling white foam to the sides behind.

Emily waved her hands, frantically trying to tell her would-be rescuer to go back. "Shark!" She pointed behind him and screamed so loud her throat burned. She held a flat vertical hand to her forehead hoping he'd recognize the scuba signal for the creature. "Shark! Behind you!"

The man waved and the dinghy kept coming. Now halfway between the trawler and the beach.

The front of the trawler jerked down, the bow dipping below the surface before it bobbed back up. The shark inadvertently severed the anchor line because the line still attached to the boat floated on the surface of the water.

The crashing water off the boat settling down got the

man's attention. He looked over his shoulder and saw what Emily saw.

Passing by the trawler, sending a wave that slapped into it broadside, a seven foot tall fin soared above the surface. A massive shadow darkened the water beneath.

The outboard motor shrieked as the man got on the gas.

But it was too late.

White water churned as the massive broad nose of the beast rose above the surface. Jaws opened revealing row upon row of shredding death. Water sluiced out between the rows, spilling down in small waterfalls to the surface below.

Emily screamed, because there was nothing she could do to help. And that somehow made it worse.

The sound came out of her mouth, but also came from a deeper place. A place that recognized the finality of the end. A place that had fought that end since the beginning of life.

The man jumped to his feet and lifted his hands as if they might somehow protect him from what was to come.

Half of the beast's body rose above the white water before it hit its target. Dark gray skin lifted above the water line revealing the lighter shade of the underbelly.

Emily wanted to turn away.

But she couldn't.

The beast came down with the crushing force of an avalanche. Wild power that knew nothing greater than itself. An animal perfected over millions of years of evolution now executing on its promise.

The back of the dinghy jumped up as the leading wave hit it. The man stumbled back. He didn't fall.

There wasn't time before he disappeared into the dark abyss.

The gaping maw simply erased him before splintering the dinghy into exploding fragments of shredded fiberglass. The broad back of the shark slipped down into the water. The dorsal fin sliced through the surface and spun away toward deeper water. With a final powerful kick of its tail, the monster sunk below the surface.

The swathe of white frothing water stood out against the surrounding blue. Bits of the dinghy bobbed violently away, riding the smaller radial waves.

It wasn't like the attack on the orca. The water didn't turn the red and pink of blood and bubbles and water.

There was no blood.

None.

It was like the man had never existed.

He was there one minute and gone the next.

Emily stared at the spot in horror as what little evidence remained slowly ebbed away. But then she noticed something that pushed the thoughts away.

The trawler was drifting. Heading straight toward the jagged rocks that crusted the shoreline to the south.

She didn't hesitate.

She ran, dragging up and into the survival suit as she went.

That boat was her way out.

If it didn't get bashed to splinters first.

Out of breath, with her heart hammering in her ears, she jumped out onto the wide band of rocks where the boat was headed.

She was going to get there first!

Emily skipped from one uneven surface to the next.

The boots of the suit doing a good job gripping the wet moss-covered rocks.

Getting there first was one thing. Then, she'd have to jump into the water, swim out to the boat and figure out how to climb aboard. All while a nightmare from the black water below waited. And before the boat hit the rocks.

Nearly across the band of rocks.

Another four carefully placed steps would do it.

Her right boot landed exactly where she intended. A flat plane of rock that was large enough to find purchase.

The rock shifted underfoot.

It rolled, yanking her boot to the left, sending her snatching for balance to the right. She keeled over and slammed headfirst into a boulder.

The impact sent an electric pain echoing down to her toes and fingertips.

Stunned.

Blinking hard trying to clear the fog.

Fighting to keep the dim edges surrounding her vision from advancing further toward the center.

A wave slammed into the rocks, lifting her up, floating, and then dropped onto the rocks again.

Her spine hit and she gasped in agony.

Ice cold seawater poured down her throat.

Emily knew this could be it, but she wasn't going to die without a fight. She paddled her arms wildly like a child learning to swim, fighting to get her feet under her before the next wave rolled in.

A crashing sound directly behind her turned her blood to ice.

The shark was there, coming to claim her.

She shifted around and saw that it was the boat, almost within arm's reach.

The side slammed into the rocks again as another wave rolled in.

She launched herself toward it and got a hold on the side. After a couple of tries, she managed to wriggle up and over only to spill onto the back deck.

A wave swept through and the stern crashed onto the rocks tossing her briefly into the air before coming down hard again.

She scrambled to her feet and dashed toward the door to the pilot's cabin. She threw open the door and held onto the frame to keep from being thrown by another wave that tossed the boat onto the rocks.

She found the wheel and the ignition and throttle next to it. Not wasting precious seconds to investigate further, she hurried over and twisted the key to the right. She jammed the button down and a the engines grumbled from somewhere below.

The warbling sputtered a few times and then caught, roaring to life.

Another wave lifted and dropped the boat onto the rocks. A terrible splitting sound shook the hull.

She slammed the throttle forward and clung to the wheel as the boat lurched forward. She steered to the right, into the oncoming waves, slicing through them with ease.

Another minute and she made it beyond the break and out into the gentle waves flowing along the surface.

Emily glanced out the side windows and back windows.

The island shrank as she continued on.

Taking her bearings from where the explosion had occurred the night before, she steered to the left and saw the compass showed that it was a southerly direction.

She scanned the gauges and noted with unbridled gratitude that the fuel dial showed a nearly full tank.

Who knew how much capacity this thing had, but it looked like the type designed to go fishing for days. Like some of the smaller boats on those reality TV shows with the captains that clearly did hard drugs and whose lives reflected the harshness of their environment.

She was about to allow herself a small smile when she noticed something odd.

The far horizon of the ocean wasn't flat like it should've been. It was canted over a little.

Rather, she realized, the boat was.

She pulled back on the throttle and boat listed further. There was a problem.

The nascent smile hardened into a frown. She should've known better. Something was always going to go wrong.

It was just a matter of time.

Emily exited the cabin and followed the lean of the boat to the aft deck. She crossed it to the far side which hung noticeably lower in the water. She leaned out over the side and gasped.

The boat hadn't escaped its encounter with the rocks without a scratch. A scratch would've been no problem.

She would've welcomed a scratch any day.

This was more like a three foot long open fissure.

And as she watched, dark blue seawater poured into the wound.

38

How long before it filled with water and dragged her and the boat under?

Had she escaped the island only to drown in the sea?

Emily gritted her teeth and spat a curse at the world.

It was a cold thing that forever sought to suck the life out of her. There was only one way to respond.

To fight.

To die if that's what happened. But not before leaving every last ounce of blood and sweat on the battlefield first.

She nodded to herself, an unspoken agreement between the split and sometimes adversarial sides in her brain. The doer and the thinker.

For now, both were in agreement.

Fight!

And that meant plugging this gash in the boat.

An idea occurred to her. A hint from the observation before. The boat had tilted further when she let off the throttle.

Of course! Going slower had dropped the back end deeper into the water. Going faster brought the back end and kept the tear at or above the waterline.

It was a theory, nothing more.

But it felt right in her gut, and when seconds could be the difference between life and death, hunches mattered as much as evidence gathered in a lab. Probably more.

Emily raced back into the cabin and slammed the throttle forward. The engines roared and the boat lurched forward. She wasn't positive, but it did seem to level some.

She spun toward the stairwell at the back of the cabin and vaulted down to the deck below. Her boots splashed into a foot of water. She passed a small room of cramped bunkbeds, then an equally small galley and dining table, and ended up in the engine room at the back of the boat. Two enormous diesel engines sat on raised platforms, both pushing out a bass thrum that echoed in her chest.

There!

In the far corner, water gushed in through the tear in the hull. She plodded over through the incoming current. The smooth hull of the boat opened into a wide wound.

It was bigger than it looked from above.

More than three feet long. Ten inches across at the widest point. Water swirled by her calves as it rushed to fill the rest of the boat.

What could patch that?

An idea came.

Desperate and probably destined to fail.

But it was something!

She hurried back to the sleeping quarters and

grabbed the lifejackets she'd seen on the way through. She looped six of them over her arm.

She was headed back through the galley when another idea came.

It could help.

She grabbed a bar stool bolted to the floor and yanked it to the side.

It didn't budge.

She braced herself on the table and reared back and let loose a side kick. Something cracked. She kicked again and again as hard as she could.

The pole holding the stool to the floor broke free and fell over with a splash into the rising water.

She dragged her haul down the short corridor and into the engine room.

The water churned around her knees.

If this didn't work, and work fast, the struggle would be over.

She fought through the incoming current and noticed the water level had climbed above the breach.

She dropped everything but a single life jacket, and thrust it under the water. The hole was easy to find because the current shoved her hand away with as much force as she pushed it forward. She pushed harder and the life jacket closed against the hull.

Water shot up into her face, blinding and choking her before the current ripped the life jacket out of her hand and swept it away below the surface.

Emily wiped her eyes clear, biting her lower lip, frantic with the knowledge that she was losing.

Another idea.

Yes! Maybe!

She scooped up the remaining life jackets and began looping their straps over and through each other, tying them off when they ran out of length. In a couple of minutes, she had a fairly well knotted together glob of life jackets.

Not anything you'd want to wear, but maybe an adequate dressing for this wound.

She tied the bunch to the flat seat of the barstool and then lifted the whole assemblage by the pole.

The water was now up to her thighs.

She drove the pole down into the water toward the gaping hole, almost like a ragged q-tip at a bleeding ear canal.

She leaned into it through the resistance of the current. At the same time, she pivoted the base of the pole pinning it against the engine platform. Another shove down on the front end and it held.

The strength of the current trying to knock her down ebbed away.

She felt under the water around the edges of the makeshift dressing.

Water was still coming in, but not blasting in like before.

She found the base of the pole and kicked it to straighten the angle and increase the pressure exerted against the hole.

She felt around the tear.

It worked!

Small streams came in here and there, but they were like the sprays of a garden hose instead of the firehose of seconds ago.

She paused and waited, not letting a smile come near her face or heart.

The fix could break loose any second.

She waited.

It didn't.

It held.

And she noticed the water level was no longer rising.

Emily pushed through the water, retracing the route to the vertical stairs leading up to the cabin. She hauled herself up and took a second to survey the situation.

The boat cut through the ocean like a water-logged arrow. At once both powerful and direct, but also dragging lower and slower than its design.

Hopefully this thing had some kind of bilge system that automatically drained water away.

But she'd rejected hope as a plan long ago.

She needed to lighten the boat. To get it to sit higher in the water because once she let off the throttle or it ran out of gas, who knew how well the fix would work.

A pungent scent in the air caught her attention.

Fuel.

She glanced at the fuel tank and gulped.

The needle pointed at just above the three-quarter mark. There was no way she'd gone through that much already.

The tank must've been punctured on the rocks.

And here she was again.

Right where life always seemed to put her.

With a choice between fighting or giving up.

Between living or dying.

Emily snarled and bared her teeth.

With her, it was never a choice.

39

BOB took a seat on the worn couch and picked at the thread-bare cushion. Flo had taken care of him on this couch just two days ago.

And now she was gone.

The madness that was Charlie Bog had swept into town and swept her away in one fell swoop.

If Bob had a bank account with a million dollars, he'd withdraw it all in ones. And then shove each bill down Charlie's throat until the bastard was crapping change. And then he'd keep stuffing more in until he was blue in the face and his eyes went dull.

What kind of lunatic bombed a police station?

The dangerous kind, that's what.

The kind that didn't abide by the same rules as every-body else.

The door to Rome's bedroom opened. A hollow voice echoed out from behind a black helmet. "What do you think?"

Bob stared at the figure standing in the hall.

What did he think?

How about that maybe this kid was crazier than Charlie, for starters?

Rome wore a full set of black tactical gear with what appeared to be a bulletproof vest along with plates that covered his waist, arms and legs. In hands covered by black gloves, he carried a semi-automatic shotgun. The clear visor showing his eyes was the only evidence that he wasn't some futuristic robot killing machine.

The black armored figure would've made even the bravest man pause to consider.

"Why are you dressed like that?"

"I told you. I'm going to kill the man that murdered my mother. I could use your help. But I'm going either way."

Bob pushed up off the couch, feeling every second of his sixty years. "I thought you meant later. Like eventually some day."

"I meant now."

"I thought you needed more ammo?"

Rome shrugged. "That bag of weed was going to get me more guns and bullets, maybe a grenade if I was lucky." He lifted the shotgun."But I still have this and enough shells to make it interesting."

Bob raised his hands in supplication. "I get it. I do. I want him dead, too. But we just escaped this morning. Shouldn't we take a few days to come up with a plan and maybe recruit some help?"

The dark helmet shook from side to side. "I'm not waiting. Before today ends, one of us is going to end up dead. And I'm gonna do my best to make sure it's him."

"You do remember that the brewery is crawling with

armed men all loyal to him? You'll never get near him before they shoot you down."

Rome knocked on the bulletproof vest. "I'm covered with kevlar plates. They'll have to get a lucky shot at my neck or underarm to take me down."

"Where did you get all this stuff?"

"You'd be surprised what you can buy online and get delivered to your door. Well, before, I mean."

Bob wasn't surprised. He'd bought plenty of things online and had them delivered to his door. Some of those things would make a call girl call it a night.

One had, in fact.

That delicious Asian treat he'd ordered like food off of a menu from OrientalOrgasms. She'd arrived at his door looking like a real professional. Like she'd seen it all before. That was until he brought out the strap-on he'd purchased online the week before.

He hadn't expected her to actually use it. The thing was a monster and glowed in the dark. It was supposed to be a joke.

But her lack of English and his lack of caring had ended with her slapping him across the face and then running out of his posh West Hollywood home, swearing at him in a language that he'd never positively identified, and yet one that was unquestionably suited for passionate cursing.

So, yeah. He knew there was a whole world of weird that could be ordered online and delivered to your doorstep.

Used to be, anyway.

There was no online anymore.

No internet. No hard-working hookers a few clicks and a credit charge away.

The world had taken a hard right turn for the worse.

Bob shook his head. "I'm not surprised. Where'd you get the shotgun?"

Rome shrugged. "Had a client that ran short on cash. Offered this instead and I accepted."

"How much weed did you sell?"

"Enough."

"Then why did you and your mother still live in this dump?"

The black-clad figure took an imposing step toward him, making Bob shrink back into the couch. "Sorry. I didn't mean it that way."

"I get it. You're an idiot. You can't help it."

Bob wouldn't have put it quite like that. He might've said he was jaded or prone to being negative or too sarcastic for his own good. But yeah, once you boiled it down, it was basically true.

"I was about to buy us a house. Had the money saved up and just had to find the perfect one. But, that doesn't matter anymore. She's dead. There's only one thing matters now. Killing the man that murdered her."

"Look, kid," Bob said, "I'm with you. I'll help however I can, but we can't just walk through the front door. They'll fill us full of bullets before we get ten feet."

"Maybe you. Not me."

Bob rolled his eyes. "Yeah, you've got some crazy super soldier gear there, but a good plan will get you further than the best gear in the world."

"What are you, Napoleon Bonaparte?"

Bob smiled. "You may not have known this, but I was an assistant producer on the A Team for several years."

"The what?"

Bob shook his head in disbelief. "The A Team! Hannibal, Face, Murdock, and B.A. Baracus! The A Team!"

Rome didn't respond.

"You know, Mr. T with the mohawk!"

"Mr. Who? Like the letter T or tee like a golf tee?"

Bob pinched his eyes shut. "Doesn't matter. Anyway, I helped the writers every now and then come up with a good plan for how the A Team would attack a stronghold. Okay, so I didn't really help. Whatever. I listened to them come up with ideas."

Rome headed for the front door. "I'm leaving."

Bob grabbed his massive arm and hauled him back. "What I'm saying is that I have a plan. A plan that has a chance of ending with Charlie Bog dead and you alive."

Rome shrugged. "I don't care if I live."

"Fine. It'll still give you a better chance to kill Charlie."

Rome returned to the kitchen table and sat down. "I'm listening."

"The key is occupying the higher ground." He dug out the car key he'd found earlier wedged down into the cushions of the couch. The one he'd been holding onto in the event Rome decided to kick him out. He held it up.

"Is that the key to the Pinto Bean?"

"Yep."

40

Bob stood at the top of the steep hill looking down at the back side of the brewery. He nodded. "Yep, this'll do it," he said as he engaged the emergency break to keep the Pinto Bean from plunging off the side of the road. The faded brown junker rattled and sputtered but didn't cut off.

A helmet-less Rome sucked in a breath of air and wiped his forehead. He slung sweat onto the pavement. "It's a thousand degrees inside this gear."

Bob nodded. "Want to take it off?"

"What's the plan again?"

Bob pointed down at the gang's headquarters. "We're going to crash this car through the back door. Take them by surprise."

Rome squinted at the building below. "Are you sure this is gonna work? It sounds like a stupid A-Team plan. I thought you said those guys always came up with awesome plans and battle buses and diversions and stuff?"

"I had almost no time to come up with this because somebody couldn't wait to get themselves shot! The A Team always had like a week or something to prepare."

"This plan sucks. The Bean just has lap belts. We'll probably die when we hit the building."

"It's better than trying to get through that wall of buses they have parked out front. Blast our way through! That's your stupid plan in a nutshell."

"It was blasting *and dodging*."

Bob rolled his eyes. "It was suicide. They would've shot us to pieces before we made it to the front door!"

Rome shook his head. "Well, this is no A Team plan. That's all I'm saying."

Bob gritted his teeth to keep his mouth shut. He longed to tell the kid where his head was and how nice it would be for him to pull it out and take a look around.

Teenagers could be so infuriating.

Instead, he took a slow breath. His relationship with Rome was already tenuous at best. A total breakdown wasn't going to help either of them.

Bob looked up at the dull glow in the sky that hinted at the location of the afternoon sun. He shrugged. "There's a chance we might die on impact. Sure. I remember that big scandal about Ford Pintos bursting in flames after a collision."

"Bursting into flames?"

"Yeah, it was when they got hit in the back, or front, or something. I don't remember."

Rome's eyes went wide. "Well, that would be a really helpful thing to remember right now! We're about to use this thing as a battering ram!"

Bob wanted to flick the kid in the forehead. "I don't

remember! Google Consumer Reports or ask Ralph Nader!"

"Ralph Nader? Who's that? What are you talking about?"

So infuriating.

"Never mind. Doesn't matter. The point is that you want to kill Charlie. I happen to agree though I doubt we're the best people for the job. But I owe your mother. And we'll get the revenge she deserves, or I'll die with you trying—"

"Are you trying to do a pre-game pep talk?"

"What?"

"You know, trying to inspire us and all that."

"What if I was?"

"Then I'd tell you it sucks."

"Shut up and let's do this."

Rome popped the hatch of the car and finished getting ready.

Bob pulled out a metal flask of vodka and spun off the cap. He drew in a slow breath. His insides twisted as the memories of the *episode* washed over him. It had started with a full bottle of vodka.

But this time was different. If he died this time, there was meaning in it. He was fighting for something that mattered. It would be a hero's death.

Not a coward's.

He brought the flask to his lips and tipped it up.

Clean fire washed over his tongue and singed down his throat. He swallowed and felt the warmth settle in his stomach. Another drink quickly followed.

If he was going to die, he'd rather do it with a good buzz.

He took a couple more drinks and forced himself to screw the cap back on. A buzz was fine. Preferred even to calm the nerves. But stumbling drunk wasn't going to help.

The reality was that he'd probably die in the next few minutes. The kid had youth and a nearly impenetrable set of body armor on his side.

Bob had old age, a weak ticker and two denim coats on. Nothing that suggested a good chance for survival.

And that was okay.

He looked up at the dull haze that blanketed the sky.

Florence, I assume you're up there somewhere. If heaven exists, you were the type it was made for. I'll help your son as much as I can. If he's lucky, he might survive.

"You praying to God?" Rome said as he slapped Bob's shoulder.

Bob looked over and again was impressed with Rome's gear. The kid was terrifying. A futuristic super soldier. Kevlar plates covering his abdomen, arms, and legs. He'd switched the visor to a dark tint that hid his eyes.

Definitely added to the sinister killing machine vibe.

Rome yanked the helmet up and cracked a can of Mountain Dew. He slugged it down in a single go.

"Ready?" Bob asked.

"Hold on." He fished another can out of a pocket and finished it in equally impressive fashion. He smashed the can flat between gloved hands. "Ready."

"Remember the plan. I'll try to get the prisoners out. You go for Charlie. If either of us succeed, the other's chances get a lot better."

Rome lowered the helmet into place. "Got it."

Bob started to turn toward the driver's door when Rome grabbed his shoulder. "I'll never forgive you for what happened to my mother."

Bob pursed his lips together and nodded. He wouldn't forgive himself so there was no reason the kid should either.

"But if we somehow survive this, maybe that means we're a good partnership. The kind of partnership you need in times like these."

Bob didn't know what to say. Rome was almost saying they could be friends. But not friends. Survival buddies? Buddies was still too optimistic. Survival associates?

Rome headed for the passenger door so Bob got in on his side. They buckled up and Bob put one hand on the steering wheel and the other on the brake release.

Rome held the semiautomatic shotgun close with the strap secured around his back. He stared out the windshield at nothing but air.

The long front hood cut off the view below, but it'd come back in a hurry as soon as Bob released the emergency brake.

"Let's kick some ass," Bob yelled. Tried to yell. His voice cracked on *some* and *ass* trickled out weak and lifeless.

He was too old for this.

41

Bob yanked the release, let off the brake pedal, and grabbed the wheel with both hands. The first job was to steer it at the back door.

The car rolled forward and the nose abruptly dropped.

The brewery jumped into view, already off to the left a little.

Bob jerked the steering wheel over and the car jerked to the left. He straightened out as they picked up speed.

They hit a bump and the front tires lifted off the ground before slamming back down.

His body tried to lift off the seat, but the lap belt kept him glued in place.

It was like taking a ride on one of those vomit comets, the planes that flew parabolic curves and gave people the sensation of weightlessness for brief periods of time.

The side of the hill wasn't a road.

It wasn't smooth.

And it was so steep that every time they bounced off a

bump in the terrain, Bob half-expected the car to launch into orbit.

He glanced at their speed.

Forty-five miles per hour!

Now halfway down the hill and Bob wondered if he should slow down. It wouldn't help to plow through the whole building and explode out the other side.

Unfortunately, there wasn't time to weigh the pros and cons. Speed versus typical building construction on a remote island that he'd never had any business being on in the first place.

It was all Malcolm Calhoun's fault. The back-stabbing, plastic-faced weasel that was his old boss. The one that had threatened to fire him if he didn't come here to personally supervise the stupid TV show.

If he ever saw Malcolm again, he was going to cut his pecker off and feed it to that idiot Pomeranian that he carried around like a purse.

An image of his wife flashed through his mind.

A particularly delicious one.

Their wedding night. White lace panties with a line of coke between her breasts. A line the size of a plastic soda straw.

God, she was gorgeous. And such a freak in bed.

He couldn't blame her for screwing his best friend. He hadn't been enough for her. It wasn't her fault.

It was her elemental nature.

She was a lioness, forever on the prowl for the strongest mate. The one that could make her submit.

I still love you, Sophie.

Bob glanced at the speedometer.

Eighty-eight miles per hour.

The brewery now thirty feet below.

The car hit a huge bump and Bob's skull tried to collapse into his spine.

The vehicle shot off the ground, veering off course, briefly showing only brown sky through the front windshield.

It came back down and landed on a trash dumpster. The heavy duty plastic lid reacted like a trampoline and launched them back up into the air.

The edge of the building's roof blurred by underneath as the front wheels crashed down. The rear wheels caught the edge and Bob slammed forward with the seatbelt trying to slice through his waist.

The back end bounced up and the windshield filled with a close up view of worn gray shingles.

Bob smashed on the brakes as the back end slammed down.

They skidded to a stop on top of the roof.

Bob's heart hammered in his chest. His knuckles ached from gripping the wheel so hard. Sharp pain pulsed from a kneecap that must've hit the dashboard.

They both stared out the windshield in stunned silence.

Rome spoke first. "Whoa! That was awesome! We're on the roof, man!"

"Yeah."

Rome turned and Bob met his gaze. "How are we going to get down?"

Bob hadn't gotten that far yet. He was still coming to terms with how the plan had gotten so messed up so fast.

A cracking sound below and the back end of the car

dropped a little and then stopped. More creaking and splintering and the roof gave way.

The Pinto Bean dropped straight down into a fog of dust and debris.

After getting over the feeling that his spine had been permanently compressed a few inches, Bob noticed movement through the thick layer of dust covering the side window. He turned expecting to see a gun and live out the final second of his life.

A hand wiped the glass clean.

Chief Stuckey peered inside. Marco Morales stood behind peering over his shoulder. "You're not going to believe this!" Stuckey shouted. He yanked open the door as Bob got the seatbelt free.

Stuckey glanced past Bob and saw the black-clad figure of doom fiddling with his seat belt release. "Is that Rome?"

Bob nodded as he leaned over and poked the button to release it.

Rome flung it away. "I'm here to kill the man that murdered my mother. I don't care about anything or anyone else." He kicked the door open. Rather kicked it off because the door fell onto the ground. The impact shattered the already cracked window. He grunted as he stepped out and his black boots crunched onto the shards.

The four met at the back of the car.

Bob recognized a few of the faces peering through the thick particulate fog. They were his fellow prisoners. The people from the meeting that had been captured the night before.

The car had apparently come down on one of the

walls of the room where they were being held. The back half inside the room and front half in the adjacent hallway.

Stuckey grabbed Marco's shoulder. "Get everyone out the back! The plan for tonight is on! Tell them to spread the word!"

Marco shook his head. "You do it, Chief. These people look up to you, not me. I'll go with Rome."

Stuckey's upper lip quivered as emotions warred within him. He bared his teeth and growled. "Okay! But you put that murderer in the grave! Got me?"

Marco nodded.

Stuckey waved to the others. "Let's go everyone! Follow me!"

Voices shouting from somewhere in the building echoed into the room.

"They're coming!" Bob shouted.

Rome grabbed the detached car door off the ground and held it in front like a shield. The door was made of thick metal and would likely stop anything that hit it.

He stepped through the gaping hole in the wall and into the hallway. Without looking back, he headed off with the shotgun tucked into his shoulder and the barrel resting on the rim of the door window.

Bob started after him, but Marco lowered his arm to block the way. He pointed toward the press of people funneling out in other direction. "You should go with them!"

Bob tried to push the muscular arm away, but failed. "I'm going with the kid! If he dies, I'm okay with joining him."

42

MARCO met his eyes and shared a look of understanding. Following Rome into the battle was only going to end one way. Even if they somehow took out Charlie, there were plenty of other gang members that were armed and all too willing to kill.

Bob stepped into the hallway and started off after Rome.

Marco followed and paused as he noticed something wedged under a section of framing lumber.

A Glock pistol.

Probably from the guard who'd been stationed outside the door. But whether he was buried under the car and debris or had somehow escaped wasn't obvious.

Not that it mattered.

Marco snatched up the pistol and inched the slide back. Yep, locked and loaded. He released the magazine and saw that it was full with fifteen rounds not including the one in the chamber.

A deafening boom shook the narrow hall.

A flash of light burned through the thinning cloud of dust.

Then another boom.

He rushed forward with the pistol raised and ready.

He approached an intersection of hallways and a man came out firing.

Marco dropped to a crouched position and put two rounds in his chest. He paused only long enough to grab the revolver from the dying man's hands. A 44 Magnum with an eight inch barrel and four rounds ready to fire. The thing would do serious damage, but it was going to kick like a mule.

He switched the revolver to his stronger right hand and the Glock pistol to his left. Now with both up at the ready, he hurried forward as the crack of small-arms fire let off like firecrackers on the fourth of July.

BOOM!

BOOM!

Rome or someone else with a shotgun added their part to the maelstrom.

The acrid taste of expended gunpowder coated Marco's tongue. The gray smoke drifted in the air.

A hand reached out from a dark room as he passed and grabbed his arm.

Marco spun around and brought the revolver to bear. He had the trigger tight and about to break when Bob's face appeared out of the gloom.

"I lost him! The kid took off like an idiot!"

"Do you know how to use one of these?" Marco asked as he held the Glock out.

"More or less. I took my ex-wife to a shooting range one time."

"Only the one time?"

"Yeah, but we stayed for a few hours."

"Whatever. Take it. Point it at what you want to destroy and pull the trigger."

Bob's lack of attention let the muzzle drift toward covering Marco.

Marco grabbed his wrist and angled it away. "Only at what you want to destroy! Got it?"

"Sure."

Marco had his doubts. The last thing he needed was to get shot in the back by someone on his own side. "Stay behind me. And don't point it at me."

Bob nodded and shuffled out as Marco spun back toward the direction Rome had gone.

The sound of an epic gun battle grew louder as they got to the end and the open doorway to the front area of the brewery.

Marco crouched and peeked around the doorway before ducking back into cover.

"What do you see?" Bob shouted behind his shoulder.

"They're firing from a protected position, behind a bunch of overturned tables. I couldn't see Rome, but I think they have him pinned down behind the bar.

The high-pitched sound of shattering glass.

The tinkling of the fragments sliding over the concrete floor.

A voice spoke into the lull of quiet. "That was Johnny Walker Black Label. The next idiot that destroys a bottle of booze is gonna get shot."

Marco recognized the madman's voice. The southern twang. The assured air of assumed superiority.

BOOM!

CRACK! CRACK! CRACK!

Glass shattered.

"Sorry, boss."

CRACK!

The thump of a body hitting the floor.

"Bet you're sorrier now. I thought I was clear on that. Nobody shoot it!"

Grumbles of agreement and understanding echoed around the large room.

"Hey, you, behind the bar! Would you mind terribly coming out where we can kill you without shooting up the bar? Wasting liquor is a mortal sin. I think I remember learning about it in Sunday school. Moses held the stone tablets and rule number one was not to waste good booze."

Marco peeked around the corner just in time to see Rome pop up and heave an expensive looking bottle of something into the no man's land in the middle of the space.

It hit and shattered into sparkling diamonds.

"I was just gonna kill you before! But now you've gone and made me mad!"

"I'm going to kill you!" Rome shouted back.

"Our mystery guest speaks at last," Charlie said with an air of amusement. "And how do you propose to go about doing that?"

BOOM!

"Well, I like simple answers but we got you pinned down and outgunned. I admire your gear. Saved you twenty times over already. But sooner or later, I'm gonna get you. And I'm gonna kill you real slow."

"You murdered my mother!"

"Your mother?"

"The bomb you set off in the police station!"

Charlie chuckled. "Oh, that little bit of mischief. I have to admit. It turned out better than I'd hoped. Think I killed the whole police force in one go." He laughed, apparently enjoying the pleasant surprise once again.

Bob tugged on Marco's shoulder. "Rome's not going to last much longer in there. He'll run out of ammo or they'll overwhelm him. We have to do something."

Yeah, but what? Nothing that had a chance of succeeding had come to mind yet.

And he was right. They were running out of time.

Voices from the front parking lot echoed through the shattered windows.

The front door clanged open.

"Boss! The prisoners! The prisoners!"

"Cool your heels and catch a breath. And try to be more specific. The prisoners is a subject without a verb, you see? It's half a thought. Something does something. That's a whole thought. You just told me something and nothing else."

"Sorry, Boss. The prisoners have escaped out the back. Lyle spotted Chief Stuckey herding 'em up the hill."

"Why do I have to do everything around here?" Charlie said with exasperation. "Alexei, you stay here and kill the nitwit behind the bar. You four! With me!"

"Yes, Boss. Okay, Boss."

Marco peeked around the corner as Charlie and his lackeys ran out the front after the prisoners.

"No!" Rome shouted as he popped up. "You can't leave!" He charged out after Charlie. The car door shield and shotgun swinging back and forth, spraying death in all directions.

Marco didn't hesitate. He yanked Bob forward and they joined the assault. The classic Smith and Wesson .44 in his hand did in fact kick like a mule as he picked a shot at an exposed foot sticking out from behind a table.

A man screamed in agony.

What had been a black boot was now a red mess.

Marco noticed Bob to his left and the flickering flower of flame as the Glock fired.

Rome didn't bother going for the front door. It would've meant running straight at a bank of overturned tables and the half dozen men with guns behind it.

Instead, he angled toward the nearest window and didn't slow down.

His weight and speed hit it like a thunderclap. The large pane exploded outward, blasting shards into the parking lot. His boot caught the sill and took him down.

Hard.

He face planted and then flopped over to his side while the car door skidded away.

Marco and Bob continued firing on the group behind the tables as they raced to follow the same escape route. They made it and jumped through as the last round left Marco's barrel.

He landed lightly and went for the shotgun harnessed around Rome's middle. He snapped it up but the sling held fast.

Glass shattered as rounds ricocheted off the pavement inches away.

Marco dropped to his belly, turned the shotgun toward their attackers and fired.

"Get up!" he shouted at Rome as he dragged him up by the shoulders.

Bob fired a couple of times and the slide locked back on his pistol. He continued to try to fire the empty gun.

Rome was on his feet, but not all there.

Marco slipped the strap off and over his own head. He hooked one arm under Rome and trained the shotgun at the men inside. He squeezed the trigger.

CLICK.

Empty!

"Run!"

There were no men standing guard on top of the buses out front. There was no one anywhere. They'd apparently all gone after the prisoners.

Rome dug into his cargo pocket and pulled out an old World War II style pineapple grenade.

Marco's eyes went wide as the kid pulled the pin and let the spoon fly open.

The tennis ball sized sphere of death sailed through the missing front window and bounced inside.

The men inside shouted in terror.

"Grenade!"

"Grenade!"

Marco waited for the explosion as they ran between two buses and saw the way ahead was clear. Something from the edge of his peripheral vision flew through the air.

Headed right at him.

He tried to duck but it was too late.

A fur ball of fury and indignation landed on his head, sharp claws digging into his scalp, harder than was strictly necessary to hold on.

Oscar hopped down onto his shoulder and bit his ear hard enough to draw blood.

"Hey buddy!" He would've given their reunion the attention it deserved, if he hadn't been running for their lives.

They kept going at a steady clip.

The explosion didn't happen.

After they turned the corner at the nearby intersection and got a building between them and the brewery, he allowed them to slow so Bob and Rome could catch a breath.

Rome yanked the helmet up and sucked down huge breaths. "You have a," more breathing, "rat on your shoulder."

"It's a weasel. Name's Oscar." Marco reached up a finger and stroked under his chin.

"Looks like a rat," Rome said.

The weasel turned to Rome and hissed.

Marco waited for them to catch their breath. Running them into the ground wasn't going to help. "Your dud grenade still did the job."

Rome shook his head. "Wasn't a dud. Worked just fine lighting joints."

Marco's mouth fell open. "That was a novelty lighter?"

Bob snorted. "You can buy all kinds of stuff online and have it delivered right to your front door."

43

Marco glanced at his watch. Emily's watch that was now his.

6:22PM

They were too late.

He grabbed Rome's shoulder and hauled him back into the shadows behind the corner.

An old Chevy truck lit up the intersection as it turned and roared by. The town had been crawling with Charlie's men ever since the attack on the brewery.

They'd returned to Rome's apartment and packed up. The plan was to get out before the fallout arrived. It was a great plan, right up until they'd left the apartment and headed into town.

Gang patrols were everywhere. The echoed reports of gunshots suggested the patrols occasionally found people. They also suggested how those people were being dealt with.

The gang's activity also suggested that the other prisoners had gotten away and that Charlie Bog was furious about it.

Good.

In leaving the town, Marco had only two regrets.

One was that they hadn't managed to kill that sociopath.

And two was that this was the last place he'd been close to Emily. She was gone and the new world wasn't like the modern world everyone had taken for granted. She wasn't a text away. She wasn't an email away. She wasn't even a letter away.

The old world and the new world had rejoined paths.

When someone went to another town or another place, chances were almost zero you'd ever see them again. Travel was again much more costly and much more dangerous.

Marco peeked around the corner and scanned the street in both directions. Clear for now. "Let's go!"

He took off across the intersection with Oscar perched on one shoulder like a living car hood ornament. He glanced to verify that Rome and Bob were right behind.

The hazy night sky cast a dim glow below. It must've been a full moon. In the old world, it would've lit up the streets on a clear night. Now, the perpetual haze cut down and diffused what light made it through.

"There it is!" Marco whispered-shouted as he spotted the marina.

The faint rumble of a boat engine echoed across the street. "Hurry up! Someone's still there!"

The plan was for everyone to meet an hour after

sunset, but they were well past that now. Two hours maybe.

They sprinted down Mission Road toward the dock at the end. They made it halfway when Oscar started chittering and zipping back and forth across his shoulders.

The unmistakable action of a pump shotgun made the hairs on the back of his neck stand on end.

"Who goes there?"

Marco raised his hands, hoping he was about to identify himself to someone on his side. Otherwise, their plan ended here.

"Marco Morales with Rome Bickle and Bob... What's your last name Bob?"

"How did you remember his last name but not mine? I'm the famous Hollywood producer. I'm the one that invited you to the show! I'm the reason you're here at all!"

The moron said it like it was a good thing. Marco answered for him. "Bob the Hollywood producer jerk," he said to the hidden voice that had challenged them.

Another voice shouted from the dock. "Marco! Get over here!"

Chief Stuckey!

Marco looked to the side as they ran and saw a man with a shotgun step behind a nearby parked boat. It was a good spot for a lookout. Cover behind the boat and trailer. Open view of anyone that passed through the narrowed neck to get to the dock.

Stuckey rolled Marco up into a bear hug that would've crushed the air out of him if he hadn't been ready for it.

Oscar jumped over to his shoulders and nibbled on the chief's earlobes as he pulled back.

"Good to see you, too!" A smile lifted the corners of his mouth. He patted Marco's shoulder and Oscar darted across it like a bridge. "Figured you didn't make it out of that shooting gallery."

Marco thumbed toward Rome. "We had a battering ram that worked out pretty well."

"Well, you three have more luck than a leprechaun because you've made it for the last ride out."

Marco scanned the dark water of the adjacent channel but didn't see movement. "Where are the others?"

Stuckey shook his head. "Not many made it. A couple hundred, maybe. Not enough time to get the word out."

"Yeah, that and Charlie's patrols have made getting through town a dangerous undertaking."

Stuckey turned back toward the shadowed faces on the nearby boat. "How's it looking, Alfie?"

"Well, engine's still leaking like a busted baby's diaper, but I think she'll make it. And if not, we've got the Zodiac and a flare kit to call for rescue if everything goes kaput."

"Good." Stuckey turned back to Marco. "All aboard. We haven't been spotted yet and I don't want to hang around to change that."

Marco handed his backpack to a woman on the boat and then climbed aboard. He turned to grab Rome's duffle bag but Bob had cut in front to get on the boat.

Bob handed him a suitcase and then accepted Marco's hand to help him over.

Marco looked to Rome next, but the kid hadn't moved. "Rome! Let's go!"

Rome dropped the duffle bag at his feet. "I can't do it."

"What?" Bob asked. "We talked about this already. We have to go. That fallout is coming and it's going to poison the whole island."

Rome covered his face with one enormous hand and pinched his temples. "No. I'm not leaving until Charlie Bog is dead."

Bob threw his hands up in the air. "I get it! I really do! That maniac deserves to die horribly, but you're killing yourself if you stay here!"

Stuckey laid a hand on Rome's shoulder. "He's right. You need to go with them. You all need to get going. The others are probably already waiting for you up at Spruce Cape."

Marco noticed the subtle suggestion in the words.

Go with them. You all.

"Is your gear already stowed, Chief?"

Stuckey chewed his lower lip. "I'm not going."

"Why?" someone on the boat said.

"There are six thousand people that live in this town. The town that I swore to protect and serve with my life. While I'm happy a few of them made it out tonight, that leaves thousands that haven't."

As much as Marco wanted to, he couldn't argue with the man. Police, the good ones, were a dedicated and honorable brotherhood. His own uncle had been a county deputy a long time ago. He'd grown up with a respect and understanding for those that worked in law enforcement.

The bad ones weren't worth the tin badges in their wallets.

Chief Stuckey was one of the good ones. One of the best ones.

"Rome, you need to go," Stuckey said. "You're not going to get a second chance."

"The only second chance I want is one at killing that murderer."

Stuckey turned to Marco. "He may not be eighteen but he is a man. He's made his choice."

Bob sighed. "I guess I'm staying too, then."

Rome shook his head. "I don't need you, old man. I can do it myself."

Bob grabbed his suitcase and slung it over to the dock. "Did you come up with the car rolling down the hill idea? Or was that me? Because I distinctly remember telling you the idea and you saying how stupid it was and how it was so not like the A-Team version of a rescue."

He kept on while Marco helped him cross over to the dock.

"And if my elderly, decrepit, failing memory has managed to remember one final thing, I recall that the plan worked out pretty well! We broke into the brewery, got the prisoners free, and somehow managed not to get killed! That's what I call a I love it when a plan comes together Hannibal A-Team moment!"

Bob yanked his suitcase off the ground and slammed it down. One of the wheels broke off and rolled away. Bob let go of the handle and it fell over. "Great! Just great!"

"Fine, I'll stay too," Marco said as he lifted his backpack.

"No," Stuckey said. "You go. You're a natural leader, son. These people will need you."

"You need my help," Marco said as he tossed the backpack over to the dock.

Stuckey grabbed it and launched it over Marco's head to the other side of the boat. He untied the line securing the boat to the dock, pushed the boat away with his foot, and tossed the line over.

The engines rumbled as the boat pulled away.

Marco appeared at the side with his retrieved backpack. He eyed the span of dark water between the boat and dock. Too far to jump. "Take us back to the dock!"

Oscar screeched in shared anger.

"No!" Stuckey roared with his command voice. The one that expected obedience.

The engines didn't spin down.

"Marco, you're still my deputy and I order you to go! There are a couple hundred people that are going to need you. I expect that my faith in you is well-placed. I expect that you will do your job."

Marco set the backpack down on the deck.

The boat turned left into the channel that ran between Kodiak and Near Island. The figures on the dock started to slip into shadow.

A voice came across the water.

"Will you do it, son?"

"Yes."

A distant pair of headlights raked across the channel before they turned down Mission Road.

The deep boom of a shotgun fired.

The sharper cracks of rifles responded.

The headlights raked across the end of the dock.

Stuckey, Rome and Bob were already gone.

"Should we go back?" someone asked.

Marco shook his head. "No. Keep going. We have to join up with the others." He reached up and stroked Oscar's back to calm him. The weasel slowly relaxed and the hairs laid flat.

Marco whispered so that only the weasel would hear. "I hope we're up to this."

44

EMILY gripped the railing lining the bow of the boat as she stared out into the darkness. Was there something out there?

Between the minimal light and the rolling surface of the ocean, she couldn't be sure.

Sometimes near and sometimes in the distance. A darker shadow than the surrounding black. A terrifying vision of the Megalodon rising up out of the water and tearing the boat apart.

Nonsense, in other words. Her mind playing tricks on her. She must've left that monster behind hours ago. But it was still impossible to stop her brain from replaying the vision over and over again.

The shadows were nothing substantial. Nothing more than tricks of light or the lack thereof.

She took another look into the distance, straining to soak up every last photon.

There!

Off to the right!

A light on the water!

A swell rolled through, sucking the spark of hope back into darkness.

Her chest tightened with worry as she started to think she'd imagined it.

The swell passed and the light appeared again.

It was real!

Someone was out on the water.

She should've been more careful, more thoughtful of the potential of meeting an unknown party in the dark of night.

But she wasn't.

All she felt was joy at no longer being alone.

She turned back for the cabin and froze as the soundtrack of her imminent rescue abruptly changed.

The rumbling of the engines.

They sputtered and guttered out.

Emily ran back inside the cabin and tried to restart them. The ignition turned over, but they didn't catch. She tried for another minute as the boat slowed and the rear dipped lower into the water.

She flipped the topside lights on and off, over and over, hoping the blinking would draw the other boat over before it was too late. She swallowed hard, knowing this moment might come.

And it had.

The sound of water crashing through the hull below echoed up to the cabin. She'd tried to reinforce the patch, but had only succeeded in making it worse. It was then that she came up with backup plan. A plan for when the current plan failed.

Something to give her a chance when the fuel ran out and the boat sank into the depths.

Emily zipped up the neck of the survival suit as a cold, dark dread settled in her gut.

It was time to get back into the water.

At night.

With no land in sight.

With nothing but water all around.

Knowing there was a monster out there.

Probably nowhere close.

Probably.

Emily gave the switch a final few flicks and then left it on before hurrying out to the forward deck.

Already it was like walking up one of the steeper streets in San Francisco.

She dragged the thing that was supposedly going to help her survive.

Constructed of all of the remaining life vests she could find, nine to be exact, lashed together with the round plastic table top secured above. It was large enough to sit on, but not lay down to sleep.

As if that would be possible.

She'd lashed a duffle bag filled with bottles of fresh water on one side and another bag containing some food she'd scavenged from the kitchen. The stuffed bags also doubled as something to lean back on, which was nice because the rest of the table had no edge, no border, nothing to separate it from the dark water that would soon be lapping at the perimeter.

The rear of the boat suddenly plunged lower into the water, almost making her fall.

She heaved her makeshift craft up onto the rail,

making sure she had the tow line firmly in one hand, and then shoved it the rest of the way over.

The sad excuse for a life raft splashed down onto the surface and steadied itself.

Before she could change her mind and decide to go down with the boat, she leaped over the rail and down onto the table.

The heel of her boot hit and shot out from under her. She careened backwards and fell into the water.

It hit her face like a thousand needle pricks at once.

She clamped her mouth shut to avoid sucking in a lungful of seawater.

Even going under, her hand shot out and latched onto one of the life preserver straps. She pulled back up and flopped over onto her belly. Pulling and kicking, she levered herself up onto the table and scooted forward to balance the load.

The emergency light tied to the suit flashed bright yellow. She snapped her eyes shut and pushed it around to her back to keep it from ruining her night vision.

She lay flat, face down for a minute or two. Trying to settle her chattering teeth. Trying to slow her racing heart. After succeeding enough at both to function, she carefully pushed up and turned to sit.

That's when she saw it.

Forty feet away.

The end of all hope.

The end of everything that made a future possible.

The bow of the boat slipped under the black surface.

A heavy feeling of despair settled onto her shoulders. A hopeless certainty that it was over.

All the struggle.

All in vain.

Emily bit down on her lip. Hard. Sliced it open and blood oozed out. She tasted the mineral tang and a flame ignited in her chest.

She spat out blood and saltwater, shifted into position between the opposing bags of supplies and tied herself in.

A wave lifted her up and she spotted the light in the distance.

Was it any closer?

The wave passed and she sunk into a valley of shadow.

She was not going to surrender.

She was not going to lay down and die.

If the sea took her, fine.

If the shark took her, fine.

If the cold took her, fine.

"But I will not give in!" she screamed at the unforgiving world. "Never!"

The fury warmed her, gave her strength as the struggle tried to sap it away.

She reached for the oar secured with straps.

It was right there. A minute ago.

But she'd noticed a minute too late.

She glanced over and saw it rise on a wave and then disappear into a valley as it drifted away. Already too far to retrieve. She clenched her jaws tight. "Never," she hissed through bared teeth.

But never could turn out to be an unimaginably long time.

Never could wait out everything and everyone.

She drifted and held on.

Her face and hands were numb from being constantly scoured with water. The driving wind sucked the heat out of her exposed skin. Her body and limbs were functioning, though they had little energy to work with.

A large wave passed beneath, lifting her high into the air.

There were several lights now!

One closer than the rest. A spotlight sweeping back and forth through the churning mist.

But still so far.

Too far.

The wave passed and she descended into a depression. The walls extended up many feet all around. The waves were getting bigger. She'd been fortunate before with calmer waters.

Even that little bit of luck was running out.

Another wave shot her up like climbing to the crow's nest to get a better view.

She squinted through the splashing and swirling mist.

The nearest light was closer yet. So close she could make out some of the boat beneath it. It shot a beam of light out across the roiling ocean surface.

The wave passed and she started down into the valley. This time was different though.

The wave fell down a dozen feet at a steep angle. The table dropped and she was suddenly floating in the air.

The restraint snapped tight and dragged her lower as the craft raced down the side. It arrived at the bottom and she slammed into it.

Head first.

Her forehead bounced off the hard plastic and

snapped back. A rush of warmth shot through her neck. Like a pulse of hot blood.

Emily reached around, hoping to find a strap to grab onto while her mind cleared. The tendons in her neck screamed. It felt like the back of her head had smacked into the center of her shoulder blades.

Gravity pressed her down onto the tabletop as another wave lifted her higher and faster, like an express elevator.

She fished for the whistle attached to the suit, found it, and started blowing as hard as she could.

The lift ended and the descent began.

Fast and furious and promising the end.

The table with her on top fell down the side more than skidded.

They both caught air and then hit. The impact dragged the leading edge under and the whole thing flipped through the air.

They somersaulted end over end and hit the water heading in different directions.

The strap securing it to her snapped as she slammed into the surface and went under.

She spun a couple of times, righted herself, and kicked for the surface.

Her head broke through and she sucked in a choking breath of air mixed with seawater.

The sound of rushing water made her spin to the right.

Just in time see the table top as it slammed into her face.

The fury of the growing storm faded away.

Emily floated.

Away from the struggle. Toward a peaceful sleep.

She took a slow breath of ice-cold water that somehow warmed her chest.

She stared down at the blinking yellow light secured to the loop at her shoulder.

Something about it was familiar.

Something she couldn't quite remember, but it made her happy all the same.

45

MARCO stood at the bow of the boat staring out into darkness. His customary fur scarf snuggled around his neck and quietly snuffling through a dream. He couldn't have been more appreciative of the little weasel. It was nice to have someone watching your back in times like these.

And the crankiness that he'd initially found so annoying had become one his favorite things about the little grouch.

He absently stroked a finger beneath his jacket and the weasel rolled in place until his belly faced up. Marco obliged and rubbed it as he surveyed the scene.

The thick haze above suffused and soaked up most of the light of the full moon. Just enough made it through to suggest the distant horizon, the line between water and sky where ancient mariners imagined ships would sail off the edge of the earth.

Where were the boats that were supposed to be waiting for them? Had they continued on already?

Marco tried not to think about the battle they'd left behind. Not knowing if Stuckey and the others escaped twisted his insides up.

Had he made the right call?

Or should they have gone back to help?

The volume of gunshots shattering the air suggested Stuckey and the others hadn't gotten away easily, if at all.

A foul taste climbed up into his throat. The bile of his churning stomach. He swallowed it down and spat out the little that got into his mouth.

The not knowing was the hardest part.

And there was every likelihood that he would never know.

Where were the stupid boats?

He was supposed to lead these people and he couldn't even find them. And what if they met up and everyone made it to the safety of the underground facility? What then? The island would be contaminated with dangerous radioactive fallout for how long?

Chernobyl was still cordoned off by an exclusion zone. Nobody could live there. Some estimates said it would be uninhabitable for twenty thousand years. How long had it taken for them to allow even brief incursions?

He couldn't remember.

But he did remember that it was still a no-go zone a long time later. Decades maybe?

He took a deep breath of the briny air and let the chill fill his lungs. It helped. A little.

He'd have to accept not knowing the fate of Stuckey and the others.

That was bad enough. But there was worse. Something he wasn't sure he'd ever be able to let go. It would be a shadow that followed him to the grave.

Emily.

Where was she?

Was she safe?

Was she getting closer to finding out what happened to her grandmother?

The second time he'd given his heart to a girl.

The second time it had gotten crushed.

And the fact that Emily didn't explicitly reject him only made it worse. There was finality with Justine. She didn't want him. There was nothing he could do about it.

But Emily was different.

They could've had a future together. As much as anyone could expect to have with the world like it was.

But the fate of her grandmother took her away.

Marco couldn't blame her, not even when he wanted to. Family came first. The irony was that most people didn't realize that back in the default everyday world.

But now?

Now that the world had been flushed down the toilet?

The things that really mattered were as obvious as needing to breathe.

Even the land he'd come to the island to save seemed distant and unimportant. His family's land. But without his family, those sweeping vistas and swaying grasslands no longer mattered.

None of it mattered without family.

"Look over there!" a voice shouted over the whipping wind. A hand pointed off to the left.

Marco looked and saw a light in the distance. The

shape of the individual boats was impossible to see from here, but it had to be them. "Looks like it."

They motored closer until the individual silhouettes of the boats started to appear.

Marco scanned the flotilla, his face full of wonder. There were at least twenty boats of every shape and size gathered together in a loose conglomeration.

A voice echoed over the water. "About time! We were about to give up on you!"

The man standing beside Marco laughed. "You're lucky we made it! Someone's got to keep this fleet from running aground!"

Something off to the right in the distance caught Marco's attention.

A flashing light in the surrounding darkness.

As he turned, it disappeared.

Had he imagined it?

He peered into the night.

Nothing.

He squinted, trying to see what lurked out in the unknown.

There!

It was on and steady now.

"Someone's in trouble out there!" Marco yelled over the wind.

The captain saw it, too. He ran back toward the pilot-house. "Get that spotlight on and get us turned around!"

The engines roared a few seconds later and the boat lurched to the right.

A blinding light clicked on sending a solid beam of brightness shooting out over the pitching waves. It was getting rougher by the second. The light traced across the dark waves as the bow cut through the water.

He waited for the distant light to reappear, but it was gone.

Their boat slammed through incoming waves and sailed off departing ones. The spotlight swept back and forth through the pale haze of swirling mist.

He scanned the surface, following the spotlight and the areas it illuminated.

It swept over something and then snapped back.

There!

A makeshift raft made of tied together lifejackets with what looked like a galley tabletop loosely hanging to the side. The spotlight kept it in focus as they drew closer.

Now thirty feet away, the engines cut off and they drifted closer.

Marco ran along the railing, leaning over looking down into the dark water.

A man joined him with a life ring and a coil of rope. "See anything?"

Marco skirted along the railing, looking everywhere. "No. Nothing."

Something caught his eye and he skidded to a stop on the slick deck. "Over here!"

Yes. There below the surface! A yellow blinking emergency light. Too far down to see who or what it was attached to.

Marco didn't hesitate.

Chief Stuckey had made him promise to protect these people. And he was going to do his best to fulfill that promise. Period.

Marco ripped off his coat and the weasel along with it. He dropped both and climbed up onto the rail.

Oscar tried to scurry up the side to reach him, but the smooth surface was too high so he slid back down.

Marco sucked in a deep breath, and dove in. The cold water hit him and nearly made him cough out the stored air. He managed to keep his mouth clamped shut and started kicking and digging deeper.

It seemed like minutes before he finally made it to the blinking light. He grabbed the shoulder of an orange survival suit and rolled the body over.

His chest pinched tight. A spasm of pain.

The flashing on and off, in and out of being, of a face he'd grown to love. Emily's. Wide, unblinking eyes staring up at nothing. Skin pale and lifeless. Her mouth open as if she was about to say something.

No!

A surge of electric terror spiked through his veins. He hooked an arm around her chest and kicked for the surface some twenty feet away.

A bank of bright lights above kicked on, bringing day to the night.

Marco kicked his legs. His chest burned. He let the breath trickle out, knowing there wouldn't be another to replace it if he gave up.

No!

A flash of movement out of the corner of his eye made him look in that direction.

His heart stopped.

The shock froze him for an instant.

An enormous wedge-shaped head with gray skin above and lighter skin below.

A shark.

Bigger than any shark could possibly be. So large the back half of it vanished into the shadows beyond the light.

A bottomless black eye peered at them as it glided by. A thick torso, wider than a semi-truck. A massive dorsal fin and eventually a muscular tail fin that thrust side to side.

Marco's brain unfroze and he kicked the rest of the way to the surface. His head broke through and he sucked in a desperate breath. The freezing air quenched the fire in his chest.

Half a dozen people leaned out over the railing. Some shouting and pointing out at the water behind them. Others shouting for him to wrap the line around them both so they could be hauled up.

Marco snatched up the line floating in the water and ran it behind his back. He pulled Emily into a hug and looped it around her. The muscles in his legs started cramping as he continued kicking to keep them both afloat. He tied off a knot to secure the rope.

It cinched tight around them as the line drew taut. It cut under his arms and into his back as it lifted them up out of the water.

"Faster!" someone above shouted. "It's coming back!"

46

The deafening report of rifles shots split the air. Several people along the railing were firing into the water.

"Oh my God!" someone shouted in horror.

"Get them up!" someone else shouted.

"It's gotta be seventy feet long!"

The rope jerked upward and Marco's boots lifted out of the water. He hugged Emily's lifeless body close, trying to block out the vision of enormous jaws cutting them both in half with a single bite.

CRACK. CRACK. CRACK. CRACK.

The intensity of the gunshots increased as the beast drew closer.

Another heave and they got close enough to the railing where several people leaned over and grabbed hold of them.

Oscar sailed through the air and landed on Marco's shoulder. He sniffed Emily's face as the emergency beacon blinked on and off.

"Get them up! Now!"

They were halfway over the railing when the shark rammed into the boat.

Screams and the sharp crack of splintering wood.

The metal railing bent and fell away and, for an instant, there was nothing but air. And then the feeling of going down a roller coaster as Marco and Emily dropped back into the icy water below.

The string securing the emergency light to Emily's suit snapped and it whirled away.

The impact knocked Oscar away and he was gone. The rope looped around Marco's arms drew tight, pinning them around Emily.

Beams of bright light shot through the water as the boat rolled onto its side and the bank of lights plunged below the surface. A blinding halo lit up the surrounding water.

A man caught in a heavy tangle of snarled railing clawed for the surface, but the weight of it pulled him down into the depths.

Fragments of the boat littered the surface. Other bits of debris floated in the water below.

People swam in all directions at once, each doing their best to survive the unfolding catastrophe.

Marco fought to free his arms, but it was no use. The rope coiled around them held tight. His lungs began to burn as he gave up and kicked for the surface.

They broke through and he gulped a breath.

Emily's head tilted to the side. Her eyes open and blank. No response.

The boat lay on its side in the water. The lights from the other side blasted a column of glowing illumination up into the night air. The few people still on the boat clung to whatever they could to keep from falling into the water.

Frantic limbs splashed and panicked voices screamed.

"No!" someone yelled louder than the rest.

"Swim! Go!"

Marco kicked his feet to spin them around and saw the shadow rising from the depths.

It cut through the light with jaws open and pale teeth reflecting white.

A man struggling at the surface looked down into the water as the shark's mouth swallowed him.

The behemoth exploded out of the water in a fury of speed and death. It's front half cleared the water before gravity pulled it back it down with a concussive splash that hit Marco's ears before a wave rolled over his head. Water shot down his throat and he gagged.

The shock of it all reached for him.

With velvet gloves and promising an end to all the suffering. If only he'd let go. It would all be over soon.

He might've accepted the offering if he'd been alone. If it was only his life hanging in the balance.

But it wasn't.

He glanced at the bloodless face inches from his own. Almost like the fairy tale of sleeping beauty. Waiting to be kissed and brought back to life.

Marco kicked to the surface again and coughed out a lungful of icy water. The water burned it was so cold. The adrenaline burned it was so hot.

The boat screeched long and slow as the balance shifted. It started rolling over the rest of the way. There was no chance for it now. It was going down.

The rope coiled around them jerked tight and dragged them under.

He twisted around and followed the taut line to where it was caught on some mangled railing. There was a section near the middle of the line that had been cut and was frayed. He yanked back to break it, but the remaining fibers held.

The boat continued to roll and the rope dragged them deeper as it went. It cut into his arms like a barbed wire python.

The boat settled upside down, now with both banks of lights shining down into the depths.

The tension on the rope eased and Marco thought it had broken. He kicked for the surface and was immediately jerked to a stop. His lungs ached as the bubbles of his last breath bobbled up toward the deck of the upside down boat.

Emily's long straight hair floated in mesmerizing waves around her head. It was beautiful. Like black silk.

Marco jerked at the rope again but couldn't get the frayed part to fail. And there wasn't enough line to get back to the surface for another breath.

They were going to drown.

If they didn't get eaten first.

He scanned the water and didn't see the shark within the halo of glowing light. But there was an ocean of darkness beyond it and the beast would be back.

Marco spotted the torn base of a railing column jutting up out of the deck nearby. The end jagged and sharp. He furiously kicked the water to swim them both to it. A few more coordinated kicks and he got the rope snagged onto the tip of the metal.

He tried to get the sharp end further under the rope, but it cut through his shirt and sliced open his arm instead.

Marco gritted his teeth and pushed again, angling the ragged blade through his flesh and finally into the rope.

Writhing back and forth, he managed to saw through it until the last fibers split and the constraining coil let go.

Fire blazed in his chest. His lungs burned to draw in life-sustaining air. He kicked and swam with one arm and held Emily with the other.

His head broke the surface as his lungs gasped for air. He reached up for something to grab, but there was nothing but the smooth hull of the boat.

A man laying on his belly across the spine of the broad hull reached down, but he was just beyond reach.

"Be ready to grab her!" Marco shouted. He lifted her up which caused him to go under. He kicked with all his might as he pushed higher and sank lower.

Her weight lifted and he made it back to the surface to see her being dragged up onto the hull.

"They're coming!" someone in the water nearby shouted.

He glanced over and saw several other boats speeding over to help.

If help was even possible.

Dark movement below.

He looked down and saw it. At the distant edge of the fading light.

The monster from the depths.

Charging up at them.

47

BOB knew he was about to get shot dead.

And he laughed.

Not about the dying part, though he wasn't overly concerned by it. It was the joke running through his head that made him laugh.

You don't have to run faster than a bear to get away, you just have to run faster than the guy next to you.

With Rome and Stuckey ahead and widening the gap, he was the slowest guy. The one that would get eaten.

It was strange how a bad joke was all that occupied his thoughts as bullets snapped through air. Some missing him by inches.

The headlights of several vehicles at the top of the road swung around and bathed the area in light.

More rounds zipped by, one so close he felt the displaced air on his forehead. They sounded like enraged hornets, and one sting would do it.

Stuckey arrived at the warehouse door and didn't

slow down. He threw a shoulder forward and crashed through it, disappearing into the dark interior.

Rome made it a few seconds later.

Bob's lungs were about to burst, which wasn't going to be a problem because his heart was thumping so hard it was going to beat them to it.

The headlights of the approaching vehicles bounced off the side of the warehouse.

Neptune Seafoods Corporation.

With a giant painted logo above it.

A cartoon of the Roman god of the sea rising up out of a cresting wave. One hand held a trident overhead while the other held a happy fish with a huge toothy grin. What once must've been bold, simple colors were now faded to dreary hues. It looked like it had been both designed and painted on the building back in the seventies. Probably a knock off of the Charlie the tunafish cartoon.

The shadowed rectangle of the open door drew closer.

Rather, Bob drew closer to it.

Only forty feet to go.

His head swam and he accidentally veered off course before getting back on track.

Any second now.

He might actually make it.

More bullets streaked by. An angry sound like the crack of a whip as the projectiles punched through a medium that had measurable density. There was all the science of supersonic flight and how air piled up and became like a thick soup of drag on a speeding object. Yeah, there was all that.

But Bob had his own proof. Experiential proof. His limbs swam through the viscous liquid that had been effortless fluidity moments before.

Now, it slowed his movement. It pulled against his progress. Encouraging him to slow to a stop.

A pale face appeared in the silhouetted frame of the door.

Stuckey. He raised a rifle and fired several shots at the approaching vehicles. "Come on!"

A bullet pinged off the metal exterior inches from Stuckey's face as he ducked inside.

Seconds later, Bob flung himself into the inky interior.

And abruptly slammed into Rome's chest and bounced off like a pinball off a bumper. He would've wiped out but Rome grabbed his arm and kept him on his feet.

Bob grabbed both knees and focused on not passing out. His head felt like a helium balloon and his limbs shook as cold sweat poured down his back. He sucked in a few deep breaths to satisfy starved lungs.

And immediately regretted it.

He gagged and coughed. "Oh, God! What is that smell?"

Stuckey clicked on a flashlight and shined it around.

Metal contraptions and conveyor belts and giant chrome tanks filled a huge space. Fifty yards or more of machinery packed into tight quarters all the way to the far walls. Metal stairs went up to a second level of exposed catwalk that offered access to the tanks and another level of conveyor belts. Metal slides connected the upper level machinery to the lower level.

A couple of the slides started smooth but then had what looked like giant cheese graters near the bottom. They flattened out below that and fed into what must've been cutting stations because they had wicked looking blades uniformly spaced across the belt.

"Fish processing plant," Stuckey said with a grimace. "Didn't smell good even when it had power and refrigeration."

Rome spat out a loogie that splatted on the concrete floor. "Smells like a fish's asshole!"

Flo would've admonished her son for the language, but she was no longer alive to hear or care. Bob knew he was a pathetic substitute for her. But he was still going to do his best to look after the poor kid.

At least until one or both of them died.

Which, judging by their current situation, would probably be any minute now.

48

The rumble of vehicles outside approached and Stuckey slammed the door shut. He grabbed a nearby mop and wedged it up under the handle to keep it from opening. It wouldn't last forever, but it might slow them down for a minute or two.

The vehicles pulled to a stop and people jumped out onto the pavement.

A knock on the door. "Knock, knock," said a voice they all recognized.

A voice that made Rome and Stuckey bare their teeth in rage. A voice that nearly made Bob lose control of his bladder.

"This is where you say, 'Who's there?', and then I say, 'CB', and then you say 'CB who?' and then I don't say anything because I'm already cutting your beating hearts out of your chests."

Rome pointed his shotgun at the door and fired.

The slug punched a hole through the metal.

Charlie laughed. "Whooo! You boys got no sense of humor!"

A spray of automatic fire punched through the metal panel wall to their right.

"Hey!" Charlie yelled. "I didn't tell anyone to shoot yet! You idiots are worse than impulsive children! First, we have to parley."

"What's parley?"

It was Red, the giant Russian bear that had somehow become CB's lapdog.

"Why, Lord? Why have you sent morons to help me? Don't I deserve better?"

"I'm not stupid! I just don't know what parley means!"

"We'll agree to disagree on that. And parley means when opposing sides in a confrontation meet to discuss terms."

"What's there to discuss? We're here to kill them!"

"Alexei, please tell me when it was that you became the boss. Because you're talking like you think that's the case."

Silence.

"Is that the case?"

"No, CB. You are." He sounded like a cowed mongrel.

"Good. Then we parley."

"Screw your parley," Rome shouted. "I'm going to kill you!"

"The voice sounds young and stupid so I'm going to assume you're the fat pimple-faced kid, right? Shut up and let your elders talk. Stuckey, you in there?"

"I am. And Rome isn't going to kill you because I'll get you first!"

Charlie chuckled. "It's nice to feel so wanted. If only

you two were a couple of horny women, then I'd be set. Bob, you in there?"

"Yeah," Bob said.

"By my count, that makes three against all of us. That's twenty or so in case you were wondering. And you're trapped in there like rats in a hole."

"Are you offering to surrender?" Stuckey asked.

"Chief, I like you. If I thought it was possible, I'd bring you to heel and give you scraps from my table. But, I suspect there would always be disobedience deep in your heart. The kind that was just waiting for an opportunity to strike. So, you've got to be put down. Which brings me to my offer. Bob and Rome, you two can make it out of here alive. You don't have to die with the chief."

"Where was your mercy when you killed my mother?" Rome shouted.

"Son, that was a simple case of bad timing. I never meant to hurt your mother."

"I don't care if you meant it or not. You killed her!"

"Bob, looks like the fat kid isn't in the mood to listen to reason. How about you? Do you want to die tonight? Or would you rather live?"

"You were never going to get that million dollars," Bob said. "Even if you beat all the other contestants, we weren't going to let you win. No backwoods Tennessee hick redneck was ever going to be the face of our show."

There was a moment of silence.

"That was rude and unnecessary, Bob. And the fact that it rings true makes me all the more upset. I'm going to enjoy cutting your belly open and pulling out your intestines while you watch. You're gonna be real surprised at how long you can survive with a wound like that."

Bob's knees went weak.

It wasn't an idle threat. He'd seen enough of the man to know that is exactly what would happen if Charlie captured him alive.

He had no intention of letting that happen.

"Well, I guess the parley's over. Fire!"

Stuckey dragged the other two toward the stairs as a barrage of bullets tore through the door and surrounding walls.

"Up!" Stuckey yelled over the cacophony of pinging, punching and whizzing rounds.

Bob's foot caught on something and he crashed to the floor. His right ankle folded as his leg collapsed under him. Sharp pain shot up his leg, radiating from his ankle. He rolled to his back, groaning and cursing at the same time.

He screamed in pain as Stuckey started to haul him up. "Stop!"

Stuckey let go. "We have to take the higher ground and find cover. It's our only chance.

"Go! I'll hide under that," Bob replied as he nodded toward part of the assembly line that hung low to the ground.

There wasn't time for discussion or negotiation.

"Stay put and stay quiet," Stuckey said before hurrying off after Rome.

Bob crawled across the cold concrete floor, gritting his teeth to keep from crying out. He squeezed under the machinery and moved to the center to improve his chances of avoiding detection. No one was going to see him unless they knelt down and looked underneath.

He fought to slow his breathing, to deal with the pulsing waves of pain shooting up his leg.

A flash of light above drew his attention. Great! There was some kind of metal grill above his head and he saw Stuckey's flashlight swinging back and forth as he and Rome ran across the catwalks of the upper level.

The gunfire tearing through the skin of the building stopped.

"Well, I reckon that gave 'em something to think about. Let's take a look."

The door handle rattled, but didn't open. It rattled a few more times, but held.

Bob watched the swinging light above until it went behind a steel pillar of the structural framework. The glowing bloom cut off a few seconds later. A multitude of tiny rays of light hung in the air from all the bullet holes punched through the exterior.

Bob tried to shift his position to get more comfortable and his ankle screamed with pain. He groaned and decided to stay put.

He imagined Stuckey and Rome in the darkness above. They'd found a good spot. They'd have cover that could stop bullets while being able to fire on anyone that approached from the exposed catwalks. It was also a perfect perch to pick off targets below that came into view.

An engine roared outside. Tires squealed.

Metal shrieked and ripped apart as a truck crashed through a panel and screeched to a stop inside the building. The headlights clicked to high and the beams bounced off the multitude of metals surfaces, dispersing reflected light to varying degrees throughout the factory. The sound of another truck scraped through the hole, adding more light to the scene.

Bob was injured. Didn't have a gun. And was stuck under some machinery.

What was he supposed to do?

Twiddle his thumbs until Stuckey and Rome got shot?

He'd never felt more useless. Never more pathetic.

Well, that wasn't strictly true.

The image of his ex-best friend screwing his ex-wife leaped to mind. When he'd opened the door with a bottle of wine in one hand and apology flowers in the other and saw them going at it like feral animals.

He'd wanted to die after seeing that.

It looked like he was finally going to get his wish.

49

MARCO stared in numb horror as the shark approached. The glow of the lights cascaded down into the water, revealing its monstrous size.

The other boats weren't going to arrive in time.

It would get here first.

And it was headed straight at them and the capsized boat.

Both banks of lights flickered and the beast winked in and out of view. With each blink, it was visibly closer.

Then they shut off. Must've shorted in the water.

There was only one thing worse than seeing a seventy foot long shark coming after you.

And that was not seeing it.

Marco peered into the depths, but could see nothing.

Unfortunately, a dark ocean wasn't going to slow it down. That was the natural habitat in which it had evolved for millions of years.

A dagger of fear stabbed into his gut.

As horrifying as seeing the massive creature had been, this was far worse.

Not being able to see it had him leaning out over the edge, ready to fall into a terrifying madness.

He knew what would happen next. He'd be eaten whole or bashed unconscious by the impact. The few people that had made it back up on top of the boat, including Emily, would get thrown back into the water.

And even if by some miracle he somehow survived the initial attack, he wouldn't be able to save her.

The emergency light was gone.

She'd sink into the depths. Or sink until the monster found her.

"No!" he screamed.

But what could he do?

A fin appeared in the water less than ten feet away.

No!

No, it wasn't a fin.

It was the outboard engine attached to the overturned inflatable zodiac.

An idea flashed through his mind.

Would it work?

He didn't know. But it seemed possible from what he could remember reading about shark behavior.

Marco powered over to the zodiac and found a strap. He dragged it across to the other side and climbed up one side, leaning back and pulling with all his weight and strength.

The boat flipped over and settled.

He scrambled in and found the emergency kit still strapped down where he'd seen it before. He wrenched the box open, loaded the flare gun, and shoved the handle between his teeth.

He stumbled to the rear and felt around until he found the ignition cord.

One pull.

Two pulls.

Three quick pulls.

And nothing.

The engine grumbled and rattled but didn't catch.

He yanked again and the handle snapped off.

But the engine caught and roared to life as he cranked the gas to keep it running.

He needed to cut the plastic gas tank open. He reached for the pocket knife he usually kept in his front pocket and cursed when he remembered it was still in his pack from the hospital visit.

What then?

He spotted the silhouette of an oar strapped to the floor. He yanked it free and smashed it against the side. The plastic end broke off leaving only the metal shaft.

Marco grasped it in the middle and raised it into the air. Twisting like a boxer delivering a knockout punch, he hammered the end into the side of the tank.

The end punctured through!

The smell of gasoline wafted in the air as the fluid poured out onto the floorboard.

Marco stepped up onto the side and steadied himself with the tiller. He cranked it up to a roar and grabbed the flare gun out of his mouth.

This was it. No time to waste on thoughts of failure.

He shifted the motor into gear as he took aim at the floorboard.

The boat catapulted forward.

He fired as he fell backwards into the water.

He went under for a second and then came back up to a thrilling orange inferno.

The burning fuel threw flames ten feet into the air as the craft bounced away over the shifting waves.

A splash behind him made him spin around.

A massive dorsal fin broke through the surface of the water and then slipped below again.

The flames soared higher as the boat slowed to a stop in the distance. The rubber must've caught because the whole thing blazed like a torch.

Lights swept the water behind him and people shouted.

"Come on!"

Marco turned and swam to the incoming boat as the engines slowed and it drifted to him. A net came down and he climbed up, searching for Emily before he vaulted onto the deck.

She was there, lying on the deck with her head tilted to the side. A woman kneeling above her administering CPR.

A screeching, chittering fury made him look back out over the water.

The spotlight swept over and landed on Oscar twenty feet from the boat.

"What is that?" someone asked.

Marco tossed a life ring out and it landed next to the irate weasel.

Oscar climbed up as Marco pulled the line taut. He scampered across the line and leaped onto Marco's shoulder and wrapped around his neck. His soaked fur made him look half as big and twice as pitiful. He shivered and chittered as Marco hurried over to Emily.

They all turned to the zodiac as the monster shot up out of the water like it had been launched from a nuclear submarine.

Liquid flames streaked through the air, leaving trails like exploding fireworks.

White water hid the beast for an instant, but then it burst through in a fury of primal aggression and force.

The shark soared through the air and slammed back down onto the water like a thunderclap.

The flames winked out and ocean went dark.

"Time to go!" someone shouted.

The engines revved and the boat spun around to chase after the other boats already headed back to the main flotilla.

Marco dropped to his knees next to Emily and took her hand. It was so, so cold. "Is she…"

He couldn't say it out loud.

The woman ignored him and kept blowing air into Emily's lungs and pumping her chest.

"Come on, Emily," he said as he squeezed her hand. "Fight, dammit! Fight!"

Seconds passed as she slipped away.

Or maybe she was already gone.

A heavy darkness grasped at his chest. Reaching to suffocate and suck the life out of him.

Emily shuddered violently and spewed out a shocking amount of seawater.

Another convulsion and more water came out.

She got the last of it out and drew a rattling breath.

"I need more light over here!" the woman yelled.

Someone obliged and Marco gasped at how white her skin was. How empty her eyes were. She whispered a word.

Even in the chaos of so many people talking and shouting and helping one another, he heard it.

And it lifted him higher into the sky than a hawk soaring over the swaying grass of his family's ranch.

"M-m-m-m-m-m-m-m-m-m-arco."

50

BOB had never been a fighter. He'd once had pretensions of being a lover, but that had turned out to be more of a delusion of grandeur than anything. So, if he wasn't a lover or a fighter, what was he?

A useless old man.

That label fit.

He hid in the shadows under the assembly line, staying absolutely still so his throbbing ankle wouldn't make him cry out and give away his position.

He pursed his lips and shook his head, disgusted with himself. Hiding under the bed like a child.

Pathetic.

Vehicle doors opened and boots smacked onto the concrete floor. "Hello! Anyone home?" Charlie yelled. His words echoed around the factory. He waited.

Did he really expect an answer?

Bob's angle gave him a front row seat. He saw a slice of truck tires and the boots gathering inside.

"Are we playing hide and seek?" Charlie shouted. "Alexei, take a few men to the upper level. The rest of you spread out. Search every dark corner! I want them found! And nobody better kill Bob! I've got a promise to keep to him."

Bob's insides turned to ice. His bladder let go before he could stop it.

Not a flood.

He was too old and dried up for that. But enough trickles to wet the front of his pants and dribble down the inside of his thighs.

If he'd felt pathetic before, and he had, he felt doubly so now.

"Hours, Bob! That's how long you'll get to watch yourself die. Maybe more if the shock doesn't get you."

Bob gulped and realized in a panic that he was losing feeling in his hands. He shook them out and tried to make fists, and maybe did, but couldn't feel them enough to be sure.

The clanking of boots on the metal stairs.

Alexei and the others going up to the second level.

"This is like hunting back home!" Charlie yelled. "Got my coonhounds on the trail. They'll track you down and tree you. And then I'll finish the job."

Bob looked up through the grill.

Alexei and three men stopped at an intersection in the catwalk that connected three pathways. He pointed at two of them and one man chose the first, two men chose the second, and Alexei took the third.

The second would eventually lead to Stuckey and Rome.

The catwalk rattled as the men ran across with their rifles sweeping back and forth. They weren't more than thirty feet from the hiding place.

When were they going to—

CRACK! CRACK!

Bob flinched and cupped his hands over his ears. The noise was deafening. His ears rang as a frequency band of his hearing died.

The first man dropped like a marionette with the strings cut. The second dropped to a knee and returned fire. Bullets pinged off the metal structure concealing Stuckey and Rome.

One of them fired again and hit him.

He collapsed and screamed in agony.

"They're on the second level. Behind that pillar over there!" Charlie shouted as he ran for the stairs. "The end of the chase is my favorite part!" He bounded up the stairs while the others ascended stairs in different parts of the building.

Stuckey and Rome didn't have a chance. They were pinned down and would run out of ammo long before their attackers did.

And what was Bob doing to help?

Nothing but getting colder in his damp underwear, doing his best not to gag on the rancid stench of rotting fish.

Bob stared in numb silence as the firefight commenced.

Charlie's men advanced on the position, firing as they went. All of them sticking to cover wherever possible after seeing two of their own go down.

The air shook with violence. A haze of smoke from expended gunpowder drifted toward the roof high above. The thunderous noise went on so long that when it finally died out, it took Bob a few seconds to realize it.

"Wooooo!" Charlie yelled. "Now this is a proper gun fight!"

There was no response from Stuckey and Rome. Were they dead?

"Why'd you stop? Run out of ammo already?"

"Come and find out," Stuckey replied.

"You, go," Charlie said to one of his men.

The designated volunteer stayed low in a crouch as he shuffled across the exposed catwalk.

BOOM!

THUMP, THUMP.

His body collapsed onto the walkway.

Movement by the trucks caught Bob's eye. A pair of boots ran up the nearby stairs.

Bob stared up through the grill and saw the man make his way to Charlie's position behind the corner of one of the enormous holding tanks. He held something in each hand.

What?

Flames flared to life from the top of the bottle in the man's hand. He used it to light the bottle in his other hand.

Molotov cocktails.

They were going to burn them out.

And there was nowhere to run.

Bob had to do something!

But what?

Something!

He glanced around and an idea came to him. If it didn't work and fast, his friends were going to be burned alive.

He scooted out from the cover of the assembly line, gritting his teeth through the pain. A few more feet and he was out in the middle of the floor, looking up at the scene unfolding on the upper level.

If any of them looked down, they'd see him plain as day.

And he knew what would happen soon after that. The horrifying vision drove him to crawl faster.

The man took aim and launched a bottle. It hit the pillar and shattered on impact. A burst of flame curled around the pillar into the hiding space. The second bottle followed and flew straight into the area behind the pillar.

An explosion of flames and screaming. Stuckey and Rome darted out onto the catwalk with parts of their clothes on fire.

Bob made it to the open door of the truck and climbed in. He glanced up through the windshield.

Charlie and Alexei were already in motion.

Alexei drove through Stuckey like a bulldozer, knocking him onto his back.

Charlie landed feet first on Rome's chest, driving him backward and down to the walkway.

Alexei held the front of Stuckey's jacket and slammed his fist into his face, again and again.

Stuckey fought the first few, but then his arms fell to the sides and offered only token resistance.

Charlie landed on Rome's chest like a gargoyle

guarding a rooftop. A blade flashed above his head as he cackled with glee.

Bob shifted the truck into gear, clicked his seatbelt, and slammed his foot down onto the gas pedal. The pain in his ankle exploded.

51

The truck roared and leaped forward like a racehorse out of the gate.

Bob saw Charlie look over before the truck crashed into the structure supporting the nearest holding tank. The framework caved in.

Metal shrieked as the enormous holding tank peeled away from the remaining supports. It started slow but picked up speed as it went sending tens of thousands of gallons of filthy, stagnant fish guts and water sluicing through the ruined structure and over the floor.

The catwalk carrying the four above jerked to the side and partially tore loose. Stuckey and Alexei fell end over end to the concrete floor. They landed hard and didn't get up. Charlie was flung off of Rome's chest and slammed into a rail.

The tank continued pulling the connected upper level structure down with it.

The catwalk twisted and bent, throwing Rome and Charlie onto one of the metal slides of the assembly line.

Rome landed on top of Charlie as they skated down the smooth surface.

Until they hit that cheese grater section.

Charlie screamed as the back of his head and neck scraped across. As his coat and shirt were shredded. As the flesh of his back was flayed away.

Their momentum carried them forward across the length of it.

Across the length of Charlie's backside.

They slammed into a wall of ruined machinery at the bottom and came to a stop.

Rome pushed up and landed short elbows into Charlie's face. It only took a few blows before the smaller man had blood pouring out of his nose and cuts on his face.

The holding tank groaned and finished its arcing collapse to the floor. A section of catwalk tore free and fell. The attached railing snapped leaving a long span with a jagged end jutting out.

It tumbled as it fell, the span rotating down.

Heading right at Rome and Charlie.

Rome glanced up over his shoulder, saw the incoming mass of twisted metal and rolled over the lip of the assembly line as the broken piece crashed down.

He hit the floor as it hit the assembly line.

Bob climbed out of the truck and hobbled over to him.

Rome lay face down in a few inches of repulsive water.

Bob grabbed his arm and managed to roll him over.

The kid coughed, blasting spray up into his face.

Bob wiped his eyes clear. "Are you okay?"

Rome blinked a few times and nodded.

Charlie groaned in pain.

Bob looked over and saw the man's face screwed up in agony. The jagged end of the railing had pierced several inches into his stomach. The top of the section hung on the edge of a bent walkway.

Rome stood up and smiled when he saw Charlie's helpless condition.

Charlie's eyes flared with fury. He reached out and then screamed from the spear pinning him down.

Footsteps from behind and Bob spun around, ready to see the gun that would end his life.

Chief Stuckey limped over.

Red hadn't moved from where they'd fallen. A fall from that height meant there was a fair chance he was dead. It was a miracle Stuckey was up and moving around.

Stuckey wrapped an arm over Bob's shoulder for balance. It felt like a tree log settling across his back. He did his best to keep most of the weight off of his ruined ankle.

All three stood above Charlie, watching.

Rome reached down and slapped the metal.

Charlie screamed as his hands gripped the railing perforating his gut.

Rome hit it again and got the same response.

"Let me have a turn," Stuckey said. He leaned forward and punched the railing.

The framework above creaked and the railing shifted half an inch, ripping through Charlie's flesh.

He howled in pain.

Charlie's expression shifted. "Please, help me. I'll give you anything you want. I'll do anything you want."

Stuckey shoved a finger into the wound. "I want you to suffer and die."

Blood gurgled out of Charlie's mouth and spewed out like lava as he screamed.

Rome looked up at the hanging section of catwalk. "Get back."

Bob followed his eyes. "What're you doing?"

"You'll see."

He helped Stuckey move back what seemed like a safe distance.

Rome climbed up onto the assembly line, standing above Charlie. He stared down with a twisted, cold expression on his face. "This is for my mother."

He lifted his huge foot and kicked the railing.

Charlie wailed louder than before as the metal screeched and moved.

Rome kicked it again and the section came loose. He leaped off the assembly line as the piece of catwalk fell to the other side like a cut tree.

The jagged end tore across Charlie's stomach before ripping free and arcing through the air. It bounced as the section hit the floor and then came to rest leaning against the assembly line.

Charlie groaned.

Bob, Stuckey and Rome gathered around him.

Gruesome didn't cover it by half.

Bob grimaced and was close to vomiting.

Charlie's middle was sliced open. His intestines spilling out like slimy, overstuffed sausage links. Mottled purple and red and slipping through his fingers as he tried to stuff them back in.

They watched him struggle for a while.

No one spoke.

It didn't take hours. Not like Charlie said it might.

But it did take more than a few minutes.

When his fingers finally stopped moving and his head slumped to the side, Rome spoke first.

"He deserved worse."

"Yes, he did," Stuckey replied. "And if there's any justice in this universe, he'll get it in hell."

52

EMILY flinched as the first drop of rain hit her cheek. She lay on the deck of the boat covered in a mountain of blankets and still shivering like she was standing naked at the North Pole. She had a fold of cloth in her mouth to keep the jackhammering from cracking a tooth. Her insides swung from numb nothingness to sharp pain and back like the jagged lines of a polygraph test.

She'd been miserable before. Plenty of times. Misery was her default state.

But this was something new. Something violently inescapable. It shook her limbs with uncontrollable quaking in fits and starts.

But it wasn't all suffering.

Because *he* was here.

Inside the burrito of blankets with her.

His bare chest against hers.

The hard planes of muscle pressed against her softer curves.

There was nothing sexual in the embrace. Her body

was too ravaged and cold. Like she'd taken the ultimate cold shower.

The connection was deeper than that. It was nurturing. It was loving. It was literally life-sustaining.

His heat burned her skin. A barely endurable pain that was all she wanted in the world.

"The rain's coming," someone nearby said.

"We're almost there," another replied.

Marco glanced down and smiled. There was masked pain in the curvature of his mouth. He leaned over and kissed her cheek. His lips felt like a hissing brand touching her skin.

But she didn't pull away.

She wanted nothing more than to be enveloped by his heat. To burrow into his core and hibernate there until Spring came and the world again filled with sunlight.

"H-h-h-h-h-h-h-h-h-h-h-h-h." She tried to speak, without success. The shivering made the words stutter to a stop on the first letter.

"Shhhh, just rest."

She wanted to know how it happened. How she'd gone under. How she was pretty sure she'd died and yet somehow woke up with him hovering above her.

Like a guardian angel.

Her guardian angel.

They lay there as the rain picked up. Not talking. Just looking into each other's eyes. Just sharing space and heat. Sharing life.

Someone came by with a plastic tarp. "Keep this over you. This rain could be radioactive." The dim figure spread it over their exposed heads and then tucked it underneath to keep it from flying away.

When she could feel her stomach, it twisted in knots every time the boat dove into another trough.

The wind ripped through harder and faster. Gusts that chilled her through the many layers of blankets.

An overwhelming drowsiness came over her. Her eyes started to droop shut.

"Emily," Marco said and his warm breath tickled her neck. "Emily."

Her eyes fluttered open. "Hmm?"

"Stay with me. Okay?"

She nodded, more from the happy surprise of seeing him than understanding and answering the question.

"There's the harbor!" someone shouted.

"I see them!" another shouted. "Look at all those trucks!"

Another few minutes of zooming up and down the roller coaster of waves and the motion began to settle.

Blinding light lit up the plastic tarp. "They've spotted us!" someone yelled.

The wind continued howling but the motion of the boat had calmed. The engines slowed to a low throttle.

"Get those lines out!"

"Sounds like it's time to go," Marco said. "I'm going to carry you, okay?"

She nodded. "O-o-okay."

The word stuttered out, relatively uninterrupted by chattering teeth.

He wriggled out of the blankets and she gasped as his skin pulled away. It felt like duct tape peeling off a bleeding wound. He wrapped the blankets around her and lifted her into the air like a child.

Like a bride on her wedding night.

She noticed Oscar for the first time, wrapped like a fur scarf around Marco's neck. The little weasel's fur wet and matted and his surprisingly lean body shivering.

Marco managed to keep the tarp wrapped over their heads. He turned as the boat bumped into the dock and a cacophony of voices competed with the howling wind.

"Get her to the nearest truck. I'll bring your bag."

Marco nodded and stepped over onto the dock. His shoulders rippled with lean muscle as he carried Emily along. He turned to leave the dock and she wondered if she was hallucinating.

There were ten or so boats already moored at the dock. Most of their passengers already climbing into one of five military style troop transports. The kind with giant knobby tires and green canvas covering the back where the people were loading up. Their headlights cast a harsh light into the surrounding darkness.

It looked like nothing so much as refugees fleeing their homeland and making it to the safety of a neighboring land.

As strange as all of it was, it wasn't the part that had her questioning her sanity.

Twenty or so soldiers carrying flashlights and rifles hurried back and forth like industrous ants. Helping people into the trucks, loading their things along with them.

It was what the soldiers were wearing that made the scene feel like an apocalyptic horror movie.

The soldiers wore bright orange hazmat suits. The oversized puffy kind that was commonly seen in every zombie outbreak movie that had ever been made. Their faces showing through the clear plastic panels was the only part that proved that they were human and not some alien race.

One of them walked by reading an instrument in his hand. It clicked audibly as he waved it back and forth through the air.

Emily had never seen a geiger counter in real life, but she knew that one was the first.

Another suited figure approached with a pen light in his hand. He stopped Marco and shined it into Emily's eyes a few times. "Come with me." He led us to the nearest truck. The one at the rear of the column.

A soldier already in the back of the truck reached down to help and then snatched his hand back as Oscar's head popped up and he hissed with anger. "What is that thing?"

"Just a weasel. He's with me."

The soldier didn't look convinced. "You need help getting in?"

Marco shook his head. "No." His arms tightened slightly.

The soldier nodded with relief and backed away.

Marco ducked under the canvas roof and sat on the empty bench seat next to the cab. Ten others were already seated and ready to go.

The man who'd directed them to the truck knelt beside Emily. He touched her forehead before digging into a white satchel filled with medical supplies. A doctor. "What happened?" His voice sounded strangely muffled coming through the plastic visor.

"She almost drowned."

He opened the bag, dug out a thermometer and

slipped it into her mouth. "How long was she in the water?"

"I don't know."

The doctor glanced up in confusion. "Did she lose consciousness?"

A soldier appeared at the back and slammed the lift gate into place. "The fallout rain is coming in earlier than expected. We have to get moving."

The doctor nodded before turning back to Marco with a questioning look.

"Yes. She was unconscious when I pulled her out."

The diesel engine rumbled and the truck lurched forward.

The doctor would've fallen over, but Marco's extended leg kept him upright.

The back bounced up and down as they picked up speed. Either this wasn't a road by any conventional sense of the word, or this truck had leaf springs made of cast iron.

After Emily bounced off Marco's lap a couple of times, he lifted her slightly so that his arms absorbed the bounce.

The doctor returned to digging through his kit, looking for something. He pulled out a bottle of pills and snapped the cap off. "Take this. It's iodide." He cracked the top off a bottle of water. He dumped two pills into Marco's outstretched hand and tucked the bottle into a fold of the blankets. "One pill for each of you."

He looked down at Emily and forced a smile. "We'll be back soon. Just hold on, okay? And no going to sleep." He turned to Marco. "Keep her awake."

Marco nodded as the doctor rotated around to pass

out pills and water bottles to the other people sharing the truck.

The patter of rain hitting the canvas surged as the storm front overtook the column of trucks speeding through the night.

53

MARCO cradled Emily above his legs so that his arms took the worst of the spine-jangling ride. He watched her like a guardian angel, ready to intervene in any way he could to make her life better.

Her bloodless skin had his stomach in knots. What if she didn't survive?

That he'd found her at all was a miracle that must have meaning. God and the universe must've had a reason for shifting the falling sands to land like this.

So she couldn't die now? Right?

She was just so pale. And so cold.

A faint smile formed on her lips and he forced himself to smile. She needed his light, his energy, his strength, and he wasn't sure he had much to offer.

Anxious dread was the only emotion he had in abundance. And it was all he could do to not let it dump out like a dam with every gate wide open.

"That bad?" she said and the smile returned.

He looked away and just as quickly returned. He coughed several times to clear his throat, to be sure his voice wouldn't break with the lie. "You look great. Seriously."

She rolled her eyes. "Terrible liar."

He laughed, a genuine response this time. Even half-dead and frozen like a human blood slushy, she still had fight in her heart. She still had a withering wit blazing pathways through her brain.

There was only one way to describe her.

"Did you know you're the most amazing person I've ever met?"

She tried to shrug but the layers of blankets mummied around her didn't allow for much movement. "Yeah."

A laugh cut short in his throat as the truck hit a crater sized pothole and the back of the truck leaped into the air. The canvas stretched over his head and, fortunately, gravity quickly prevailed and he landed on the seat with a knuckle punch to the coccyx.

The coccyx. The vertebrae that comprised the final four in the spine. They typically got no attention until they took a shot and radiated electric agony through the pelvis.

Like Marco's did now.

He somehow managed to hang on to Emily while he got his feet planted, groaning through the pain.

Oscar had stayed put by digging his claws into Marco's skin. The indignant weasel chirped and chittered before settling back in to his favorite position.

As the pain in Marco's pelvis ebbed, the stinging of

the furrows Oscar had dug into his skin grabbed his attention.

The truck lurched to a stop and the other passengers sprawled on the floor picked themselves up.

The doctor climbed up to the bench seat and plopped down. The rubber suit squeaked as he looked around in confusion.

With the engine idling, the pounding of the driving rain hitting the canvas took center stage. It was like a river falling out of the sky.

A soldier appeared at the tailgate. "Sorry about that. The rain is tearing up the road and I didn't see that hole until it was too late. We're going to take it slow from here. Everyone hang on."

Seconds later, the truck rolled forward again.

Now at what must've been less than fifteen miles per hour.

"Hey, doc!" Marco yelled over the clanging orchestra of ambient noise.

He paused picking up various supplies from the floor and glanced up.

"How long to get to your base?"

"Normally around fifteen minutes. But probably another thirty at this rate."

The truck steered left and right as they went, crawling around the worst parts of the road.

But getting closer.

Closer to Project Hermes. Closer to help for Emily.

Her eyes fluttered and Marco's chest squeezed tight. His heart rate spiked.

He touched her cheek. "Hey there, no snoozing."

She blinked awake and nodded. "Right."

Was she just exhausted and needed rest? Or was it something more? Something lethal? Something that merited the bubbling acid in his belly?

The truck jerked to a stop and a rushing sound like an avalanche coming down on the truck made everyone look around with fearful eyes, seeing nothing but the olive green canvas and the dark blanket of nothing out the back.

The front of the truck dropped several feet.

Marco slid forward and caught the back of the cab with his feet to avoid Emily's head taking the impact.

The diesel engines thundered like Thor sending down a storm of lightning. The vibration ran up through the metal bench and continued on through his belly and chest.

The tires spun throwing mud like firehoses.

Glops of thick goo smacked into the green canvas, punching at it like an angry mob.

The truck jumped backward, but Marco was ready with his feet out wide for support. It hurled back a dozen feet and skidded to a stop.

The same soldier appeared at the back. "The road's washed out! The other vehicles already made it by, but it nearly took us along for a ride!"

The doctor's eyes went wide. "What are we going to do?"

"Keep your head on straight, doc! We'll loop around to the back entrance. It's a longer route, but we'll get there."

"How much longer?" Marco yelled over the pouring rain.

"From here, forty-five minutes or so. Assuming we don't run into anything else." He was gone and the truck got moving again soon after.

54

Exactly forty-three minutes later by Marco's watch, that caveat came back to bite them.

The poison rain had slowed and the truck had been moving along at a fast clip for the last twenty minutes. It now slowed to a crawl and turned to avoid something in the road.

Road?

Path was more accurate.

Suggestion of a path more accurate still.

Each time the doctor shined his flashlight out the back, there seemed to be less and less of anything that resembled a road.

BAM!

Something slammed into the truck, causing it to tilt over on two wheels.

Marco pressed into the backrest and his head into the canvas as the truck leaned over.

Oscar's claws dug into Marco's skin as the weasel fought to stay anchored.

The people sitting on the opposite bench flew face first into the other side. Fortunately, no one was sitting directly across from Marco and Emily.

The truck stopped at the peak of the arc, perfectly balanced, but only for an instant. It creaked and moaned and then slammed down on its side.

Marco's head smacked through the canvas onto the road. He rolled to his side, doing his best to cradle and protect Emily.

Oscar leaped away and landed on all fours, ready to attack. His nose twitched and he hissed with fury.

CRACK CRACK CRACK CRACK!

Automatic rifle fire split the air.

A soldier appeared at the truck's gate, his face as white as a sheet except for the gash on his cheek leaking red. The first soldier appeared with two others at his side. "Everybody out! Now!"

He spun around and emptied a magazine into something outside. He replaced it while one of the soldiers threw the gate open and helped people out.

Marco and Emily were the last to exit. As he climbed out and stood up with her in his arms, Oscar leaped up onto his pants and skittered up to perch on his shoulder. He rose on two legs and sniffed at the air.

Someone screamed.

A hideous, soul-crushing wail of terror.

The sickening sound of a body being torn apart. The wet ripping of living flesh.

The soldiers fired while screaming to each other.

"What the hell is that thing?"

"It's one of those giant lizards!"

A strange clicking echoed back and forth through the darkness.

"There's more than one!"

"Target at nine o'clock!"

The lead soldier dragged Marco forward and shoved a flashlight in his hand. "Take this!" He yanked the pistol out of his holster and shoved it into Marco's other hand. "And this!" He pointed at the entrance to a cave further up the hill. "It's in there! Go!"

Marco didn't need a second invitation.

He knew what was out there.

He'd seen one before.

The terrible beast that the ancient men were hunting. The one that had an uncanny ability to camouflage itself into its surroundings. An ability so profound and adaptive that the lizard almost looked like rushing water as it moved over the ground.

What had Emily called it?

Megalania. That was it.

It had taken a small tribe of hunters to take one down.

And now there were more than one. Possibly many more out there in the darkness, beyond the reach of the truck's headlights.

Two soldiers ran a screen on one side as all of the passengers ran toward the cave. The one in the lead fired at shifting, blurred air and then went down under a mouth full of sharp teeth.

He shrieked in agony as the thing bit his arm off.

Another lizard appeared and tore through the flimsy suit and into the man's belly.

Fueled by the terror of letting them get Emily, Marco ran like he'd never run before. Emily bouncing in his arms, a pistol in one hand and a flashlight in the other. A weasel clinging to his shoulder, riding it like a bucking bull.

Marco's head swiveled back and forth, waiting for the night to shift and ripple and take them.

One of the other passengers, the closest one behind, screamed and went down. The horrifying sounds of being eaten alive followed.

The monsters weren't far behind.

The cave wasn't far ahead.

Just had to get there.

And then a thought nearly made him trip and wipe out. He didn't know what was inside the cave. Was the door directly inside? What if it was closed and locked? Which presumably it would be.

Then they'd be trapped, backed into a corner with insufficient firepower to have a chance at escape.

The monsters were gaining.

They were fast. What had Emily said? They could run up to twenty-five miles per hour. Was that right?

It didn't seem possible for such a lumbering beast, but then again he remembered being shocked by how fast the one he'd encountered had moved.

The sound of pounding ground behind.

Not from boots.

Marco raced into the mouth of the cave, half-expecting to turn the corner and slam straight into a door. He didn't.

Instead he turned into a large cavern that went back into a man-made corridor carved into the rock. He would've kept running in that direction...

Except for the rock he didn't see before it was too late.

The toe of his boot smacked it and he flew forward, carrying Emily like Superman carrying Lois Lane.

Only this ride was short-lived and it wasn't going to be a soft landing.

In mid-air, he pulled her in and spun around. An instant later, he landed hard on his back and Emily bounced out of his grasp.

Oscar squealed as he was flung away.

The flashlight hit the ground and blinked out, dropping the cave into an inky darkness that may as well have been a black hole.

Marco tumbled end over end and side over side before flattening out and cracking his head on the dirt floor.

Got his bell rung.

Because it sounded like that. Like he'd shoved his head into the Liberty bell and Thor had hit it with his hammer. The sound vibrated through his skull and down to his toes.

He hurt everywhere at once.

But his chest hurt the most. Terror shoved an icy fist straight into it and twisted, hard. "Emily!"

He rolled onto his stomach and swept his arms in wide arcs back and forth. "Emily!"

She groaned from somewhere to his left.

On all fours, panicking more than thinking, he scrambled in the direction of the sound. His hands sliding back and forth over the ground.

His fingers hit something cold and he recoiled from the unknown an instant before realizing what it was. He found it again and picked up the pistol.

He swept the other hand through the dirt, hoping to find the flashlight nearby.

No luck.

From somewhere nearby, Oscar chittered softly.

Fear.

Something he'd never heard from the weasel.

He listened for Emily to make another sound. She moaned and he moved his head back and forth like a radar to localize on the direction.

CLICK.

CLICK CLICK.

Something clicking. Like two rocks smacked together.

The sound of something heavy dragging through the dirt.

His pulse spiked and he wanted to scream.

One of the lizards was in the cave!

The clicking continued.

He swung the pistol around and listened in the direction he thought it had come from. Then swung to face another direction. Then again another.

The sound echoed off the rock, making it impossible to localize the source.

Emily groaned again and the heavy dragging picked up speed.

The monster had found her!

The horrifying sounds of her getting torn apart. The shrieks of agony while being eaten alive.

The imagined scene flashed through his mind and dissolved his reason.

"I'm here! Come get me!" he screamed into the shadows. He pounded his fist into the dirt. "Here!"

More of the clicking. Getting louder. Closer.

Oscar's plaintive chittering an ominous warning of what was coming.

Marco swung the pistol with each click, but the next click always seemed to come from a different direction. He couldn't start firing in random directions because he might hit Emily.

His heart hammered in his chest, a fast and furious beat that echoed in his ears.

"Marco?" Emily whispered from the void.

He spun toward her voice as the heavy dragging sound and clicking stopped.

Silence.

Even the weasel had gone quiet.

"Don't talk and don't move!" he shouted. "There's one in here with us. I'm here! Come get me!"

He waited for the inevitable rush of speed and power. To be crushed under the massive beast. To feel its rank breath wash over him before it tore him to pieces.

But there was nothing.

Only silence.

No movement. No clicking.

Was it gone?

Had he imagined the entire thing?

"Emily?"

"Here," she whispered. "I have the flashlight."

He was about to tell her to keep it turned off, but was a second too late.

The light clicked on.

There was a reason why people were afraid of the dark.

A very good reason.

55

EMILY lay on her back and gripped the flashlight the with both hands. It had been sheer luck that her hand had bumped into it in the darkness. She clicked it on, knowing it was better to be able to see than not.

The light shot a beam up to the ceiling and bounced its glow around the cavern.

Oscar stood a few feet away, low to the ground on all fours. Looking at her and hissing with his teeth bared.

There was Marco!

Ten feet away on hands and knees like an animal, holding a pistol in one hand. His eyes saucer wide as he stared in her direction.

Why?

CLICK CLICK.

The nearness of the sound startled her.

She looked behind her and a scream died in her throat.

A mouth full of long teeth cracked open and a forked

tongue flicked out. Rough like sandpaper scratching at her cheek.

Its nostrils flared and blew out air. The smell of death enveloped her, knocking her senseless. Like a weaponized nerve agent.

Its jaws started to open.

"Get down!" Marco shouted.

She collapsed to the ground, as much from her limbs going numb as following the instruction.

Marco fired shots at the beast's head as he sprinted over.

Oscar leaped through the air and landed on the monster's back.

The shots had some effect as the twenty foot long lizard thrashed to the side. Its massive tail slammed into the wall, the impact a sonic boom in the enclosed space.

Marco scooped her up with one hand and kept firing with the other. He pinned her against his chest and darted down the corridor. "Come on, Oscar!"

The flashlight swung from Emily's death grip as he carried her.

They went around a curve in the narrowing corridor just as the lizard's head snapped up and turned in their direction.

A comparatively tiny weasel ran up on top of its head and leaped off.

The lizard snapped at the air, but the weasel had already landed and was racing to catch up.

The clicking again and the creature was after them.

Marco kept running, but the sound of the pursuit grew louder. The heavy shuffling and pounding.

It appeared around a bend and hurled forward.

It was unbelievably fast.

Too fast.

Another few seconds and it would take them down.

Emily shined the light in its eyes, hoping that might slow it down, but it didn't work.

Oscar circled back and leaped onto the lizard's back, causing it to twist to the side and crash to the ground. The insane weasel darted away as the lizard's jaws just missed.

Oscar raced ahead and suddenly darted left and disappeared into an almost invisible cleft in the rock wall.

Marco skidded to a stop to follow. He crouched low and pulled Emily into his embrace as he crawled through the narrow fissure.

Her blanketed legs scraped over uneven rock as they emerged into a small space.

Marco spun them around and they looked back at the entrance.

The lizard's head poked into the narrow crevice, but its wide shoulders caught as it tried to crawl through. Its mouth bit at the air. Its tongue flicked in and out. It struggled to bulldoze through.

Bits of rock crumbled from the sides but it held.

Oscar charged at the entrance, snapping and clawing at the air. Wisely, he stopped short before getting too close.

The lizard thrashed and clawed for a few minutes trying to get to them.

Marco lowered Emily to the ground while he kept the pistol trained on the beast.

Not that it would've helped. He'd fired three shots

into the lizard's face and, other than being temporarily distracted, it didn't appear to be that fazed.

But the fissure was too narrow for its bulk to squeeze through. After a few more minutes, it apparently realized that fact and gave up. It backed out of the gap and turned its head to the side.

One small eye stared at them.

And then it was gone.

Possibly gone.

Not that they were going to go out and check.

Oscar's defensive display quieted and he sat back on his hind legs, not taking his eye off the entrance. Guarding it like a well-trained dog might.

Emily turned and shined the flashlight around the room. A natural open space in the rock. The walls smooth and showing none of the carved lines of the corridor beyond.

Empty.

Wait.

She stopped the light on a relatively flat expanse of wall at the back.

There were markings.

Manmade.

Was it writing?

Something called to her. Something she couldn't put in words, but felt in her soul.

She shrugged out of the blankets and crawled over. She was about to read the message when she noticed something else.

A small silver ring on a narrow ledge below the message.

She picked it up and her chest shuddered with a spasm of recognition.

The cold metal burned her palm.

Not knowing how it was possible, and already knowing what would be there, she tilted the ring to read the inscription on the inside of the band.

With this, you'll never lose Hope.

Emily's chest clenched so tight she couldn't breathe.

Her father's wedding ring.

The one on his finger when he'd left her embrace over ten years ago. The ring he'd worn when he'd disappeared a few days later.

Vanished out of her life forever.

And he'd somehow ended up here.

Hot, wet tears welled in her eyes and spilled down her cheeks. Her fingers closed around the ring as she held it to her heart. She looked up at the wall, wiping at the tears blurring her vision.

There was a message for her. Many of the letters not fully formed. Scripted by a finger in a crusted brown paint.

Only it wasn't paint.

Her heart wrenched painfully as she realized the paint had once been brighter, redder.

A message recorded in her father's blood.

CHICKPEA IM SORRY. I DIDNT KNOW HOW TO HEAL. I WISH I COULD COME BACK TO YOU. ID NEVER LEAVE AGAIN.

DONT LOSE HOPE. DONT GIVE UP. YOURE STRONGER

*THAN YOU KNOW. ILL SEE YOU AGAIN SOMEDAY. I
LOVE YOU. DADDY*

Over ten years of guarding her heart, of locking it in a cage so she could make it through another day, came crashing down.

Wracking, shuddering, sobbing cries escaped her chest.

All the pain.

All the loss.

All the times she'd awakened in the middle of the night and, for the briefest instant, thought he was sleeping in his room down the hall. Her spirit soaring in that second.

And then the crushing loss as reality surfaced and dragged her into the abyss. The crushing weight of sorrow, again, as if for the first time.

All of it came out in a flood of sorrow and suffering.

She collapsed, but found strong arms pulling her close. They held her as the dam broke and a torrent of tears gushed out.

She sobbed uncontrollably.

Wild. Primal. The deformed depths of her twisted soul pouring out.

Parts of herself she'd thought had long gone numb and cold came to life. Shocked awake like defibrillators zapping a heart.

The returning feeling agonizing and exquisite at the same time.

She didn't know how long she cried.

It wasn't forever, but it felt that way.

The shuddering sobs finally ebbed and the tears slowed.

She lifted her cheek from Marco's chest and melted at the tenderness in his eyes.

The hurt he felt for her.

The concern.

The love.

"Are you Chickpea?" he asked.

She'd never told him about the nickname or how she'd got it. She nodded and raised the ring to show him. "My father's wedding ring." She shifted around so that she could see her father's final message. She leaned back and let Marco hold her. Support her.

"Do you think that was written in blood?" she asked.

"Yes."

"Which means he must've been dying. His final thoughts were of me."

Marco didn't respond.

"I always wondered why he didn't come back. When I was younger, I thought I'd done something wrong to make him not want to come back."

"You did nothing wrong."

"I know. When I got older, I realized it wasn't my fault. But knowing that didn't make it hurt any less."

"You've had to endure too much for one person."

Her heart squeezed tight and her voice cracked as she replied. "I have. But my father was right. I've survived. Somehow, I've survived it all."

"That's because you're strong, Emily. The strongest person I've ever known."

She didn't feel strong now.

She felt emptied out. Raw. Insides scoured by a firehose.

She felt different.

For the first time in as long as she could remember, she felt something new.

Peace.

Some measure of it, at least.

She slipped the ring onto her thumb and it fit perfectly. She pushed up and Marco helped her up to her knees.

She scooted forward and touched her hand to the word *DADDY*.

The blood spilled from her dying father's body. Now dried and crusted. Bits of it flaked off onto her skin.

"I love you, too."

Oscar screeched and then raced around in a tight circle before stopping and sitting back on his hind legs. He chittered with excitement.

Voices echoed from somewhere nearby. They got louder.

"We're in here," Marco shouted.

It took a while, but they eventually arrived.

A soldier stopped near the narrow fissure and spotted them. He climbed through and stood, his rifle pointed low while he did a quick scan of the space.

There was just the two of them.

Oscar darted behind Marco and peeked out from the side.

Well, the three of them.

And the ring. And the message.

He nodded with a somber smile. "It's okay. You're safe now."

56

DR. YONG marched into the cafeteria doing his best to appear calm and confident. The fact that his palms were soaked and his stomach churning proved otherwise. But hopefully no one would notice.

He was the director of Project Hermes.

Not by choice.

Not by desire.

But by the unfolding of events that some called fate and others called a random roll of the dice.

The nearly two hundred people that had made it from the town of Kodiak crowded around long tables devouring plates piled high with scrambled eggs and wedges of wheat toast slathered with butter. Only eight days after the end of the world and it looked like most of them had already run into food scarcity problems.

The project's staff had been told to stay away from the cafeteria this morning in order to accommodate their new guests. Two hundred people filled the available space and then some. The only members of the staff present were a number of soldiers that formed the security detail.

He'd briefed their supervisor that no rifles were allowed and no weapons were to be brandished unless a serious security risk arose.

Zhang was pleased to see the half-dozen soldiers had followed instructions. A few of them even had plates in their hands and were scarfing down a breakfast of their own. A little too relaxed, maybe, but it was probably for the best.

The important thing was to make these people feel like welcome guests, not suspicious strangers.

He didn't expect any trouble, but he also didn't know any of them and they'd all been through the most traumatic experience of their lives over the last eight days.

The end of the world was more than enough to unhinge even the most stable mind.

He scanned the room for Emily Wilder and Marco Morales. The two had somehow survived the onslaught of the Megalania pack and made it to the back entrance of the facility. No one else from their vehicle had survived.

The project had lost four good soldiers and their best doctor, not to mention the civilians that had escaped the chaos in Kodiak only to die before making it to safety.

He spotted the two sitting together.

Emily in a wheelchair with a tray in her lap. Marco seated next to her, spooning soup into her mouth.

The little weasel he'd heard about perched on Marco's shoulder like it was his guardian angel.

Emily looked better than when they'd brought her in last night. More color in her face.

There was a strange serenity in her expression that was found nowhere else in the room.

He hadn't had a chance to speak with her yet, but he would remedy that soon. Now that fate had brought her here, to the very same place her father had ended up ten years ago, she deserved to know the truth.

Deserved to know what happened to her father.

And there was no top secret vetting procedure to put a lid on it this time. The time for secrets was over.

The time for truth had arrived.

"Good morning, everyone," he said in a voice that didn't come out nearly as loud and commanding as he'd intended.

The hum of conversation filling the room didn't so much as stutter.

He cleared his throat a few times and swallowed. He balled his hands into fists and let out a slow exhale until his lungs were empty and aching for a refill.

It was time to be a leader.

He walked to the nearest long table and tapped on the shoulders of the two men seated at the end. "Excuse me," he said as he stepped up onto the bench seat and then up onto the table.

They scooted their plates away and stared up at him like he'd lost his mind.

"Everyone! I need your attention!"

It came out loud and strong this time.

The chatter of voices petered out.

Emily and Marco watched as he offered a smile in their direction.

"Thank you," he said as he scanned back and forth to make everyone feel included and involved. "My name is

Dr. Zhang Yong. Please call me Zhang as there is no need for formality. I am the director here at Project Hermes. I would first like to welcome you to our facility. You are both brave and wise to risk the journey and I hope to be able to make it worth your while."

He looked around the room. Every single person had stopped eating and was watching him.

Waiting for him to solve their problems.

They were about to find out that while he could solve some, he would invariably bring others into their lives.

That was the nature of reality.

Especially this one.

He was no messiah come to bring heaven down to a ravaged earth. He was a man. A man with an idea and the duty to attempt to pull it off. It could mean their salvation.

If they agreed.

And if it worked.

"I hope everyone is enjoying breakfast," he said with a wide smile.

A chorus of cheering broke out and he let it settle naturally.

"Wonderful," he said after the noise died down. "I'm here this morning to give you a brief overview of what's happening in the outside world. As much as we know, anyway. And also to make you an offer."

Voices whispered back and forth and he waved the room back to silence. "Some of what I'm about to say will shock you. You will find it hard to believe. You may reject it outright, but let me assure you that this is no joke. Everything I will tell you is absolutely true. And you will see the truth of it if you choose to."

"Get on with it, doc" someone yelled.

Zhang didn't know whether to laugh or to be offended. He chose neither and continued. "Eight days ago, the world changed forever. World War Three. We don't yet know what started it and we may never know. We do know that every nuclear-capable country launched most of their arsenals at their enemies. And their enemies launched their arsenals in the opposite direction. The United States had the largest arsenal by far, and, if reports are to be believed, deployed over ninety percent of it."

There were gasps of sucked in breath and similar expressions of disbelief and awe.

"The result was exactly what you would expect. The end of the world, for all intents and purposes. For humanity, at least. You've seen the brown skies since that fateful day. It is getting thicker. Soon, the world will plunge into a nuclear winter that will suffocate and starve most life on this planet."

A commotion broke out and he again waved them to silence to ensure he would be heard.

"I'm sorry to have to bring you such news. But the simple and tragic truth is that mankind has destroyed its own future on this planet. As a species, we will go extinct if we stay here."

"What do you mean *if we stay here*?" someone said.

Zhang pointed at the woman who spoke. "Good question. And one that brings me to my next point." He again looked around the crowd to include them all. "This facility was founded long ago to research the possibility of faster than light travel."

"What?" a man in the back with dreads hanging over

his shoulders. "You want to build ships like in Star Wars or something?"

Zhang chuckled. In those early days, he'd often thought of their work in similar terms. Though Star Trek was more his speed. "Something like that. But, it turned out that Einstein was right. Or at least, not wrong that we have yet discovered. We couldn't crack the code for it. But we did stumble upon something else."

"Let me guess," the Star Wars guy said. "You found a little green guy with big ears who always spoke in riddles and said things backwards. Discovered the secret of the universe, we have."

His Yoda voice wasn't half bad.

"No. We created discontinuities in the time-space continuum."

That got blank looks.

"In other words, we opened windows to the distant past."

"Light speed to the dinosaur age!" the dreaded guy shouted. "Cool! Sounds like an awesome movie!"

"It's no movie and we haven't opened a window that far back. But essentially, yes."

It took several minutes to get the chattering voices to quiet down. He waited until every last person was silent and listening. This was too important to miss.

"Which brings me to my proposal. Our time in this world is doomed. But we have gates to other times. Think of it as a do over. Humanity evolved too quickly. Our technology outpaced our wisdom. That would typically end in oblivion. But perhaps not this time. We are going to attempt to colonize the past. The goal is to move as many of us from this time back to other times and restart civilization with a clean slate. If we are successful, humanity will have its second chance. It will have many second chances in independent timelines."

They hadn't conclusively proven the independent part, but modern theories in the field of quantum mechanics coupled with his gut feeling made him believe that it was true.

"My offer is this. You can have a new future that starts in the past. You can be part of the first group to go back and begin to build a better tomorrow."

He expected another wave of conversation. Confusion or excitement or disbelief.

Something.

But no.

Not a single person spoke. There was nothing but the constant background hum of the air exchangers keeping the air breathable.

It stayed like that for a minute or two. And then one voice pierced the suffocating silence.

"I'll go."

57

BOB drew the sleeping bag up over his shoulder. The military issue collapsible cot creaked under him. He rubbed the crust out of his eyes and blinked them open. He looked up at the perforated off-white ceiling tiles above. If he'd had a sharp pencil, he would've put money on being able to stick it up there on the first try.

The tile above the desk in his office, old office, used to require replacing every few months because he'd chew it up with thousands of throws. He used to think of it as his exercise for the day. Sure, it wasn't running or yoga or whatever, but he was too old and lazy for that.

Running would've killed his knees and yoga would've made him feel like a new age freak.

So, he'd thrown pencils at the ceiling. Ten tries at a time, at least ten times a day. He'd gotten so good that there were days when he'd stick every last one.

Part of his assistant's job was to knock them down, resharpen them, and put them back on his desk for the next round of throws.

Veronica.

Her sultry lips and curvy hips rose in his mind and he took his time remembering every inch of her long legs. His loins stirred with interest, but then slumped into disinterest.

She was a million miles away.

And probably dead. Ashes spread across Los Angeles.

She deserved better than that.

She'd deserved a better boss than him, but there was nothing he could do about that now.

But while he couldn't change the selfish jerk he'd been for as long as he could remember, he didn't have to continue being that person.

That old saying about old dogs was BS.

An old dog could learn new tricks.

His *episode* and Flo's death had taught him that.

But what did a new and better Bob look like?

He didn't know. It wasn't a path he'd travelled before.

I'll just keep walking, trying to do the right thing whenever I can.

Chief Stuckey, wearing a face full of ugly bruises, pulled up a chair and sat down next to him. He held out a steaming cup of something. "Glad to see you wake up."

"Why? Did you think I was going to die last night?"

"With all the moaning and groaning you did over a sprained ankle, I was kinda hoping you would."

Bob pushed himself up against the cool cinder block wall and winced a few times from the ankle, but the bandage wrapped around it kept it from moving too much.

He looked over and saw Rome sleeping on a nearby cot. His wide girth spilled over the edges on both sides.

His head hung off one side with his mouth open and a long tendril of drool dangling halfway to the floor.

Kids could fall asleep like that. Any which way on any kind of surface.

What Bob wouldn't give to feel like that again. But no, he'd left those years behind long ago.

His back and shoulders were pinched up tight and he knew from experience that it would take a couple of hours of movement to work some relief into them.

Getting old sucked.

But the alternative was worse.

He realized that now. After the *episode*.

"You want it or not?" Stuckey said.

"Sorry and yes." He accepted the cup and discovered that it was black coffee. Not a latte like he would've preferred. Not a latte made by his gorgeously curvaceous assistant like he would've preferred even more.

But it was coffee.

And it was hot.

He took a sip and burned his tongue.

He took a long slow breath, letting the burnt earthy aroma fill his chest.

"Hey, how about a refill over here?"

Bob turned and saw the two old men from the diner, huddled up in the corner, sitting in chairs with a lantern glowing on a table between them.

They'd run across the two last night on their way here.

The two idiots had been sitting in their usual booth in the ruined diner. Drunk as drunk skunks. Drunker.

Yelling and laughing and carrying on like they didn't have a care in the world.

Stuckey had dragged them along for their own good.

The one with cracked tectonic plates for skin pointed at his cup. "This cup isn't going to fill itself."

Stuckey grabbed the nearby pot and stood. "Careful, Earl."

The man with the giant fuzzy caterpillars for eyebrows laughed and then groaned. "Don't make me laugh. My head hurts."

Stuckey sauntered over and filled their cups. "Serves you right for getting stupid drunk."

His bugbrows dipped and hid most of his eyes. "What are you? The morality police? We survived the end of the world. That's cause for celebration." He screwed off the cap of a hip flask and poured some booze into his cup before doing the same in Earl's cup.

Stuckey held out his cup for a splash. "Come on, then."

The old man complied with more than a splash.

"Thanks, Jim," he said before returning to the chair by Bob.

"You?" Jim said as he held the flask up.

"No, I'm fine with this," Bob said as he treasured the hot cup and the warmth ebbing into his stiff fingers.

The muffled sound of rain made it through the second story above.

After they'd finished with Charlie last night, they'd discovered that Red and the rest of the gang had disappeared. That was a problem for another day, though. There was a more immediate threat.

The rain.

The fallout.

Upon leaving the processing plant last night, the rain

drops had started coming down. They hadn't had much time and Stuckey had decided to shelter in the nearby high school. It had two floors and a few interior rooms on the first floor that didn't have windows or other access to the outside.

After picking up Earl and Jim, they'd all made it inside before the drops had turned into a downpour.

Bob took another scalding sip. "How'd you make this?"

"Don't tell the principal, but I had a small campfire going in the break room sink earlier this morning."

"Your secret is safe with me." He took another sip. "How's the kid?"

"Banged up six ways to Sunday but he'll be okay. How about you?"

"You mean aside from my mangled ankle?"

"Yeah, besides that."

"I'll survive. You look pretty good for a man that could've died several times yesterday."

He didn't look that good, but Bob was trying on his good guy role. It felt like a suit made for someone else. The collar itched. The sleeves were too short and cut into his armpits.

Nobody ever said change was easy.

Just that it could be done.

Stuckey shrugged. "I've been through worse."

"Is that madman really dead?"

The chief nodded.

"But Red got away."

He scowled. "Yep."

"What's our next move?"

Stuckey looked up as if he could see the rain pelting

the roof of the floor above. "Have to wait this out for starters. After that, we'll see. There are a lot of folks that didn't make it to the marina last night. They're going to need help."

Bob took another sip.

"Thanks for doing what you did with the truck. I don't know if Rome and I would be alive if you hadn't helped."

"Just doing my job."

The chief laughed. "When I met you, I thought you were a worthless piece of human garbage. And I'm a good judge of character."

"Are you saying you've changed your mind?"

Stuckey shrugged. "I'm thinking about it."

The two sat quietly for a few minutes, listening to the rain, listening to Rome snore, listening to the two old men slurp their spiked coffees.

"Bob, how would you like to be a deputy on the Kodiak police force?"

Bob took another sip of coffee, luxuriating in the cheap bitter brew. He closed his eyes and breathed in the acrid scent.

For such a terrible turn of events, there was still good in the world.

A few minutes passed in silence.

Stuckey cleared his throat. "Well? What do you say?"

Bob grinned. "I'm thinking about it."

58

EMILY didn't know why she was the first to volunteer. Not in the moment, anyway. It just came out. People had looked at her like she was crazy. Most of them.

Not Marco.

He understood, probably before she did.

She scooted up and adjusted the pillow to help her sit up. He was picking up their lunches and would be back soon. They hadn't had a chance to discuss it because she'd passed out as soon as the meeting in the cafeteria ended.

Not actually passed out, but close enough. Her eyes had blinked and she'd drifted off to sleep for several hours.

And when she'd woken up, he'd been right there in the chair next to the bed.

A warmth spread in her belly and rose up into her chest. Even in this dangerous, desperate, ruined world, she felt safe with him by her side.

A knock at the open door.

She looked up to see Dr. Yong standing in the doorway.

"May I come in?"

"Sure," she said as she gestured at the empty chair.

"Thanks, but I can't stay long. There's too much to do." He paused and stared at her, measuring her. For the task ahead, no doubt.

Did she really understand what she was getting herself into?

Of course not.

How could she?

Mankind had grown to inhabit every corner of the world because intrepid explorers had pushed beyond the known world and risked everything to see what was beyond.

And all that they had done paled in comparison to what she faced. Going back in time to help restart the human race.

Never had the stakes been so high.

Never had the destination been more unknown.

"Emily, I wanted to talk to you about something."

Was he about to refuse to let her go?

Was she too beat up to take part in the mission?

Now that she'd committed, she wasn't about to back down.

"I know I don't look like much right now. But I'll survive and I'm as strong and capable as anyone else you're considering."

He stared at her another minute and then responded. "I have no doubt of that. But that's not why I'm here."

Her brows knitted together in confusion. And then it hit her. In the chest.

"I was here the day your father died."

A painful lump formed in her throat. She knew he was gone. Long before finding the ring and the message written in blood. He would've come home otherwise.

She choked down a swallow. "What happened?"

"He was attacked by a short-faced bear."

"Arctodus."

He nodded. "We found the bear dead in the cavern. A spear lodged in its head. We found your father at the security entrance. We tried to save him but he'd sustained fatal wounds. It was a miracle he made it as far as he did."

Emily looked down, spinning the ring around her thumb. There was deep sadness, like there always was. But there was also something else.

Something that put a floor under the bottomless pit that usually dragged her down.

The knowing.

Finally. Knowing what happened.

Saying it was closure would've put it in too positive a light. It wasn't like she stopped hurting and missing him. She wasn't ready to relegate him to the past and merrily skip into her future.

But there was comfort in knowing.

Dr. Yong touched her shoulder. His eyes glistened. "I'm sorry it took so long for you to find out the truth. I know the hollow pain of losing a loved one and not knowing their fate."

Emily couldn't speak. The lump had returned and hardened like concrete in her throat.

Marco appeared at the door carrying two trays piled high with food. His ever present and once-again fluffy furred companion perched on his shoulder. The little weasel's head bobbing up and down as it tracked the trays like prey.

Emily wasn't able to eat much yet, but Marco had proved at breakfast that it wouldn't go to waste. "Am I interrupting something?"

Dr. Yong slid the table over for Marco to set everything on. "No. I was just leaving." He turned back to Emily with a sad smile. "We'll talk more later. Okay?"

She nodded, still unable to dislodge the boulder clogging her throat.

He turned and left without another word.

Marco swung the table around so it slid over the bed in front of her.

Oscar leaped down onto the bed and hissed at her. His needle-like teeth showing for an instant before he turned back to the food.

She still had no idea what she'd done to deserve such ill will.

Marco uncovered a bowl of eggs and placed them at the foot of the bed.

Oscar pounced on them before the bowl touched the sheet. He fell into the bowl and began shoving egg-filled paws into his mouth.

"You need to learn some manners, you animal," Marco said.

The weasel's head popped up with a bit of yellow egg hanging out of his mouth. His upper lip curled back into a snarl and then he dove back in.

Marco shook his head and turned back to Emily. "What was that about with Zhang? Everything okay?"

Emily reached up for him with both arms and he leaned down into the embrace.

His broad shoulders and hard back covered and protected her like a turtle's shell.

She pulled him closer, needing to draw his warmth into her soul.

He pressed against her, bracing himself so that they came together with the perfect weight of connection.

They stayed like that for a few minutes. Sharing breath and touch.

He lifted up and looked into her eyes. His hand cupped her cheek, thumb touched her lips. "Are you okay?"

She reached behind his head, slipped her fingers through his wild hair, and pulled him closer.

His eyes burned into hers. A line of invisible current that made her brain buzz with need.

His full lips inches away.

Soft breaths caressing her skin.

"I will be."

She pulled him down to close the unbearable distance and their lips touched.

Soft and hard at once.

The thing she feared most and the thing she needed most at the same time.

The walls around her heart began to crack and crumble.

And for the first time since losing her mother, then losing Hope, then losing her father, she let it happen.

More.

She embraced it.

Whatever the future held, they would face it together.

THE END OF BOOK 2

I hope you enjoyed the story! I'm working hard on the next book, *Sole Refuge*, right now. If you'd like to be notified when it's released, tap below to sign up to my Readers Group.

TAP HERE TO SIGN UP

You'll also get free copies of *The Last Day*, *Sole Prey*, and *Zomburbia*. One novel, one novella and one short story, all for free. As a member of the Readers Group, you'll receive exclusive discounts on new releases, freebie short stories and best of all... you'll get to know me!

Thanks for reading!
- Will

Want a free short story set right after the end of this book? It's called *Zomburbia* and it's 9000 words of mind-boggling, wonderful zombie fun!

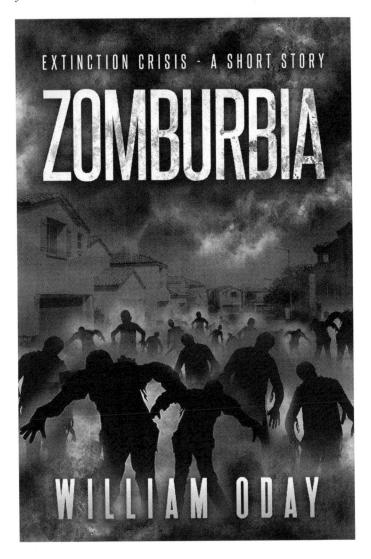

Take everything awesome about the 1980's and add zombies!

Bob Randy, a top Hollywood producer and degenerate of the highest order, fights to keep his latest TV series from being cancelled. Will he succeed? Told as a story within a story within a story. Get ready to have your brain melted...or eaten, as it were.

This story is exclusively available to the Readers Group. It is not available for sale on any retailer. If you want a free copy, sign up below.

As mentioned, joining gets you free copies of *The Last Day*, *Sole Prey*, and *Zomburbia*. One novel, one novella and one short story, all for free. You'll also receive news on discounted new releases, freebie stories and best of all... you'll get to know me!

TAP HERE TO SIGN UP

WANT BOOKS FOR FREE?

Join the Readers Group to get a free copy of *The Last Day*, *Sole Prey*, and *The Plunge*. One novel, one novella and one short story, all for free. You'll also receive exclusive discounts on new releases, freebie short stories and more!

Go to WWW.WILLIAMODAY.COM to find out more.

OTHER WORKS

Extinction Crisis series
SOLE CONNECTION, a Short Story
SOLE PREY, a Prequel Novella
SOLE SURVIVOR, Book 1
SOLE CHAOS, Book 2
THE TANK MAN, a Short Story
THE PLUNGE, a Short Story

Edge of Survival series
THE LAST DAY, Book 1
THE FINAL COLLAPSE, Book 2
THE FRAGILE HOPE, Book 3

The Best Adventures series
THE SLITHERING GOLIATH
THE BEEPOCALYPSE
THE PHARAOH'S CURSE

Short Stories
THE GENDER LOTTERY
SAINT JOHN
SHE'S GONE

QUESTIONS OR COMMENTS?

Have any questions or comments? I'd love to hear from you! Seriously. Voices coming from outside my head are such a relief.

Give me a shout at william@williamoday.com.

All the best,
Will

THE GOAL

I have a simple storytelling goal that can be wildly difficult to achieve. I want to entertain you with little black marks arranged on a white background. Read the marks and join me on a grand adventure. If all goes well, you'll slip under the spell and so walk alongside heroes and villains. You'll feel what they feel. You'll understand the world as they do.

My writing and your reading is a kind of mechanical telepathy. I translate my thoughts and emotions through characters and conflict in a written story. If the transmission works, your heart will pound, your heart will break, and you will care. At the very least, hopefully you'll escape your world and live in mine for a little while.

I hope to see you there!
Will

MY LIFE THUS FAR

I grew up in the red dirt of the Midwest, the center of the states. I later meandered out to the West Coast and have remained off-center ever since. Living in Los Angeles, I achieved my Career 1.0 dream by working on big-budget movies for over a decade. If you've seen a Will Smith or Tom Cruise blockbuster action movie, you've likely seen my work.

The work was challenging and fulfilling... until I got tired of telling other people's stories. I longed to tell my own. So, now I'm pursuing my Career 2.0 dream—a dream I've had since youth—to write stories that pull a reader in and make the everyday world fade away.

I've since moved to a more rural setting north of San Francisco with my lovely wife, vibrant children, and a dog that has discovered the secret to infinite energy. His name is Trip and he fits the name in four unique ways.

WILLIAMODAY.COM

Printed in Poland
by Amazon Fulfillment
Poland Sp. z o.o., Wrocław

53782616R00208